The Mistletoe Dare

The Daring Daughters Book 8

By Emma V. Leech

Published by Emma V. Leech.

Editing Services Magpie Literary Services

Cover Art: Victoria Cooper

ISBN No: 978-2-492133-37-4

Other Works by Emma V. Leech

Daring Daughters

Daring Daughters Series

Girls Who Dare

Girls Who Dare Series

Rogues & Gentlemen

Rogues & Gentlemen Series

The Regency Romance Mysteries

The Regency Romance Mysteries Series

The French Vampire Legend

The French Vampire Legend Series

The French Fae Legend

The French Fae Legend Series

Stand Alone

The Book Lover (a paranormal novella)

The Girl is Not for Christmas (Regency Romance)

Audio Books

Don't have time to read but still need your romance fix? The wait is over…

By popular demand, get many of your favourite Emma V Leech Regency Romance books on audio as performed by the incomparable Philip Battley and Gerard Marzilli. Several titles available and more added each month!

Find them at your favourite audiobook retailer!

Acknowledgements

Thanks, of course, to my wonderful editor Kezia Cole with Magpie Literary Services.

To Victoria Cooper for all your hard work, amazing artwork and above all your unending patience!!! Thank you so much. You are amazing!

To my BFF, PA, personal cheerleader and bringer of chocolate, Varsi Appel, for moral support, confidence boosting and for reading my work more times than I have. I love you loads!

A huge thank you to all of Emma's Book Club members! You guys are the best!

I'm always so happy to hear from you so do email or message me :)

emmavleech@orange.fr

To my husband Pat and my family … For always being proud of me.

Table of Contents

Dedication

For Roy Kelly

My dear friend.

King Sanglier

I will miss you.

Family Trees

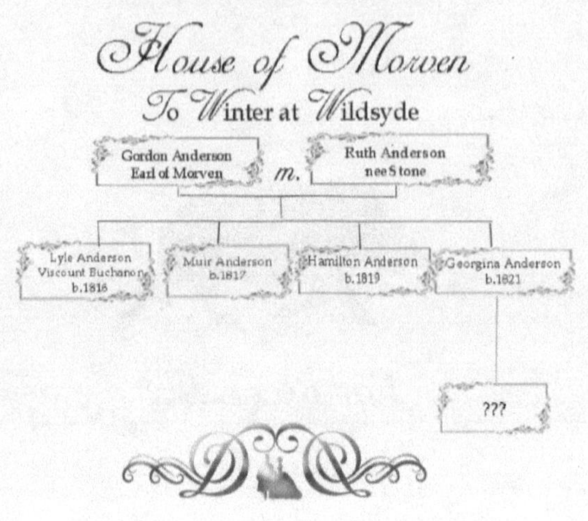

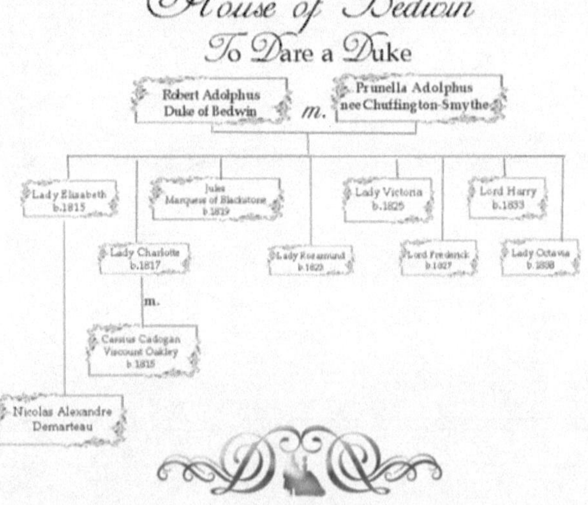

House of Hunt
To Steal a Kiss

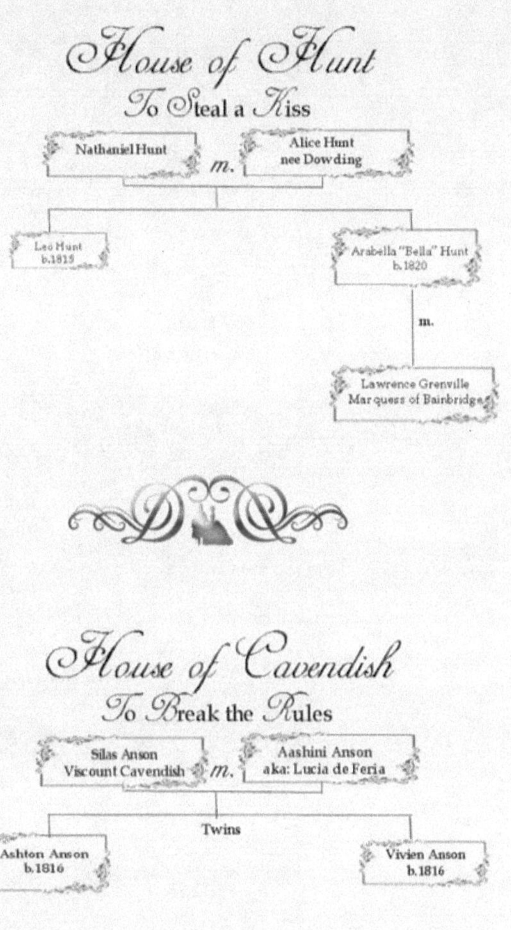

House of Cavendish
To Break the Rules

House of Trevick
To Follow her Heart

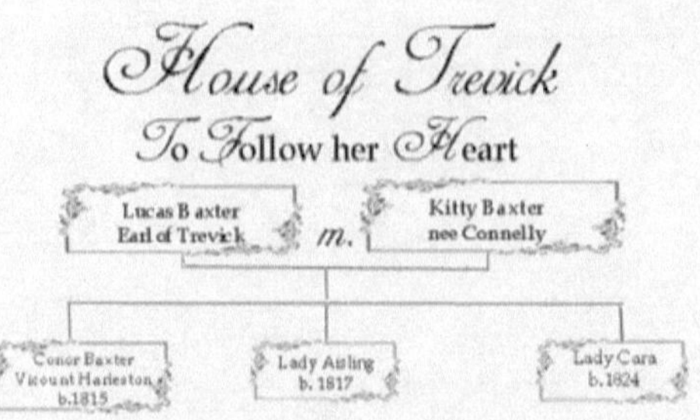

House of St Clair
To Wager with Love

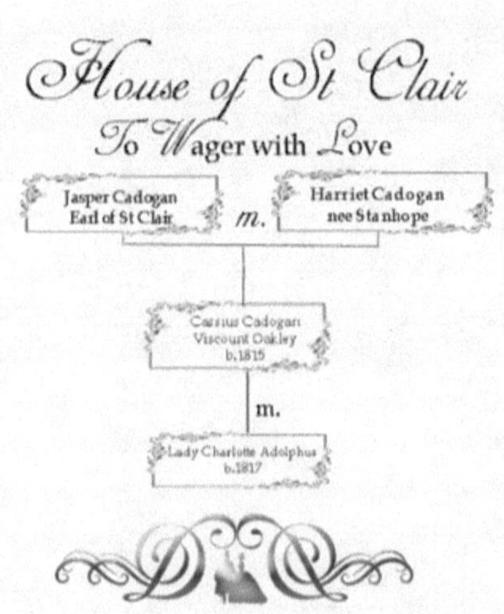

House of Cadogan
To Dance with a Devil

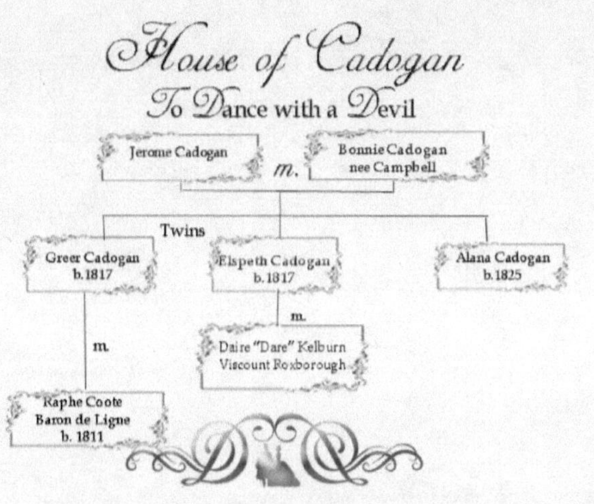

House of de Beauvoir
To Experiment with Desire

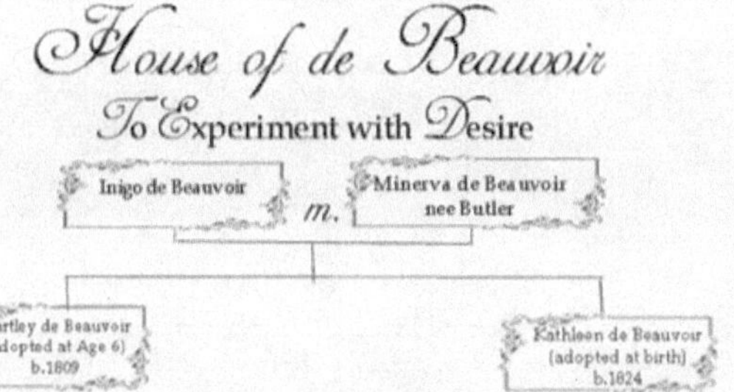

House of Rothborn
To Bed the Baron

House of Knight
To Ride with the Knight

House of Montagu
To Hunt the Hunter

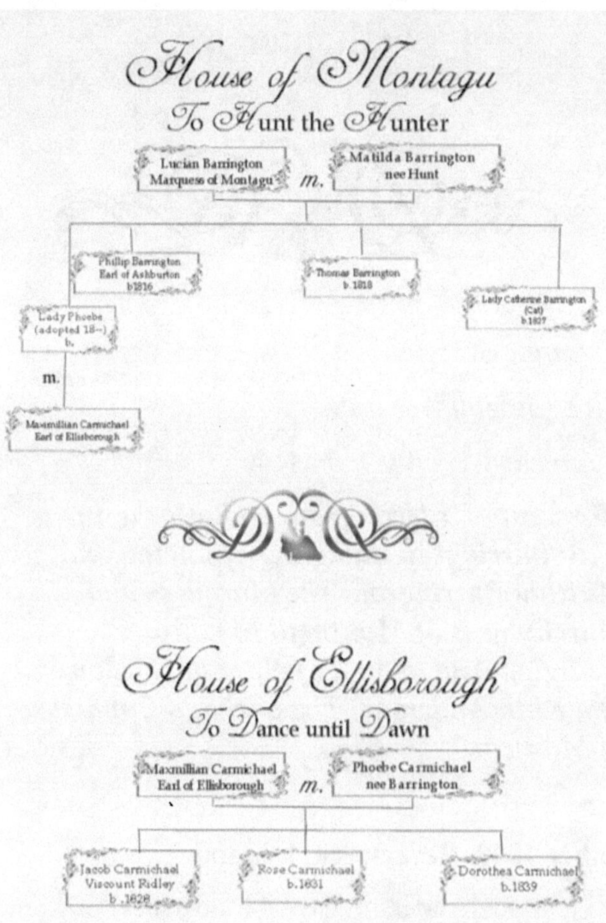

House of Ellisborough
To Dance until Dawn

Chapter 1

Dearest Georgie,

It's Christmas at last!

You know what you must do.

—Excerpt of a letter from Lady Catherine 'Cat' Barrington (daughter of Lucian and Matilda Barrington, The Marquess and Marchioness of Montagu) to Lady Georgina Anderson (daughter of Gordon and Ruth Anderson, The Earl and Countess of Morven).

7th December 1840, Beverwyck, London.

Lady Georgina Anderson gave a little squeal of excitement as the huge London residence belonging to her godparents finally came into view. Beverwyck, home to the Duke and Duchess of Bedwin, appeared before them in all its unapologetic grandeur.

"We're here!" she exclaimed with unconcealed delight. She felt like a child, jittery with excitement for everything to come.

Her maid let out a heartfelt sigh of relief.

"Thank the Lord," she grumbled. "'Tis nae wonder if my behind is flat as a pancake. I lost all feeling two days ago."

Georgie shook her head and ignored the comment, as she had ignored the greater part of Meg's grumbling and complaint on the slow and lengthy journey from Scotland to England. It was easier than in her parents' day, at least. Parts of the journey could be done by train now, which meant it was a deal quicker than it had ever been before, but Meg was a homebody and, given the opportunity, would never even set foot outside the castle gardens at Wildsyde. Though it was one of the smallest properties owned by Georgie's father, the Earl of Morven, it was home and where the family preferred to spend most of their time. Georgie loved it dearly, but she also hungered for more, for entertainment and amusement, and an absence of her three overbearing older brothers. She loved them, like Wildsyde, despite their many, *many* faults, but the idea of an entire three weeks without them and in the company of her friends was nothing short of miraculous.

She slipped her hand into the fur muff about her neck and touched the little slip of paper nestled there. Her heart skipped. She had carried the scrap about for months now, ever since the summer when she and Mama had visited the Marquess and Marchioness of Montagu. Matilda was one of Mama's dearest friends and her youngest daughter, little Cat, with her big brothers away from home, had been bored. No doubt the two handsome devils were cutting a swathe through the female population somewhere and leaving a trail of broken hearts. Well, perhaps not Philip. The eldest was much like his father; he kept his thoughts and feelings to himself and was scrupulously discreet. Georgie suspected he wasn't half as perfect as he appeared. She hoped not, anyway. Still, in the absence of her brothers, Georgie had kept the little girl amused, and had inevitably given in to her demand to take a dare from the wretched hat.

Kiss a man under the mistletoe.

It was a simple enough dare on the face of it. Or at least it would have been if there was a single man of her acquaintance that Georgie *wanted* to kiss. And the devil of it was the dare had a time limit, for if she did not complete it this Christmas, she'd have to wait an entire year to try again. The chances of her finding anyone to kiss at Wildsyde, where her family always spent Christmas, were slim to none. Of course, she could cheat and kiss her father or one of her brothers on the cheek, but that didn't feel right. In desperation, she had confided in her mother, who had understood at once. Well, she would, seeing as it had been a dare that had propelled her mama to do something as outrageous as propose to a complete stranger. Still, that had worked out beautifully. So, Mama had persuaded her father to allow Georgie to spend Christmas with the Duke and Duchess of Bedwin in London, where there would be society—and men—aplenty. *Trust in the dare,* Mama had said. *It will lead you where you need to go.* As if there were magic in the writing. Silly, obviously, but… Georgie shivered all the same.

The carriage rolled to a halt, and a footman opened the door, putting down the step for her and moving to offer his hand. Before he could, Georgie had leapt down, running into the grand entrance hall with a cry of delight as she saw the duchess and two of her daughters waiting to greet her.

"Auntie!" Georgie exclaimed, throwing herself into the duchess's arms. Though they were not blood relations, Prue had been Auntie to all the Anderson children and would allow nothing more formal.

"Darling girl," the duchess said, hugging her tight. "I am so happy to have you here." Georgie straightened and looked down at Prue, chagrined to discover that she was a full head taller than both her aunt and her daughters.

"How well you look, Georgie."

She turned towards the soft voice and smiled at Lady Rosamund. At almost eighteen, she had turned into a lovely young woman with dark hair like her father and thickly lashed brown eyes. "I am well, and you are a beauty, Ozzie. Whatever has happened since I saw you last?"

Ozzie laughed good-naturedly and gave a shrug. "I grew an inch and filled out a bit," she admitted.

"Only an inch, you lucky thing," Georgie lamented with a quirk of her lips. "I wish I could shrink a little."

Her mother, Ruth, was a tall, big-boned woman and her father, Gordy, an enormous bear of a man. This was excellent for his sons, who had followed in his footsteps. Sadly, Georgie had as well and was far too tall for a woman and built with statuesque proportions that either intimidated men or attracted entirely the wrong attention.

"You look quite magnificent," Aunt Prue said sternly. "Shrinking, indeed! I should think not. The more of you there is, the better."

"You can't have too much of a good thing," Ozzie said with a giggle, taking her arm.

Georgie pulled a face. "Actually, I think you can, but I'll take the compliment anyway."

Prue and Ozzie laughed and bore her off up the stairs. "Come along. Let us get you settled. Everyone is arriving today, and you'll want time to wash and change."

"And eat," Georgie said desperately, clutching at her stomach. "The last stop we made seems an age ago."

Prue nodded. "We'll have tea and cakes sent to your room."

"Oh, heaven," Georgie said with a happy sigh, and followed her godmother up the stairs.

Alden Seymour, the Duke of Rochford, looked across the carriage at his companion and resisted the urge to sigh. A more unlikely pair of friends would be difficult to imagine. Sprawled across the seat opposite him lounged Jules Adolphus, the Marquess of Blackstone. At seven and twenty, Rochford was five years older than Blackstone. That was hardly extraordinary, but where Blackstone possessed a face and figure handsome enough that young women stopped and stared, Rochford did not. At least, yes, they stopped and stared, but not because he was handsome. Nicknamed the Monster of Mulcaster Castle by those local to his ancestral home, people did not stare at Rochford for his beauty.

Standing six feet and seven inches high and built with all the finesse of the castle he'd inherited along with his title in the wilds of Cumbria, he was an intimidating figure, and he knew it. Add to his hulking stature a deep, ugly scar that cut through his lip and over his cheek and he cut quite a grotesque figure. The scar narrowly missed his eye before travelling up into his hairline, leaving a patch where the hair did not grow properly. It also twisted his mouth into a permanent sneer. Then there was the pockmarked skin from a severe bout of measles that had almost killed him as a boy. The results were hardly pretty. He'd heard young women snigger and comment that his was a face only a mother could love, but even his own mother couldn't stand the sight of him, which showed how bloody much they knew. Not that he cared. He was a duke, he was wealthy, and people had to suffer his company whether or not they liked it. Mostly, they didn't.

He had run into Blackstone during a tavern brawl two years ago. It had been a low dive with a lower clientele and a place the young man had no business going. Recognising Bedwin's heir and realising the duke would owe him a debt if he hauled his son out of trouble, Rochford had stepped in. He had assumed he'd escort the young cub home, ensure Bedwin knew about the favour he owed, and be done with it, but much to his surprise he'd discovered Blackstone to be an entertaining companion and they had caroused together until the early hours. They'd been friends ever since, though why Blackstone continued to seek him out, Rochford could not fathom.

Blackstone stirred on the seat, stretching and yawning. "Are we there yet?"

"Yes, so you'd best straighten yourself up. You look like you slept in your clothes," Rochford observed in disgust.

"I did," Blackstone replied, smirking.

Rochford raised an eyebrow. "And do you wish for your darling mama to know it?"

Blackstone pursed his lips. "A fair point," he admitted, and set about straightening his attire. He glowered a little at Rochford. "Why aren't you crumpled?"

"Because I don't slouch and sprawl like an indolent cat."

"No, true enough. You're too uptight. That's your trouble, Rochford. One day you'll remove that giant stick from your arse and feel a deal better for it."

Rochford returned his attention to the passing scenery. "Ah, yes. Now I remember why I keep you around. Such an intelligent and witty conversationalist."

Blackstone snorted as he tried to retie his cravat, using his reflection in the window. "It's too damned early for wit and intelligence. Give a fellow a chance to wake up."

"It's ten thirty, you idle fop. Hardly the crack of dawn."

"Too early when you've not been to bed," Blackstone grumbled. "Why aren't you tired, damn you?"

Rochford shrugged. "Stamina."

"Stamina, my eye. You're not normal. Made a deal with the devil, I reckon," Blackstone grumbled, but halted any further observations about supernatural dealings as the carriage drew up outside his home.

The two friends made their way up the steps of the imposing residence and Rochford wondered once again what on earth had possessed him to accept Blackstone's invitation. The next three weeks promised to be full of gaiety and entertainment, goodwill to all men and festive cheer, all of which were things that would usually have him running in the opposite direction at speed. Rochford did not like gaiety. He wasn't the least bit good humoured, and he preferred ill will because then he knew where he stood, dammit. Yet the idea of returning to the vast castle in the wilds of Cumbria that he called home had sent a chill through him, the like of which he'd never known. It had made him feel hollow and cold, and a good many emotions he was not about to analyse. So here he was, with no one to blame but himself, so he'd better bloody well endure it like a man.

Once Georgie had bathed and changed, eaten two large slices of cake, and washed it down with several cups of tea, she felt much more herself, though a headache nagged at her temples still. The journey had been long and fatiguing, and she promised herself a good night's sleep and a lie in tomorrow. She sent Meg off with strict instructions to have a nap before she did anything else, aware she would suffer the consequences if her maid did not get some rest before she needed to get ready for dinner later. Meg had a clever hand for hair and was the only one who seemed able to contain Georgie's riot of thick, dark curls with any success. However, she could be ruthless and a little vindictive with hairpins, particularly if she was in a bad mood.

Meg had informed her that several guests had arrived, including Evie Knight, one of Georgie's best friends. She had not seen Evie since the spring and was looking forward to catching up with her. Not least, she was on pins to set eyes on the mysterious Louis César de Montluc, the Comte de Villen, about whom she'd heard so much. His illegitimate half-brother, Nicolas Alexandre Demarteau, had married the duke and duchess's eldest daughter, Eliza, causing a terrific stir among the *ton*. The duke and duchess had disregarded this, welcoming Nic into the family and, along with him, the comte.

Evie had confided how she had befriended Louis César, a circumstance which Georgie found both scandalous and intriguing.

That Evie, an unmarried lady only just turned eighteen, had for the past two years apparently been a friend and confidante to a man many years her senior, seemed astonishing. Georgie could not help but wonder why Lady Helena had allowed it, but then she was a sensible woman and presumably she knew best. Whenever anyone but Evie wrote and mentioned the Frenchman, though, all they could speak of was how dreadfully beautiful he was, how deliciously seductive. Phrases like *fallen angel*, and *the handsomest man in the country, perhaps even the world*, were repeated often, yet Evie never mentioned him in such a way, insisting they were friends and nothing more. It was all most enthralling.

Making her way down the stairs, Georgie headed towards the library. It was her and Evie's favourite place at Beverwyck, and she knew Evie would go there to find her when she arrived. A footman had informed her no one else had yet come down, so she would have the plush library all to herself whilst she waited. She pushed open the heavy oak door, inhaling the scent of the grand room as it enveloped her. It was a subtle blend of old books and cigar smoke, polish, and centuries of power and knowledge. Though it was a grand room of vast proportions, with the higher shelves accessed by galleried walkways, it still felt cosy. This was partly thanks to the way some of the doubled sided shelves cut into the room, creating smaller, private spaces. There were snug little nooks to curl up, and window seats where you could look out over the expansive gardens, never suspecting you were in the city at all. She could hear the crackle of a fire blazing in the enormous fireplace and could hardly wait to find an interesting title to sit down with and warm her toes. Suffused with good humour, Georgie shrugged off her tiredness and hurried towards the section she wanted—the novels—and collided with a huge, dark object.

Georgie was not given to hysterics. She had three large, intimidating brothers, and could hold her own with all of them. However, expecting to find herself alone and walking headlong into a stranger was daunting to begin with. Looking up and finding a bear of a man staring at her with cold grey eyes the colour of slate and a face that was hardly friendly was enough to make her give a shriek of alarm.

She stumbled back, tripped on her own skirts, and fell hard on her backside.

"Ouch!"

The man looked down at her in silence, his expression about as warm and welcoming as the Loch of Wester in February.

Georgie took him in, noting quickly the quality of his dress, his bearing, and the large cabochon ruby glinting on his little finger. A guest. A wealthy and powerful guest. One she'd just made a complete fool of herself in front of.

Still, he was hardly acting the gentleman, staring at her in disdain rather than offering her a hand up.

"If you wouldn't mind?" she said, her tone irritable as she held out a hand to him.

He quirked a thick dark eyebrow, the sneer at his lips leading her to expect a derisive comment. She was not disappointed.

"Are you certain you can bear it?" he asked, and his deep voice rumbled through her.

"Bear what?" she asked in confusion.

"The touch of my hand, as you damn near broke your neck in your haste to run away."

"I wasn't running away, you—you merely startled me, that's all."

He snorted, and the contemptuous curl of his lip made her too-ready temper spark to life.

"If you go about lurking in dark corners, I wonder you don't expect such a reaction," she retorted. "Perhaps you did it on purpose?"

"You think it my habit to linger in the shadows and frighten maidens? Ah, yes. I see what manner of man you have painted me as. No doubt I eat small children for breakfast?"

"I never said that!" Georgie exclaimed in outrage, wondering why he was so damned touchy. She was the one sprawled on her backside and looking like a fool. Oh, what was the use? She scrambled to her knees and got up without his help, brushing her skirts smooth with sharp, agitated movements. Glaring at the big brute, she lifted her chin and hurried past him towards the shelves reserved for novels. Her heart was still beating too fast, but Georgie did her best to calm herself, making a show of perusing the titles on offer but far too aware she was being watched. His gaze seemed to burn her back through her gown, and she lasted precisely two minutes before she reacted, turning to meet his gaze. Instead of looking guilty for staring, or at least looking away and pretending he hadn't been doing anything of the sort, the arrogant devil just continued to watch her.

"Was there something you wanted, sir?" she demanded, folding her arms. Goodness, but he was a mountainous size, and she was used to being around hulking Scotsmen. She realised now that what she had believed to be a sneer was a scar that scored deep into his cheek and tugged his lip out of line. He wore a beard, the hair thick and dark, and she wondered if he did it to cover his skin, which was badly pockmarked. He was not a handsome man, but certainly compelling.

His grey eyes never wavered from her face.

"Being alone with me is inadvisable. You ought to leave," he observed coolly. "Or have you no concept of polite manners?"

Georgie could not help the snort of amusement that escaped her. "Polite manners? This from a man who won't offer a woman his hand to help her up."

He shrugged, unimpressed. "I would have offered. I was only ensuring you wouldn't swoon if your dainty hand touched mine."

"Nonsense. You were enjoying looking down on me and feeling superior."

"I wasn't, but I might now, considering I have never in my life met a more ill-mannered, sharp-tongued harpy."

Georgie's mouth fell open in shock. She was used to trading insults with her brothers, but for a man she didn't know from Adam to speak to her so…!

"You should leave," he said again, his voice firm. "For I'll not have you ruined and the blame laid at my feet, if you're considering trapping a rich husband."

Georgie closed her mouth with a snap before her jaw hit the floor in outrage.

"Trap *you*," she repeated faintly, "into *marriage?*"

She gave a startled laugh before she could think better of it, and then tried her best to smother the next, and then the urge to laugh was so strong she could not help but give into it. Georgie laughed and laughed, clutching at her sides until tears rolled down her cheeks.

She tried to stop. Truly, she did. Except every time she looked up and saw his expression of disgust and the icy glare in his eyes, it set off another bout and she went off into whoops.

"When you've quite finished," he said, sounding as if he'd happily pick her up and throw her out of the nearest window, given the opportunity.

"I beg your p-pardon, sir," she stammered, doing her best to smother her laughter, but her voice quavered with amusement.

"Your *grace*," he said, growling the words with obvious relish.

Georgie blinked, stunned into silence. The word *grace* and this man did not belong in the same sentence. Wait. Your grace. *Your grace?* He was a *duke?* Little by little, the colour leached from her face. She felt it go, along with any vestige of warmth she'd regained since she'd arrived at Beverwyck. Lud. She'd been in town for five minutes and she'd insulted a duke. Oh, good heavens. Her mother would kill her.

"Do run along," he said, his grey eyes glinting with a look that suggested she ought to do as he said, or else she would not like the consequences.

Finally intimidated, but refusing to be entirely cowed, Georgie turned back to the shelf, snatched up the nearest title, and stalked past him with her nose in the air.

Rochford let out an uneven breath as he heard the library door close. He raked a hand through his thick hair and glowered at the bookshelf in front of him as if it had personally offended him.

Damn her.

He had not expected to feel at home here, in this place of happy families and friends and warm welcomes. Bedwin and his duchess had always acted kindly towards him, no doubt hoping he'd be of use to them at some point, or perhaps in gratitude for saving their son's neck. To discover that even here they viewed him as a monster, however, was hard to bear. He'd assumed Blackstone's parents would have warned all their guests of his presence, no doubt apologising and asking them to endure his company as best they could. Well, the warning had not gone far enough for that young beauty.

When she had hurried around the corner, almost throwing herself into his arms, for a moment his breath had caught. It had barely lasted a second, yet he could recall every damned detail. She was glorious. She was extraordinarily tall for a woman, and her skin was impossibly pale, like alabaster. Her dark curly hair had tickled his cheek and the delicious scent of vanilla had invaded his senses. Her long, thick eyelashes swept down over eyes the colour of whisky, and her body… God. Statuesque was hardly an adequate description. Desire uncoiled deep in his gut as he remembered the lush curves of her hips and full breasts. Abruptly, he made himself remember the look in her eyes as she'd seen his face, the shock and revulsion.

Remember that, you damned fool.

A woman like that might marry him for his title, or his money, but she'd need a bloody strong stomach to endure it.

Chapter 2

August,

For the love of God, leave your witless female relations to cause havoc by themselves if they must. They don't want you interfering and tying yourself in knots over their dreadful scrapes. Keeping them out of trouble will only give you a nervous collapse. It's your darling mama's responsibility to keep them in line and, bearing in mind she's the worst of the lot, you ought to do yourself a favour and wash your hands of them. They'll all be happier, and you'll likely live longer.

Come and stay with me for a bit. I want to show off my wife. If you've a lick of sense, you'll find one for yourself and settle down. I highly recommend it.

—*Excerpt of a letter from The Most Hon'ble Lawrence Grenville, The Marquess of Bainbridge to The Right Hon'ble August Lane Fox.*

7th December 1840, Beverwyck, London.

Evie laughed as she looked down at the note, slipped under her door.

Evie, you little twit. I would never lie to
you. Surely you know that.

Meet me in the library at midnight
tonight with the monstrous dress. For
God's sake, make sure no one sees you.

Really, Louis César was foolish if he thought he could make her believe she was a great beauty. She had enough examples of feminine perfection among her friends and family to know what men considered beautiful. Even gorgeous Georgie did not meet the *ton's* exacting requirements, simply because she was too tall, whereas Evie was too short, and plain, and plump.

Evie had to admit she had improved a great deal over the past months, but she had a weakness for sweet things, and she did not have the stature to carry off the extra pounds that seemed to accumulate with startling ease. The fact had never much bothered her before, though. She had always been at ease in her own skin. Until recently. Though Evie made light of it, the words of the sought-after modiste, Madame Blanchet's, about her weight had undermined her confidence and made her unhappy. So much so that she'd even taken the wretched woman's advice and begun following the lowering diet she had recommended. According to Madame, if she stuck to it, the weight would fall off her in no time. What she didn't say was that the diet would make feel Evie wretched and light-headed, but she had lost eight pounds so far, so perhaps it was worth it. She wondered if Louis César would notice the change in her.

It had been months since she'd seen him, and then only once or twice during the summer, and she worried he was avoiding her. They corresponded regularly, at least twice a week, but she had noticed his letters changing. They were always amusing and full of news and gossip, but he did not confide in her as much as he once had, and that troubled her. He had no close friends that she knew of and, since his brother had married, he spent more time alone than was good for him. It had been a tremendous relief to her when he had finally given in and accepted the duchess's invitation to come for Christmas, for Evie could not bear the thought of him spending the festive season all by himself. Well, whatever the problem was, she would discover it over the coming weeks. Somehow, she had to find what made poor, dear Louis so unhappy, and fix it.

🎩 🎩 🎩

"Evie!" Georgie squealed with delight at the sight of her friend and ran down the last few steps to haul her into an embrace

"Georgie!" Evie's muffled voice exclaimed from Georgie's generous bosom. "Can't breathe!"

"Oh, I'm sorry." Georgie let her go, and returned a sheepish grin.

Evie laughed, a little breathless, and then hugged Georgie again. "It's lovely to see you. My, but you look well, so…."

"Big?" Georgie suggested sourly. She ought to be used to towering over all the other delicate young ladies by now, but though she loved all her friends dearly, they made her feel like an Amazon. They were all so petite and ladylike, and she… wasn't.

"I was going to say beautiful," Evie scolded, and then gave a wistful sigh. "And I'd happily steal a couple of extra inches from you, so don't go lamenting them on my account."

"You, my lovely Evie, are small and perfectly formed," Georgie said firmly. Evie might not have been a classical beauty, but her goodness shone from her, and she had the most startling green eyes, thickly lashed and so expressive. Evie gave her usual snort of amusement, her response to any kind of compliment about her appearance, and Georgie shook her head. "You are, you know. Any man would be lucky to have you."

Evie shrugged and took her arm. "Yes, but would I be lucky to have them? That's the trouble. Oh, Georgie, I know it's dreadful of me to say so, but it's so hard to find anyone of interest. It's not like I'm short of offers, but I know most of them are in love with my enormous dowry, not with me. They just seem so false, and you know I cannot abide people who say one thing and mean another."

Georgie nodded, understanding the problem all too well. "It's impossible to get to know any man when you cannot spend any proper time with them. At the parties they are all on their best behaviour and perfectly charming. What are they like when they wake up with a head cold and find the cat's been sick in their slippers, though? That's the real test."

Evie spluttered with amusement, her eyes glittering. "Oh, we should arrange something of the sort, like those fairy tales where the hero has to complete five tasks to win the princess's hand in marriage."

"Oh, yes. What else should we ask of them?" Georgie asked, enjoying herself thoroughly now she was with her friend again.

"Umm. Oh, I know. How they react if a beautiful woman goes past and gives them a come-hither look."

"Oh, yes, because if they go hither, they are definitely out," Georgie said, nodding.

"Exactly." Evie grinned.

Georgie looked up to see the duchess gesturing to her from the other side of the hall. "Come along. Everyone is waiting in the drawing room. We're dreadfully late."

They hurried to where everyone waited, drinks in hand, smiling and greeting each other with familiar warmth. Georgie saw the glowering duke she had run into so disastrously earlier. He was standing silently, somehow apart from everyone, even though he stood with Jules, the Marquess of Blackstone. Jules lifted his hand to wave at her and Georgie smiled at him, refusing to catch the duke's eyes, and then her breath caught, and she almost stumbled as another man appeared in the door.

"Mercy," she whispered, stopping in her tracks, unable to do anything less than gape in astonishment. Whoever he was, he was utterly gorgeous. Tall and lithe with broad shoulders and thick dark hair, his blue eyes were the colour of an exotic sea. He was effortlessly stylish, his evening clothes moulded to his impressive physique and showing long, long legs. Turning towards them, his sensuous mouth tilted up at the corners and his blue eyes sparkled with warmth.

"Louis!" Evie exclaimed in a whisper, making as if she would run across the room to him.

Shocked, Georgie held on to her, giving her a warning glance. Evie coloured, but gave a small nod, and they moved sedately towards him. The man's gaze followed Evie as she came closer, full of amusement.

"*Bonsoir soirée, ma petite*," he said to Evie, the words spoken quietly enough that only she and Georgie could hear the far too familiar greeting.

Georgie shivered as the sound of his deep voice swept over her. Good heavens, the Comte de Villen was everything everyone had said about him.

His azure gaze swept over Evie, and a slight frown creased his brow. "Are you well, Miss Knight?"

"Of course," Evie said, beaming at him. "All the better for seeing you, you dreadful man. Where have you been? It's been months."

Before the comte could answer, the butler appeared and announced that dinner was ready. Evie sighed in frustration, narrowing her eyes at the comte.

"Don't think you've escaped," she warned him. "I want to know everything you've been up to."

The man's lips twitched, but he replied with apparent sincerity. "*Oui, Mademoiselle.* I know you do."

"Oh, Lou—Monsieur Le Comte, please allow me to introduce my dear friend, Lady Georgina Anderson. Georgie, this is Louis César de Montluc, Comte de Villen."

"*Enchantée,*" he said, bowing over her hand. "A pleasure to make your acquaintance, my lady."

Georgie blushed and curtsied, quite unable to withstand his proximity, those blue eyes and that devastating French accent all at once. She could not think of a single intelligent thing to say, so for once she was sensible and kept her mouth shut.

"You here again, Georgie?"

George turned at the familiar voice and grinned at Jules. "Good evening, Jules, and yes, like the proverbial bad penny, I've turned up again."

"Good show. It's been too dashed quiet here of late, since my two dreadful sisters have married and left home. We need someone to cause a bit of chaos, liven things up a bit."

Georgie glared at him, wishing she could kick the devil for speaking so. Embarrassed, she shot a nervous smile at the comte. "He's only funning, monsieur. The marquess has a remarkably peculiar sense of humour," she assured him, before the man thought she was an ill-mannered hoyden.

"No, I don't. You always liven things up by doing something dreadful, you know you do," Jules protested.

"Be quiet," she gritted out through her teeth, before turning back to the comte, and Evie, who was struggling not to laugh, well aware of Georgie's mortification.

"May I have the honour, Miss Knight?" the comte asked Evie, offering his arm to take her into dinner.

"You may," Evie replied, her cheeks dimpling as she smiled up at him.

"Well then, looks like you're stuck with me, George, old girl," Jules said, smirking at her. He stuck his elbow out at her and Georgie sighed, taking it as there were no better options.

"I'd forgotten how annoying you were," she grumbled as Jules led her through to the dining room.

"Funny, that's what my sisters say whenever they come back to visit," he remarked, winking at her.

Georgie rolled her eyes and then noticed ahead of them that the ill-mannered duke she'd encountered was escorting Aunt Prue.

"Who is that awful man, Jules?" she demanded.

Jules laughed as he saw who she was gesturing towards. "The Duke of Rochford, and he's an ill-tempered devil, I'll grant you, though not as dreadful as he makes out."

"I beg to differ," she muttered crossly.

Jules gave her an alert look. "You know him?"

"No, but I ran into him in the library earlier and he was horribly rude to me."

"Why? What did you do?"

Georgie's mouth fell open for the second time that day. "What did *I* do?" she repeated in outrage.

"Well? Out with it," Jules persisted.

"I did nothing!" Georgie said, keeping her voice low and urgent, for they were almost in the dining room. "He was lurking in a dark corner of the library, and I didn't know he was there. I walked into him—which is akin to walking into a brick wall, I might add—and the impact threw me off my feet. There I was, sprawled on the floor in front of him, utterly humiliated and all he did was stare at me like I was something unpleasant he'd stepped in."

"Really?" Jules said, looking thoroughly entertained.

"Yes, *really*," she said, flushing with embarrassment as she remembered. "He didn't even offer me a hand to get up."

"Why not? What did he say?"

Georgie rolled her eyes at him. "He said he would have offered, but he wanted to ensure I wouldn't swoon at the thought of touching him, or some such nonsense."

A thoughtful expression flitted over Jules' face as he considered this.

"What?" she demanded, but they lost any further chance at conversation as they had to find their places.

"I'll speak to you another time, George," Jules promised cryptically.

Frustrated and curious, Georgie had to be satisfied… until she turned to discover she was seated next to the Duke of Rochford.

Rochford smirked inwardly as he saw the young woman look at the place cards, scowl, and look up at him.

Yes, my pretty little dove, they've sat you next to the mangy cur and there's damn all you can do about it.

He watched, admitting himself impressed, as she gathered herself, put up her chin and moved to her place.

"Good evening, your grace," she said with impeccable politeness, drawing out the honorific with such emphasis that he wanted to smile. She curtsied, offering him a peek of her splendid décolletage and, for a moment, Rochford forgot anything resembling manners, too riveted by the sight and a lurid daydream about burying his face there. She looked up, catching him ogling her like some panting, overheated schoolboy. He felt bad about it until he remembered the way she'd sprung away from him like he'd the pox. Anger and resentment overtook any feelings of guilt and he leered at her, ensuring she was not in doubt she'd been right in thinking him a vile monster. She stiffened and refused to look at him again.

Rochford endured the evening, as he'd known would be inevitable. Everyone here was related or an old friend of the family, and the atmosphere was warm and convivial. The conversation flitted past him, witty and fast-paced and covering many eclectic topics. But Rochford let the noise wash over him. It was always this way, with him on the outside even if he was in the centre of a crowd. Once upon a time, it had bothered him. Once upon a time, he'd been fool enough to try to belong. No longer. With an inward sigh, he wondered if he might have been better off alone at Mulcaster than sitting through weeks of evenings like this. A chill ran down his spine as he considered returning to the castle alone. No. No, this was far from perfect, but it was better than that.

"—then Rochford stepped in and saved my sorry arse."

"Jules! Language," the duchess scolded, though her eyes danced with mirth.

Jules grinned at her, not looking the least bit chastised. "Sorry, Mama, but it's true, I swear. Isn't it, Rochford?"

Rochford glanced up, discomforted, to find everyone at the table looking at him.

"If it's coming from your lips, I highly doubt it," he muttered, concentrating on cutting up a slice of roast beef.

A murmur of laughter rippled around the room.

"A fair remark, but all the same, they outnumbered me five to one, and the fellows were cut-throats to a man, I swear. I thought my number was up, I don't mind telling you."

"Oh, Jules, have a care for your poor mother!" the duchess said with agitation, swiping up her wineglass and taking an unladylike swallow.

"There, there, Prue. He survived and was a deal wiser for the experience," Bedwin said, from the other end of the table.

"Anyway, Rochford arrived like an incoming tide," Jules said, apparently enjoying himself enormously. "For a moment, I wasn't certain what side he was on, as he didn't look exactly friendly himself, but then… *then…* he picked the first fellow up, over his head, and flung him halfway across the room. I swear to God, I've never seen the like before or since."

The entire room fell silent, gawping at Rochford, and his skin prickled with unease. Well, let them look. They looked and saw a great beast capable of violence and destruction, and why not? He *was* capable of such behaviour, right enough. Fighting their expectations certainly didn't get him anywhere.

"What happened next, Jules?" his sister, Lady Rosamund, asked with wide eyes.

"The other fellows took one look at Rochford and ran away," Jules said, laughing. "So I bought him a drink to thank him for his help, and the surly devil took a liking to me."

"I never did. You just won't take no for an answer," Rochford grumbled.

"Ah, there he is, my dearest pal." Jules gestured affectionately across the table towards him.

Rochford shook his head in exasperation and returned his attention to his dinner. A moment later, he felt the unmistakable sensation of being scrutinised, one which he would usually ignore. People always stared at him and whispered to each other, and he was past caring what they thought. Yet this time the sensation nagged, and he turned to discover the woman at his side studying him. He glowered back at her.

"Thank you," she said.

Rochford sat back, surprised. "For?" he demanded, wondering if it was a trick.

"For keeping Jules out of trouble," she said, and Rochford felt a surge of resentment for the familiar way she spoke about his friend.

He wondered if perhaps there was an understanding between them and had to batter down an unwelcome flood of bitterness. She was beautiful and well-bred, no doubt an ideal bride for the handsome young man. Blackstone had told him she was Lady Georgina Anderson, daughter of the Earl of Morven, though whoever had the raising of her had been wise enough to work the Scottish accent from her speech. The *ton* did not tolerate such differences, like a face that was scarred and twisted. Irritated by her gratitude, though he did not understand why, Rochford turned to look at her.

"He was a damned fool for going to such a place."

She stared at him, narrowing her eyes. "Perhaps he was. I was only thanking you for your kindness in helping him."

"I didn't do it to be kind."

Her gaze upon him was steady. He had to give her credit for that, for unless they were whispering about him from a safe distance, most women would not meet his eye.

"Then why?"

"I knew Bedwin would owe me a debt of gratitude if I saved his heir's neck."

He watched her, waiting for her contemptuous expression, when she realised he'd done it for his own gain and not out of any sense of fair play.

"Well," she said, after a long moment. "Whatever your motivation, I am grateful for it." She returned her attention to her dinner and did not speak another word to him all evening.

Chapter 3

Evening of the 7th of December 1840, Beverwyck, London.

Evie hesitated at the top of the stairs as she heard muffled voices from below. Footmen spoke in hushed tones before walking off and going about their business. She held her breath, cursing to herself as her stomach rumbled ominously. Drat the thing, if her stomach made a racket and got her caught, that would just be typical of her luck. She'd barely eaten a thing at dinner, which had been utter misery as she'd watched all the mouth-watering courses come and go, but she was determined to do her best. Louis had promised to fix the horrid pink gown she was wearing, or burn it, but if she were just a few pounds lighter, it would make the job much easier, surely?

Evie waited until she was certain the servants had carried on their way, then picked up her skirts and ran down the steps, the material billowing and rustling as she went. She could not help but grin as she ran through the darkened corridors and rooms on the way to the library. There were stunningly beautiful women of all ages who would go to extreme lengths to be alone with Louis César and here she was, plain little Evie Knight, meeting him in private. Of course, there was nothing the least bit romantic in their meeting, but it amused her to imagine their reaction should any of those women discover it. Not that they ever would. No one must ever know, for it would be a shocking scandal and then poor Louis would have to marry her. That would never do, though she wished she could find a nice, kind woman who would love and care for him as he deserved. She had tried, but no one ever seemed to be quite right. Yet, anyway. But surely there must be someone for him. Georgie, for example, was very kind and loving, and the sight of Louis had certainly made an impression on her. Evie remembered her friend's stunned expression with amusement.

She quickened her steps as she reached the library door and, with one last furtive look over her shoulder, she slipped inside.

It was dark, apart from the warm glow cast from the hearth, where a fire burned low.

"Louis?" she whispered. As there was no answer, she moved towards the fire to wait for him. A few minutes later, the ornate grandfather clock that stood in the entrance hall chimed the hour as the door opened silently and a tall figure entered the room.

"Louis!" Evie exclaimed, and ran to him, hugging him tight.

"Evie, you little wretch," he said with a sigh as his arms closed around her. "You nearly did that earlier in front of everyone and set them all talking."

"I know, I am sorry," she said sheepishly. "Only it's been months and months, and I've missed you."

"I've missed you too, *ma petite*." He hugged her briefly before letting her go. "Now, let us have a proper look at this offensive gown and see what we can do with it."

Evie waited, holding onto a chair as she felt a little lightheaded. She was curious to know what on earth he had in mind for the ugly gown she was wearing. Louis crouched by the fire to light a taper and then went and lit the lamps. When he was satisfied there was enough light, he turned back to her. As they had done earlier, his brows drew together. Well, it *was* an ugly gown.

"Evie? Are you certain you are quite well?" he asked, moving closer to her.

"Yes, of course," she said, impatient to know his opinion of her horrid pink dress. "Now, what do you think of it? Isn't it vile?"

She turned in a circle to give him a good look and gasped as the room tilted.

"Evie!"

Strong arms caught her around the waist, and Louis hauled her against his muscular, warm body. Evie gasped in shock, still too dazed to respond, as he lifted her as though she weighed nothing, which was certainly not true.

"I—" she said, disorientated and giddy. She put her hands to her temples and closed her eyes, too weak to protest as Louis carried her and laid her carefully down upon a settee.

"*Merde!* What the devil have you been up to, you little fool?" he demanded, his voice hard and angrier than she had ever heard it.

"Nothing!" she protested, not understanding what she'd done to deserve such a scold.

"*Rien!*" he retorted, shaking his head. "That is a lie. You barely ate a mouthful at dinner, and don't tell me otherwise, for I was watching. You've lost weight, far too much, and you're so pale. *Mon Dieu*, Evie, what were you thinking?"

Evie's eyes prickled with embarrassment and humiliation at his words. "W-Why shouldn't I try to lose weight? Everyone else does it and Madame Blanchet said—"

"Madame Blanchet? She told you to starve yourself? Well the wretched woman can go to the devil, and so I shall tell her," he raged, his eyes sparking blue fire.

"Oh, no! No, Louis, you must not," she said, reaching out to clasp his arm. "Think of the scandal. It's not at all appropriate."

His expression was rather daunting as he turned on her, for she had never seen him angry with her. "And since when do you give a damn about propriety? You are here alone with a man who could ruin you, and do you care?"

Evie put her chin up. "You would never hurt me."

"So much you know," he said savagely, tugging his arm free and walking away from her. He stood staring down at the fire, his shoulders rigid.

"Louis?" she said, uncertain now, never having encountered her friend in this kind of mood before. There was a long silence, followed by a muttered curse. Louis ran a hand through his hair and then turned back to her.

"I am sorry, Evie," he said, his voice low. "I beg you will forgive me. I ought never have spoken to you so harshly."

"It was nothing, please, let us forget it..." she began, but Louis crossed the floor and knelt beside her, taking her hand.

"Non! It is not nothing, and neither is that dreadful woman making you feel anything less than beautiful nothing. She has no right to make you unhappy, and neither do I. My only defence is that it makes me furious to see you make yourself ill, and for what? To look like another dull little debutante, just like all the others, when the world already has its fill of those."

Evie felt her eyes burn again and looked away, embarrassed. She had long been accustomed to being the plain, plump one among a bevy of beautiful women, but to have to discuss it with Louis… How mortifying. Yet, he was her dearest friend, and who else would she speak to?

"I was j-just tired of the constant comments. 'Oh, Evie, you'd be so much prettier if only you'd lose some weight.' 'Oh, Evie, I found the most wonderful diet—I've lost six pounds, you must try it!' 'Oh, Evie, do you think you ought to have another piece of cake? It's dreadfully fattening.'"

She blinked hard as her vision blurred, startled to hear a volley of furious French as Louis muttered beneath his breath.

"What?"

"Nothing," he said, his voice terse.

She waited as he took a deep breath and let it out again. Despite her best efforts, she felt a tear slide down her cheek. Louis saw it and his jaw set again, but he reached out and wiped it away, his touch gentle.

"Evie, do you trust me?"

"Of course, I do. You know I do."

He snorted and shook his head. *"Oui,* far more than you should, *ma petite,* but if you trust me, you will heed my words and believe them. Do you promise?"

Evie frowned. "Well, I shall try, but I don't know what they are yet."

Louis shook his head. "That is not how this works. You will listen, and you will believe me, because I am telling you the truth. You are every bit as beautiful as any woman you wish to compare yourself with."

Evie let out a huff of laughter. Well, if he was going to be silly about it….

"I am serious," he said, and her breath caught at the anger in his eyes. "You. Are. Beautiful. Inside and out, and anyone who cannot see that does not deserve a moment of your time, and certainly not your tears."

It was hard not to believe his words whilst those blue eyes stared at her with such sincerity, but Evie could not help but feel sceptical. She was a practical girl, after all, and aware of her own attributes. That's not to say she had none. She knew she was fun to be with and could hold an intelligent conversation, and she had pretty eyes and hair, and she'd be an excellent wife and companion to anyone who wished to marry her. But to suggest she could compare to the great beauties of the *ton* was simply ridiculous. She knew Louis meant she was a beautiful person because he thought she was kind-hearted, but that was not at all the same thing. She simply wasn't the type who made men wild with desire or prompted them to write sonnets or fight duels. Not that she wanted anyone to fight a duel on her account, for that would be horrible, but it would be nice to see *some* evidence of desire or jealousy. She had seen the possessive looks on the faces of Arabella's and Florence's husbands, the pride and the heat in their eyes as they looked upon their beloveds. It would be nice to think some man might feel like that for her one day, but she felt a little dubious, no matter Louis' words.

"You don't believe me, do you?" Louis said, his tone flat.

Evie gave a rueful smile. "I believe you are fond enough of me to see me with a kinder eye than most, and I am grateful for it, but please, Louis, let us speak of something else. What are we to do about this wretched dress?"

Louis sighed, shaking his head. "Very well. Can you stand without swooning?" he asked, his tone a little impatient.

Evie nodded, so he gave her his hand and helped her up. Louis stood back and muttered something that did not sound complimentary about the dress as he walked around her, studying the gown from all angles.

"I hate pink," Evie said, wishing she didn't look such a wretched sight.

He shook his head, studying her. *"Non,* I disagree with that, at least. The colour is good. You have a complexion most women would kill for, all that creamy white skin and here…." He moved closer to touch a finger to her cheek. "The faintest flush of rose," he murmured.

Evie flushed a deal harder at his words. The way the French rolled the r on rose was rather delicious after all. Louis smirked. "Not so faint."

"Well, perhaps the colour isn't to blame, but it's still dreadful," Evie grumbled, folding her arms about her middle and feeling increasingly self-conscious.

Louis took her wrists, uncrossing her arms and staring at her bust and midriff with such concentration she wanted to die of embarrassment.

"Louis," she said, uncomfortable.

"The cut is all wrong," he said, interrupting her. "This neckline is far too high and unflattering. It does not make the most of your assets."

"My… what?"

"Your assets," Louis repeated impatiently.

"Do I have, er… assets?" she asked doubtfully.

Louis tsked, giving her an incredulous glance. "Your bust is magnificent, Evie, and it's being hidden beneath that high neck when it ought to be on display. I cannot understand what the woman was thinking. Perhaps she was jealous."

Evie snorted in amusement, too entertained to be scandalised by the comment. "I hardly think—"

"What kind of corset are you wearing?"

"Wh—" Evie began, and then gave up, staring at him in outrage. "You cannot ask me that!" she whispered, stunned.

Louis rolled his eyes. "You wanted my advice, my help, *oui*? Well, whatever is under that dress is not doing what it ought. *Tiens,* never mind. You must send me your measurements and I shall deal with that too."

"But—"

"Hush." Louis silenced her as he stood back, contemplating.

Obediently, Evie hushed, too confounded to say another word. Louis studied her critically.

"The cut of this neckline needs to be low, and these dreadful frills must go. They are all wrong for you. You need a much simpler style, with some small pleats for emphasis, I think… *Oui,* that run from the shoulders to here."

Evie blinked, a little stunned, as he traced a line in mid-air, from her shoulder to low on her décolletage.

"There?" she squealed in alarm. "I'll fall out of it!"

"No, you will not," he assured her.

"B-But everyone will stare at me," she protested, flushing hot as she considered the idea.

Louis shrugged. *"Oui, naturellement."*

"I'm really not sure—"

"You said you trusted me," he replied, watching her with unnerving intensity.

"I do. Of course, I do, but…" Evie sighed at the implacable look in his eyes. "Oh. Very well."

"You will have the gown sent to my room and I will see to the alterations."

"Yes, Louis."

He nodded, apparently satisfied. The sound of the clock chiming one, echoed in the distance. Evie sighed in disappointment. "I suppose I had better go to bed."

"*Non*, not yet," Louis said, taking her firmly by the hand and leading her to the door.

"Where are we going?" she asked, brightening to think the evening was not yet over, and curious to know what he had in mind.

Louis looked over his shoulder at her, a determined glint in his eyes. "To get you something to eat."

🎩 🎩 🎩

8th December 1840, Beverwyck, London.

Georgie came down late to breakfast the next morning after a luxurious lie in. Nearly everyone but Evie had already been and gone ages ago, but she was content enough, sipping a cup of delicious hot chocolate. She gave a little sigh of pleasure and licked her lips, setting the cup down and turning to Evie, who was smothering a yawn.

"Did you not sleep well?" George asked her in concern.

Evie flushed and returned a nervous smile. "Umm, no, not very well. All the excitement I expect."

"I slept like the dead. Meg had to shake me to wake me up, or I'd still be snoring," Georgie said, grinning, though her smile faded as she noticed the Duke of Rochford sit down at the opposite end of the table. He was scowling at her. She resisted the temptation to stick her tongue out at him and returned her attention to Evie.

"Aunt Prue said I might go to the kitchens and make shortbread. Do you want to come?"

Evie bit her lip. "Actually, I have a bit of a headache. I might go for a walk and get some fresh air. Clear the cobwebs away."

Georgie nodded. "As you wish. I hope you feel better."

Evie smiled and got up, leaving the table. Georgie reached for a fresh bread roll and tore it in half. She had buttered one side and begun on the other before she realised Rochford was still there.

"You cook?" he asked, surprising her.

She had assumed he would ignore her and had been quite happy with that. Conversing with him did not seem wise, but she could hardly refuse to answer a direct question.

"I do."

He frowned at her, apparently unhappy with this answer. "Why? You are the daughter of an earl. If you want something, you need only snap your pretty fingers."

"And do aristocratic men *need* to go out and shoot birds and deer?" she countered.

He waved this away with disregard. "It is not considered a respectable hobby for a lady, I think. It is too menial."

Georgie stared back at him. "I don't care. I enjoy it."

His thick, dark brows drew together.

She gave a tut of irritation. "If the *ton* suddenly disapproved of men hunting, would you stop?"

"I don't hunt anyway, so I should not care."

She stared at him in surprise.

"You don't hunt?" The surprise in her voice was audible.

He shot her a contemptuous look. "No doubt you imagine me murdering the wildlife with my bare hands, but no, my lady. I do not hunt."

The bitterness of his tone took her aback, and Georgie looked at him with interest. "You certainly look capable of doing that," she admitted. "But I do not understand why you should think I imagine you doing so."

"Do you not?" he said, and she wondered if he was really sneering at her, or if it was the scar at his lip that just gave that impression. She ignored his comment and concentrated on piling jam onto one half of the roll.

"I like to cook. It gives me pleasure, both to make things and to see people enjoy the results. Obviously, I do not need to do it, but I find it… soothing."

"Soothing?" he repeated. "What in God's name do you need soothing for? You're young and rich and beautiful. A charmed life, I would think."

Georgie glanced at him, wondering why he seemed so dreadfully cross with her when he did not know her at all. Though she noted he thought her beautiful and was alarmed by the little jolt of pleasure the words gave her. He was a peculiar fellow, this duke.

"Indeed, a charmed life. I am very fortunate, but so are you, I think."

His lip curled. This time it was deliberate, she was certain.

"Indeed," he echoed, a private note to his voice she could not decipher.

A footman appeared at her elbow to refill her cup of chocolate and she smiled, recognising the handsome young man. "Good morning. Roberts, isn't it?"

"Yes, my lady," he said, beaming at her, clearly pleased to be remembered.

"How are you settling in? You had not long been here when I last visited. Are you happy?"

Roberts flushed with pleasure at her inquiry. "Oh, yes, my lady. The duke and duchess are most kind and everyone has been very welcoming. I've been fortunate."

"And how is your mother? She was unwell, I think? I do hope she has recovered."

Roberts gaped at her in astonishment, but nodded. "Yes, my lady, she is fit as a flea—I mean, she's well, thank you. She'll be that made up to know you asked after her."

"Well, then I am glad on both counts," Georgie said, before thanking him for the chocolate.

Roberts moved away down the table and Georgie once again felt the weight of the duke's scrutiny. Heavens. Now what? She looked at him and raised her eyebrows.

"You ought not be so familiar with the staff," he said, his voice cold. "It causes problems."

"Problems for whom?" she demanded, matching his icy tone. "Not me."

"No. For them. For if they do not know where the line is, they overstep and jeopardise their situation."

"Perhaps in your employ, not in my mother's, nor my Aunt Prue's," she retorted.

He made an impatient sound. "They are not your friends. They work for you."

"That does not mean we must treat them as if they do not exist," Georgie snapped, her temper rising.

Her mother had instilled that lesson into her. Georgie knew, as her mother had discovered in her time, that it was not done to thank servants, or even acknowledge the fact that they existed. As the daughter of a vastly wealthy self-made man, the aristocracy had not accepted her mother, viewing her as an imposter in their select ranks. The *ton* had reviled her for her lack of breeding and laughed at her befriending the staff, implying that like was drawn to like. Despite this, she had refused to follow their lead and blend in by acting as they did. She had always known the names of her staff and whether they were happy or well, and as much about their families and situations as they wished to share. She also thanked her staff for a job well done. Every one of Georgie's father's great estates ran like clockwork, and the staff were happy and well-treated. That was down to her mother, so this pig-headed, mean-spirited duke was not about to change her mind or her ways.

"They will not respect you if you speak so freely with them. They'll take advantage. Did you not see the way that boy looked at you?"

Georgie blinked at him. "What way?" The duke made a disgusted sound and threw his napkin down on the table as he stood.

"Ignorant child," he muttered under his breath.

Georgie flushed. "I am not the least ignorant, and you are rude and unkind, and I don't care if you are a duke, you are not a gentleman."

Rochford snorted at that, staring at her for a long, uncomfortable moment. "No. I'm not."

He stalked out of the breakfast parlour without another word, leaving Georgie to seethe in his absence.

Rochford walked back towards Beverwyck, the frost hardened grass crunching beneath his boots. He was still simmering after his confrontation with Lady Georgina, though why she'd annoyed him so he could not fathom. She was just another brainless debutante, except this one had an urge to be a do-gooder. Her kindness would get her or a member of staff into trouble one day, but she'd not heed him, so he might have saved his breath.

A delicious scent drifted upon the cold air as he drew closer to the house. Rochford stopped, sniffing appreciatively. He'd been walking for some time, trying to shake off a growing sense of restlessness, and had found himself on the side of the house where the kitchens and utility buildings lay out of sight of the grander parts of the property. Not that they were shabby. Everything about Beverwyck was immaculate and revealed a sharp eye for beauty and detail. The sound of a door opening had him turning, and he muttered a curse as he saw Lady Georgina step outside. Typical. Just what he needed. He was considering ducking behind a well-placed oak tree in order to escape her when she looked up. She stiffened at the sight of him, a reaction which only irritated him further, though heaven alone knew why. It wasn't as if he wanted the blasted woman to *like* him. No one liked him. They respected him, feared him, and damn well did what he said, but they didn't like him. He didn't have friends who liked him. Well, apart from Blackstone, but he had a warped sense of humour and was somewhat eccentric, so he could be excused for his judgement, which was clearly unsound.

The kitchen was set on the lower floors and, as he could not now escape, Rochford waited as she climbed the stairs back up to ground level. Her cheeks were flushed from the heat of the kitchen and her thick, curling hair was escaping its pins on all sides. Rochford had a sudden and unwelcome vision of how she might look beneath him as she cried out in passion, her lovely skin pink for an entirely different reason. He stamped on the image at once, but it was too late and his body reacted, his skin feeling two sizes too small as desire flared with an accompanying rush of heat.

"The famous shortbread, I surmise," he said, jerking his head at the tin box she carried.

"Yes," she replied, looking wary, as well she might.

The scent of butter and sugar clung to her, and Rochford's mouth watered. Damn the shortbread, she looked good enough to eat.

She hesitated for a moment before tugging the lid off and offering the tin to him. "Try one."

"I don't like sweets," Rochford growled, aware he sounded ungrateful and churlish but unable to stop himself.

"Try anyway. You'll like these," she predicted, annoying him further.

He'd just told her he didn't have a sweet tooth, hadn't he? She waved the tin under his nose, clearly not about to take no for an answer. Rochford gave a long-suffering sigh and looked at the biscuits, which had been made in the shape of a thistle. He picked out a golden piece, studded all over with sugar, and put the whole thing in his mouth, chewing reluctantly. Butter and sweetness and a crumbly, rich texture filled his mouth, and it was all he could do not to moan with pleasure. He was damned if he'd let her know that, though. He scowled and shrugged.

"It's a biscuit."

She gave a derisive snort and glared at him in outrage. "It's not just *a biscuit.* It's shortbread!"

Rochford regarded her with amusement. He'd never guessed someone could get so furious over a biscuit.

"Shortbread is a superior biscuit. It is the king of biscuits and you enjoyed it, you're just being stubborn."

Rochford felt his eyebrows go up. "The king of biscuits?" he repeated sceptically.

She flushed harder but put up her chin. "Aye."

Ah, and there was the Scottish accent she hid, emerging because she was flustered.

"Aye," he repeated, smiling. It was a mistake. He'd not meant to mock her, but she clearly took it as such.

"Aye," she repeated, her voice louder and harder now as she crammed the lid back on the tin. "So awa' n bile yer heid!"

Rochford's mouth fell open, though he was uncertain whether he was more stunned by the thick Scottish accent or the fact she'd just told him to go boil his head. He had no opportunity to react or retaliate, though, as she turned and stalked away, and he could do nothing but watch the mesmerising sway of her glorious backside as she went.

Chapter 4

Dearest Aisling,

Do you remember when I last visited you and I joked about you making a love potion and you said such things really existed. Do they work? And could you make one? Only, I know how clever you are with herbs and medicines, and I just wondered because —

—Excerpt of a letter from The Lady Rosamund Adolphus (daughter of Robert and Prudence Adolphus, their graces, The Duke and Duchess of Bedwin) to Lady Aisling Baxter (daughter of Luke and Kitty Baxter, The Earl and Countess of Trevick).

8th December 1840, Beverwyck, London.

The rude, aggravating, impossible man! Georgie seethed all the way back to her room, flinging the tin of shortbread down and snatching at the ribbons of her bonnet.

"Stop tugging at them like that, ye'll get them all fankled," Meg scolded, moving closer to smack her hands away.

Georgie huffed but stood like an obedient child as Meg removed her bonnet and took her coat. Her maid gave her a squint-eyed look and correctly interpreted her mood.

"What's got ye crabbit now? You were in a fine mood when ye went down the stairs."

"Rochford," Georgie said, folding her arms.

"Ach, he's a fine, big fellow, so he is," Meg said with a dreamy sigh. "A face like a slapped arse, I grant ye, but ye need not look at him in the dark, hen."

"Meg!" Georgie exclaimed. She was well used to Meg's rather forthright manner of speech, but still.

Meg looked back at her, all innocence. "What? Don't tell me he doesn't get your heart going pitty-patty when ye consider those big, brawny arms about ye. Why he could lift ye like a feather, and there are few men ye can say that about, for you're a fine, braw lassie, but no delicate flower."

Georgie ignored the observation about her stature, having heard it often enough before. "He's rude and arrogant and the most annoying man that ever walked the earth!"

"Give him something better to do than flap his gums, then. I could think of better uses for his—"

"That's enough," Georgie cut in, horrified.

Meg smirked, sashaying off with her bonnet and pelisse to put them away. Good heavens, what a thought. Her and Rochford, of all men. Georgie shook her head, incredulous at the idea of kissing a man like Rochford, at the thought of those muscular arms going around her, that huge, powerful body pressed to hers. She imagined those cold grey eyes staring at her with warmth, and that overbearing man who looked like a brutal warrior treating her with gentleness and affection. A surge of heat swept over her, stealing her breath and making her feel giddy. Good Lord. Surely, she couldn't be attracted to that bad-tempered devil. No. That was… it couldn't… it wasn't possible.

Oh no!

Georgie sat down on the bed with a thud and tested the theory again, cautiously imagining the duke of Rochford sweeping her into his arms and kissing her. With horror, she realised her heart was racing, a fine prickle of sweat flushing her skin, and a strange aching sensation had begun deep inside her.

Oh, dear heaven. This was a disaster. Rochford? Of all men, she had to find herself wanting that great ill-mannered oaf? Georgie groaned and put her head in her hands. This was bad. This was very, very bad.

Gathering herself, Georgie took a deep breath. Very well. She was utterly deranged and found the great ox appealing. It wasn't the end of the world. She just needed to stay away from him and ensure they were never in close proximity, never alone together. Besides which, he clearly couldn't stand the sight of her. He thought she was a mannerless, ignorant hoyden, *and* he'd mocked her accent when it had slipped, the beast. So, unless she threw herself at him—which she was certainly *not* going to do—she ought to be safe enough.

Comforted by the thought, Georgie steeled her spine and went back downstairs.

She found the family in their favourite parlour, one which they only allowed very close friends to enter. All the furniture was comfortable and worn just enough to make it clear this was a well-used space. Books and magazines littered the tabletops, and drawing pencils and sketchbooks lay abandoned next to half-finished pieces of needlework. It was warm and cosy, especially as the bright morning had gradually clouded over into a grey late afternoon, and a fine drizzle of rain fell as the daylight waned.

Everyone was playing charades, and Ozzie had just begun her turn, with everyone shouting at once and giving completely opposing suggestions.

Georgie grinned as she entered, amused to see everyone taking part. Everyone except for Rochford. He stood apart, leaning back against the low windowsill, watching the proceedings with a frown. She got the impression he hadn't the least idea what was going on.

"Turning," Jules shouted at Ozzie, who threw up her hands in frustration. "Well, you are turning round and round," Jules retorted.

"Dizzy?" Aunt Prue suggested.

"Lost! She's lost," seven-year-old Harry said.

Aunt Prue ruffled his hair affectionately. "What a good guess!"

Georgie looked back at Rochford. He'd crossed his muscular arms over his chest and was still scowling. Like a big angry bear. Yet, the longer she looked, Georgie could not help but wonder if he was more puzzled than angry. It was so hard to tell when he appeared so fierce all the time, and that scar gave him a look of permanent disdain, making him dreadfully intimidating. Despite her annoyance with him for mocking her earlier, and in opposition of her better judgement, Georgie went to stand beside him.

He straightened at the sight of her, his arms falling to his sides.

"Have you never played charades?" she asked.

Rochford returned an incredulous expression.

"No," he said, terse as ever, confirming her suspicions.

She wondered at that. How could he never have played? It was such a common pastime.

"Not even as a boy?"

He snorted. "Especially not as a boy."

Georgie frowned. "Why not?"

She was unsurprised by the impatient huff of irritation but stared at him, awaiting his answer.

"I inherited the title when I was seven years old. Dukes don't play games. They've more important things to occupy themselves with."

"At seven years old?" she returned incredulously, before pointing at the Duke of Bedwin, who was trying to guess the charade with as much enthusiasm as everyone else.

Rochford shrugged, and the sight of those enormous shoulders rolling momentarily diverted Georgie's attention as the muscles shifted beneath his tight-fitting coat.

"My home bore little resemblance to his one."

"You've *never* played charades?"

He shook his head.

"You must have played games, though?" she pressed, appalled at the idea of a childhood with no games.

"I played hide and seek," he admitted, but there was a darkly amused look in his eyes that unsettled her.

"Oh?"

"Oh, yes. I hid from my mother's lover, so he couldn't thrash me for putting maggots in his tea or dead mice in his boots."

Georgie stared at him.

"Yes," he replied dryly, sneering. "I'm certain you are not shocked to discover I was just as charming and ugly as a boy as I am now, though I didn't get the measles until I was six, and the scar not long after that."

The words *you're not ugly* burned on Georgie's tongue, but she didn't know how to say them. It seemed far too intimate, and this man already posed a threat of sorts. She must not encourage any familiarity between them. Yet, she considered a boy of seven losing his father. No wonder he had taken it out on his mother's lover. Why had he even known the man existed so soon after his father's death? Hadn't his mother protected him? He must have been so angry and confused. Compassion stirred in her breast, but she pushed it aside. A man like this would hardly thank her for such sympathy. He had obviously crushed any feeling of tenderness or sympathy a long time ago. So, instead, she ignored his comments.

"Well, it's easy enough to play," she said briskly. "The player, or players, choose a title of a book or play, or perhaps a nursery rhyme or a saying, and then they must try to act out the words in a way that the others in their team can guess it. I think Lady Rosamund said hers has two words and is the title of a book."

Rochford frowned, watching as Lady Rosamund mimed screwing a corkscrew into a bottle.

"Twist," he said. "Oliver Twist."

"Oh!" Georgie exclaimed, staring at him in delight and then calling out. "Oliver Twist!"

Ozzie exclaimed in relief. "Oh, thank goodness. Well done, Georgie."

"Oh, it wasn't me," Georgie replied, giving Rochford a wicked grin. "It was his grace."

Rochford shook his head. "No," he said, his tone brooking no argument as he realised the dreadful creature had set him up. Revenge, he didn't doubt, for mocking her accent. Not that he had been. He'd thought it charming, but it was obviously a sore spot and he'd hit it.

"Don't be such a stick in the mud," she said, rolling her eyes. Her expression softened, and she lowered her voice. "It's fun. Come on, Rochford, I'll help you if you like. We can do it together."

For the briefest moment temptation shimmered at the thought of doing anything with Lady Georgina but making a complete twat of himself in front of the entire household was not an occupation that appealed.

"Forget it. I'll not make an arse of myself for your entertainment, much as you might like to make a fool of me," he said coldly, and stalked away from her and out of the room. Irritation simmered under his skin, and he strode along the corridor towards the front door. He needed to get outside, into the fresh air, and away from all these bloody people.

"Don't you run away from me, you pig-headed devil."

Rochford's steps faltered at the sound of the imperious voice echoing down the corridor. He turned, admitting himself astonished to discover Lady Georgina had followed him—and had called him a pig-headed devil.

"Are you going to instruct me to boil my head again?" he asked dryly.

She flushed but did not back down, instead closing the distance between them.

"Quite possibly," she retorted. "But I want a word with you first. Are you really so high in the instep that you cannot lower yourself to have fun with these people? The duke and duchess were playing, for heaven's sake, or do you consider yourself better than them?"

It took a deal of effort not to laugh in her face at the idea he might consider himself better than the Duke and Duchess of Bedwin. Everyone liked and admired the duke and duchess, and people were happy to laugh with them if they chose to behave foolishly. If Rochford did it, he'd be crucified. He knew that well enough.

"I don't want to play the fool game," he snapped, for he was hardly going to articulate any other motivation for running away.

The woman stared at him, studying him. No one ever looked at him so directly. "Very well. If it makes you so uncomfortable, you need not take part, but do come back to the parlour."

There was a softer look in her eyes now, one that looked horribly like sympathy. Understanding. *Damn her.* He'd not be treated like a child.

"Why should I?" he snapped, too angry to moderate his voice.

She hesitated and Rochford snorted, aware she could not think of a good reason. The soft look vanished abruptly, and she scowled at him, which was a blessed relief. "Because you should be with everyone else. I feel quite certain you spend more than enough time on your own."

"That's because I prefer my own company to that of a pack of damned fools," he retorted, before he could think better of it. Naturally, the words offended her, as they'd been meant to do, but now he wished he could take them back as her face shuttered up.

"Well, if you despise us all so, I wonder you came at all," she threw back, tossing her head as she turned and stalked away from him.

"Hell and the devil! Wait, damn you," he said, striding after her.

"Why? So you can insult me and the people I care about some more? No, I think not."

Rochford clenched his fists in frustration. "Argh, you blasted hellcat! I—I didn't mean it."

Her footsteps slowed but didn't stop.

Rochford gnashed his teeth, but there was obviously no other option. "I'm *sorry,*" he ground out, incensed at having to apologise to the chit.

She stopped and turned to look at him.

"For?" she pressed.

For a moment, he toyed with the idea of throwing her over his shoulder and depositing her in the nearest body of water, preferably a lake, but that would only lead to another apology.

"For calling you all a pack of fools. I didn't mean it. Well, Blackstone is a bloody fool, but he'd tell you that himself."

Rochford studied her, waiting to see if he'd humiliated himself enough to gain her forgiveness, though why the hell it mattered he didn't know. He thought perhaps her lips twitched at his words, but he couldn't be certain.

She nodded, apparently accepting his apology. "Thank you."

As they stood staring at each other, the atmosphere prickled and became increasingly awkward.

"Well, then," he said gruffly. "I'll see you tomorrow."

He turned to leave, desperate to get away before the situation became utterly intolerable. The sooner he got outside in the cold, the better.

"Wait," she said, reaching out and grasping his sleeve.

Rochford froze, staring down at her slender hand upon his arm. She wore no gloves, and he saw her fingers were long and elegant, the nails buffed to a shine. He looked up, his gaze meeting hers, and she snatched her hand away as if she'd been burned.

"I… umm," she dithered, and he wondered what she was looking so uneasy about. Her cheeks were flushed, but he could not fathom why. "Aren't you coming to the rout party tonight?"

Rochford's eyebrows went up. "I don't go to parties," he said tersely, wondering if she was mocking him. Everyone knew he didn't go to such events.

"Why not?"

He scowled at her. Surely, she was taunting him. "Do you think I would find it entertaining to stand about while all the pretty debutantes squeal and pretend to swoon if I glance in their direction?"

"Good heavens, no," she said, looking genuinely appalled. "They don't, do they?"

Rochford studied her. Did she really not know he was about as welcome as a dose of the clap at *ton* events? Angry now, he closed the gap between them, staring down at her.

"Look at my face, Lady Georgina. What would you expect the young ladies to do on seeing it?"

He had to give her credit, she did not flinch away from him but studied his face intently. He knew it was ugly. Christ, he'd been told often enough without the evidence of his own eyes. The ragged scar twisted the skin of his face, pulling at his mouth and eye. If that wasn't bad enough, what skin wasn't scarred was pockmarked. Thank the lord he could grow a thick beard, which hid most of it, but the hair was sparse both there and above his ear where the scar ran through it. Yes, he was a pretty sight, was he not?

"I admit it—it is striking at first sight, so I suppose it ought not surprise me they stare. I am perhaps guilty of doing so to begin with, but anything more than that is simply foolishness and shows a lack of intelligence."

To Rochford's utter astonishment, she reached a hand up, as if to touch him. He grabbed her wrist before she could and she gasped, her gaze flying to his. Fleetingly he saw fear waver there, and he expected her to snatch her wrist free, but she relaxed in his hold, making him feel foolish for the second time that day.

"Are you really so terrified of a mere female? I would not scratch your eyes out, you know. No matter how provoking you are."

Perplexed, Rochford let her go. Her hand hung suspended in mid-air, and then she closed the space, tracing the ragged line of the scar that deeply scored the right side of his face. His breath caught and held, his lungs trapped in a vice as emotions he neither recognised nor welcomed ran riot inside him. Her touch was gentle, so careful, and he wasn't certain if he wanted to howl with rage or weep for the feelings she stirred inside him.

"You were lucky not to lose your eye," she observed, studying the scar, her voice soft.

"Yes. Lucky," he replied bitterly, though he could not have moved if his life depended on it, bespelled by the gentle warmth of her fingertips.

"It's really not so fearsome," she said, and then her whisky coloured eyes met his. "And I think perhaps… neither are you."

Longing exploded inside him, so fierce and overwhelming that it terrified him. He'd spent too much of his life learning not to want or need anyone. He was damned if he'd start now and let this sly chit get under his skin. Who the hell did she think she was, touching his scars and looking at him as if he didn't repel her? Well, she might be a damned fine actress—all those years playing bloody charades, no doubt—but she didn't fool him. Rochford pushed her hand away and stepped back, putting distance between them.

"I don't go to balls, and I don't suffer fools, Lady Georgina, so whatever little game it is you're playing at, forget it. If you're angling to be my duchess, you're barking up the wrong bloody tree. I won't marry you, so cast your lures elsewhere."

"My lures?" she repeated faintly, blinking up at him as if she'd just snapped out of a trance. "You think I…."

A blush scalded her fair skin, so fierce he could feel the heat of it rising from her.

He frowned, mystified once again by this bewildering woman, for he *knew* she couldn't have been sincere.

She put her chin up.

"You really are an obnoxious arse," she said, and hurried away from him.

But not before he'd seen the tears in her eyes.

Rochford stood there for a long moment after she'd gone. He hadn't the faintest idea what had just happened, though the realisation that he'd behaved badly—again—was more unwelcome than usual. He always *acted* like an obnoxious arse and, he reminded himself, he didn't give a damn for the consequences. Except, it seemed like he gave a damn this time and that… that was troubling. No, not troubling, it was bloody unnerving.

Gingerly, he raised his hand to his cheek, to the place where her fingers had lingered so carefully. He let out an uneven breath, wondering what the hell it all meant, before turning on his heel and hurrying outside.

Chapter 5

Dearest Cat,

I hope this letter finds you well. Are you having a splendid time this Christmas? We are. Eliza and Lottie are both back at Beverwyck with their husbands, and we have Georgie and Evie staying, too, as well as Aggie. She sends her love, by the way. I hope we get to see you soon.

Everyone is off to a rout party this evening, but at least Victoria and Aggie and I may stay up late and play games instead of going to bed like the babies.

—Excerpt of a letter from The Lord Frederick Adolphus (younger son of Their Graces, Robert and Prunella Adolphus, Duke and Duchess of Bedwin) to The Lady Catherine Barrington (daughter of Lucian and Matilda Barrington, The Most Hon'ble Marquess and Marchioness of Montagu).

8th December 1840, Beverwyck, London.

Georgie stalked back to the parlour, as cross as a baited badger. Oh, the nerve of the man. And to think she'd been feeling sorry for him, the aggravating lout. Well, good. At least now she could put aside any unruly and inappropriate feelings for him. Currently, the only thing she wanted to do to him was hit him with a heavy blunt object, not that it would dent his thick skull. Still, it was all for the good, for there had been a disconcerting moment when she had stood looking up at him, her fingers tracing the line of that ugly scar. She had been certain they'd had a connection, that for a moment she had glimpsed beneath the angry façade and what she'd seen had made her heart ache, had made her want to kiss him. Thank God she hadn't acted on it. The horrid creature would have believed it proof positive she was trying to seduce him for his title! As if she'd want to spend the rest of her days tied to a fiend like that.

Everyone looked up, staring at her as she flounced back into the room. It took her a moment to realise she had done nothing to disguise her fury. Her cheeks were flushed with irritation and she no doubt looked ready to do murder—after having flown from the room in pursuit of the Duke of Rochford.

Oh.

Deciding it was best to go on the offensive, she turned on Jules. "What were you thinking, inviting that beastly man to come for Christmas?" she demanded.

Jules' eyebrows flew up. "I didn't want him to be on his own," he said, candid as ever.

Georgie huffed and folded her arms. "Perhaps there's a good reason he's alone," she groused, aware she hardly sounded as if she was full of goodwill to all men. Though she was, she truly was, just… all men *except* the Duke of Rochford.

"Undoubtedly," Jules agreed, watching her with interest but offering nothing more concrete.

"He's too bloody proud to even join in a game of charades," she said, brushing irritably at a curl of hair that had escaped its pins. "He can see Uncle Robert playing, but no… he won't lower himself."

"Perhaps he's shy," Aunt Prue suggested mildly.

A tea tray had arrived in Georgie's absence and the duchess was pouring out steaming cups.

Georgie stared at her. "*Shy?*"

For a moment she considered the duke, all six foot seven of him. He was hardly slow in telling her how she ought to behave. He wasn't shy about that, now, was he? Nor was he shy in calling her friends a pack of fools, or accusing her of wanting to marry him for his title.

"He's not shy," she muttered crossly.

Aunt Prue handed her a cup, made just how Georgie liked it. "Then, perhaps he doesn't know how to play games."

Georgie gave a reluctant shrug. "He doesn't. He said he never played games as a child."

"The poor man. How dreadfully sad," her aunt said, watching Georgie intently. "I wonder what kind of life he's had, to be so alone, and not know how to play games?"

"A bloody awful one, from the bits I've pieced together over the years," Jules said, his expression thoughtful. "That's why I invited him. He's got this huge draughty castle down in the wilds of Cumbria, but he never speaks of family, and I know he hasn't any friends. Well, except me."

"Why *are* you friends, Jules?" Georgie asked, wondering how two such unlikely men could get along.

Jules shrugged, rubbing the back of his neck. "Ah, well. He's a good fellow underneath all that growling and bluster. You just have to persevere. He's not an easy man, I'll grant you. He's irascible and prickly, and bloody-minded and—good Lord, why *am* I friends with him?"

His mother laughed and reached over to ruffle his hair as if he was a small boy. "Because you have a kind heart," she said affectionately.

Jules grumbled and made a show of smoothing down his hair, but Georgie suspected he didn't really mind. She took her tea back to her chair and sat down, frowning into the golden liquid. With a sigh of frustration, she took a sip, and then another. By the time she'd finished, she didn't feel quite so out of sorts, just a bit… unsettled. Feeling eyes upon her, Georgie looked up to see her aunt was still watching her. Prue smiled.

"Perhaps the duke needs another chance," she suggested.

Georgie snorted at that. "I'm certain he's already had at least three, and I only met him yesterday."

Prue chuckled and set down her teacup. "Well, I think Rochford might need a lot of chances, perhaps to make up for all the ones he's missed until now."

Georgie groaned inwardly. Well, now she felt guilty, and the wretched man had been utterly vile. Surely she could be furious with him? Yes, she decided. She could certainly be furious with him, but… but perhaps Prue was right. Perhaps he deserved a few more chances. Just in case.

🎩 🎩 🎩

"Nobody wants me there, for the love of God. Why must you keep harping on about this damned party?" Rochford groaned.

His patience was wearing thin, but Blackstone seemed determined to break it entirely.

"In the first place, you ought to show your face in society now and then, because it might stop people from believing you are some mad beast who eats small children for breakfast."

Rochford snorted. "Well, that's a steaming pile of horse shite. What the devil do I care what they think? What's the second place? Get it over with, so we can abandon this farce, will you?"

Blackstone gave a long-suffering sigh, but carried on. "In the second place, I think perhaps there is someone who wants you there."

"If you say *you,* I'm going to toss your sorry carcass out the nearest window," Rochford warned, getting up and stalking to the whisky decanter.

They'd retired to the comfortable suite of rooms the duke and duchess had assigned him for his stay, and Blackstone had sprawled in a chair by the fire, looking every inch the pampered, indolent aristocrat.

"God, you're violent," Blackstone complained, tutting at him. "And of course I want you there, but—"

He made a staying motion as Rochford turned back to him with a challenging glint in his eye.

"—but that's not what I meant. I think Lady Georgina wants you there, too."

Rochford was so startled he nearly dropped the decanter and wasted a good deal of very fine whisky. "Have you lost your mind? The woman hates me."

"And why would that be?" Blackstone asked, his tone conversational.

Rochford avoided his all-too-knowing gaze and made a production of pouring the drinks. He handed one to his friend, still avoiding making eye contact, and sat down. He took a large swallow and stared down into his glass.

"Well?" Blackstone persisted. "Spit it out."

Rochford made a harrumphing sound and rubbed the back of his neck. "She… I… I might have been somewhat… ill-tempered."

"*You?*" Blackstone said, feigning astonishment. "Ill-tempered? I don't believe it."

"Sod off."

"Such charming company I keep. In what way were you ill-tempered, Rochford?"

Realising he would not get a moment's peace if he didn't tell all, Rochford capitulated. "I suggested she was trying to… lure me."

"Lure you?" Jules said, sitting up straighter. "What the devil did you mean by that?"

"Into marrying her, dammit. I suggested the chit was after my title," Rochford said, feeling ridiculous now, which only irritated him all the more.

Jules stared at him, so clearly astonished that Rochford felt a prize twit. As if a woman like Lady Georgina would ever consider him, even if it was only for his money and his title. She'd have no trouble making a fine match, and without having to spend the rest of her days enduring his ugly mug.

"You think Lady Georgina was trying to flirt with you, hoping to become a duchess?"

"I never said it made any sense, did I?" Rochford retorted. "But that's why she hates me."

"I should think she does! Well, that certainly explains why she came back into the parlour with her feathers all on end. The questions is, though, what made you think that was what she was after?"

Rochford scowled down into his whisky, wishing it wouldn't keep putting him in mind of Lady Georgina's beautiful tawny eyes. "She was kind to me," he grumbled.

"She was kind to you," Blackstone repeated, *sotto voce.*

"Yes." Rochford glared at him, wondering why the idiot didn't understand plain English all of a sudden.

"She was kind to you, and so you accused her of trying to lure you into marriage?"

Rochford rubbed a hand over his face. "Yes! I said so, didn't I?"

"Rochford, I'm kind to you, but I assure you—"

"One more word," Rochford said, pointing a finger at him.

Blackstone subsided with a smirk. "Very well, but really, Rochford, what were you thinking? Georgie is a dear creature with a kind heart. Why shouldn't she be kind to you, too? What makes you so special that she *wouldn't* include you? She's kind to everyone, even me."

Rochford frowned. He hadn't considered that. Perhaps the foolish girl was simply deluded. One of those poor, simple beings who thought all God's creatures were precious, even the slithery, crawling ones. Well, that made some sense, perhaps. He'd heard of young women getting fanatically religious and wanting to be nuns, and going about doing good works at all hours of the day and night. Perhaps it was something of that sort.

"She's perfectly sane, Rochford," Jules said dryly, proving something that Rochford had suspected for some time. The devil knew him too well.

Rochford swallowed his drink and got up to pour another.

"So, you'll come tonight?"

"I never said I would," Rochford retorted.

"No, but you need the opportunity to apologise to Lady Georgina for being a—"

"An obnoxious arse," Rochford supplied for him. "Her words, not mine."

Blackstone snorted and headed for the door. "Well, she's got your measure, that's for sure. Be ready to leave at seven thirty."

Rochford gave a groan of frustration, but didn't argue.

Chapter 6

Dearest Evie,

I hope you are well. It seems an age since we saw you last. Do come and visit soon. Even Hart is cheerful when you are around. So, you <u>must</u> be welcome.

Have you lots of celebrations and parties to attend this Christmas? Poor Mama must juggle between accepting the right amount to be polite and not make Papa and Hart utterly miserable. They bear it with good grace and rarely complain, but they really don't have the patience for polite society. Heaven help them when I come out, for I shall want to go to every ball I can. Not to catch a husband, for I'm in no hurry for that, but I do love to dance. They'll hate every minute, the poor dears.

—Excerpt of a letter from Kathleen de Beauvoir (daughter of Mr and Mrs Inigo and Minerva de Beauvoir) to Miss Evie Knight (daughter of Mr Gabriel and Lady Helena Knight).

Evening of the 8th of December 1840, Mrs Barclay's Rout Party, Grosvenor Square, London.

"How have you been?" Nic asked his brother. "I feel you've been avoiding me these past weeks."

Louis César's beautiful face was impassive, revealing nothing. The damned mask he wore was firmly in place tonight. Nic wondered when the last time was he'd seen it slip. Once upon a time, he and Louis had been inseparable, hiding nothing from each other. In fact, Louis had hated not having him around. He never had borne being alone well, but recently Nic barely saw him.

"Very well, as you see," Louis replied, though he didn't turn to look at Nic, just watched the room.

"I'm glad you decided to come."

Louis did turn then, quirking one elegant eyebrow just a little. "It was a decision, was it?" he asked mildly.

Nic shrugged. "We wanted you here. The duchess wanted you here, Aggie and your Miss Evie wanted you here."

"She's not *my* Miss Evie," Louis snapped, glaring at him.

Nic raised his hands in a surrendering movement. "*D'accord,* if you say so."

"Who says otherwise?" he demanded.

Nic's eyebrows went up, a little surprised by his brother's defensiveness. "No one, you just always seem thick as thieves, that's all. You still write to her, don't you?"

Louis shrugged, which Nic took to be a yes. He had long been puzzled by Louis' close relationship with Evie Knight. She seemed an unlikely confidante for Louis, because Louis always had access to the most beautiful women for company. No, that was not quite correct. He could understand Louis being *her* friend. His brother was inherently kind and always had a soft spot for a waif or stray… hence Aggie. Not that Evie was a waif or stray, but she did not fit the mould of the usual debutante either, and Louis would always recognise another outsider. It was what they both were. Oh, Louis might look as though he belonged here among the *ton* for he was handsome and titled and rich, but underneath was a different matter. Underneath, he was still a boy dressed in rags, who got tossed scraps to eat and slept on the kitchen floor. Louis might not realise Nic knew that was still true, but it was. Even so, he had not expected Louis to make Evie of all people his closest friend, yet Nic was certain he had, which was both puzzling, and a worry.

It could ruin Evie and, if that happened, it would destroy Louis.

Speak of the devil. Here was the young lady herself.

"Monsieur Le Comte," she said, beaming at Louis. "Will you come and play cards, please?"

Nic watched with interest as the stern lines of Louis' face softened in her presence and the mask fell, amusement glinting in his eyes.

"Surely, I taught you a lesson the last time we played, Miss Knight? I am not good-natured enough to let you win."

"I should hope not!" she said indignantly, and with such vehemence that Louis smiled. "I shall beat you fair and square or not at all."

"Well, if you must learn the hard way." Louis held out his arm, told Nic he would see him later, and escorted Miss Knight to the card room.

Nic watched them go, lost in thought.

"Why, Lady Georgina, I believe you have made a conquest."

Georgina looked at Jules in consternation. "What are you talking about? What conquest?"

Jules gestured to the other side of the crowded room where people were milling about, drinking and chatting. There would be dancing later, but for now there was a concert going on in the ballroom, some famous opera singer by all accounts. Georgina did not feel like sitting still, though, and she had avoided the card room for the same reason. She felt fractious and out of sorts, though she wasn't sure why, and Jules making cryptic comments was not helping her temper. Georgie craned her neck, able to see over the heads of much of the crowd, unlike most of the female guests, not that the new arrival was hard to miss.

Her mouth fell open, and she turned to stare at Jules.

"You cannot be serious?"

"Why not? He *never* attends parties or balls, or any of the *ton* events. Yet you want him to come and *voila,* here he is." Jules put his hands out as if to say, *you explain it.*

"Who says I wanted him to come?" Georgie demanded, flushing scarlet.

Jules smirked at her. "He told me you said he should come."

"Only so he wouldn't be all by himself, because the company might be good for him. I didn't *ask* him to come. Not for me. Not because *I* want him here. I didn't ask him because I wanted to see him. That would be ridiculous. You know I can't stand him!" Georgie subsided, aware she may have run on rather longer than was necessary.

Jules merely quirked an eyebrow at her. Georgie simmered and promised herself the pleasure of stamping on his foot if the words *methinks the lady doth protest too much* dared pass his smug lips.

Despite herself, Georgie could not help but glance back to where the duke was making his way across the room. People parted in front of him, conversations falling silent, gasps and whispers moving around the room like a breeze rustling long grass. Georgie gritted her teeth. The duke might be an obnoxious arse, but they had no right to treat him so. Yes, he was certainly *striking*, but… but he was also rather splendid. There was not another man in the room who could match him for height and breadth, and Georgie couldn't help but find him magnificent. She also had a something of an idea of how he felt. She'd seen the way some of the young men looked at her, smirking and laughing. They made lewd jokes about her size and made her feel ridiculous, too big, too ungainly in a world where fragility and fainting seemed prized in a woman. It made her angry too. It made her hate those people because they hurt her and made her feel wrong and unfeminine.

"Oh, give him a chance, Georgie," Jules whispered in her ear. "Like Mama said. He just doesn't know how to play nicely yet. No one ever taught him."

"Well, why do I have to be the one to do it?" she asked, folding her arms. "I'm likely to get scratched to pieces for my trouble."

"Oh, no. Only a little bruised," Jules said, chuckling. "Come on, Georgie, you're made of stern stuff. You'd need to be to survive those hulking brutes you call brothers."

Georgie smirked. "You're just still smarting that Muir knocked you out cold."

"I wasn't ready!" Jules retorted, nettled.

"Dear me, that was, what, ten years ago, and it still rankles, doesn't it, Julie?" she said, aware she was waving a red rag at him. It's what had begun the fight in the first place.

"Don't call me that," Jules warned, narrowing his eyes at her.

"Then stop trying your hand at matchmaking. It won't work," she retorted, and stalked off.

Georgie took a turn about the room, and then saw the duke still hadn't found Jules and was standing awkwardly in the middle of the room, glowering at anyone who got near. Oh, drat it all. She'd better speak to him, but if he was rude to her, she was leaving him to flounder on his own.

Deciding she wasn't above a little mischief, Georgie crept up behind him and tapped him on his left shoulder, before darting right. He looked around, frowning as he found an empty space.

"Good evening, your grace."

He jumped and turned back, scowling at her.

"Oh, you're here," he said, not sounding pleased to discover it.

"Well, you knew I would be," she said, keeping her smile in place.

He made a harrumphing sound.

"You, on the other hand, were very certain you would not attend."

"I didn't want to," he grumbled.

"And yet, here you are," she replied sweetly.

Another harrumphing sound.

"You don't like me," Georgie observed with amusement.

"No more than you like me," he countered.

Georgie batted her eyelashes at him. "Does anyone like you?"

He frowned, looking genuinely puzzled. "Why would I want them to? I'm a duke."

"You're a man."

"No, I'm not. I'm a title and an estate, I am history and the future, and thousands depend on me."

She stared at him in outrage. "How pompous you sound."

"I'm a *duke,*" he repeated slowly, as if she were a half-wit.

"Pfft. You're still just a man, and an ill-tempered, rude one at that."

He bristled, his eyes glittering. She had the sudden notion he was enjoying himself. Stranger still, so was she.

"And you are a graceless, mannerless, baggage."

"Probably," Georgie replied cheerfully. "But at least I'm happy about it."

"What is that supposed to mean?" he demanded.

"That you're not. You're unhappy and cross but you don't know what to do about it, and so you take it out on the rest of us because you envy us."

"Envy… *you*?" She might as well have accused him of being an imposter, he was so outraged.

Georgie grinned at him and shrugged. "I tell you what. As an act of charity, for it is Christmas after all, I shall teach you to play a game."

He folded his massive arms, rendering her speechless for several seconds. "I don't want to play a game."

Georgie forced herself back to the conversation. "That's because you don't know how. Now, I shall begin. I say, 'I went to the shops and bought a book,' then you must repeat the sentence but with another object. I will tell you if the object is correct or not, but they must have something in common."

"What in common?"

"Ah, that is what you have to figure out, that's the game part of it."

"This is ridiculous."

"Of course it is. That's the point of a game. It's fun."

"I want to go home."

"Oh, for heaven's sake. I give up." Georgie said in exasperation and turned to walk away from him, startled to find a large hand dart out and snare her wrist. Goodness, but he was fast.

Sensation prickled up her arm, making her cheeks burn, and he dropped his hold on her like she'd burned him.

"Don't go," he said, his voice all low and gravelly, sending shivers down her spine.

"Why?" she demanded, wishing that hadn't sounded quite so breathless, but he had startled her, that was all.

He gave an irritated huff before admitting, "I don't know where Jules is, and I don't know anyone else here I can bear talking to."

"You mean you can bear talking *to me?* Why, your grace, I may swoon." Georgie placed a hand over her heart and fluttered her eyelashes at him.

Rochford snorted. "Yes, yes, very amusing, I'm sure. You should be on the stage. Think of it as another act of charity, why don't you?"

"Yes, I suppose I can do that," Georgie said gravely. "Like reading to a doddering old man whilst he dribbles into his soup."

"Charming."

"No, you're not the least bit charming. Frankly, I'd rather take the toothless soup drinker, but that's life. No one said it was fair."

He stared down at her and she thought she saw amusement in his eyes. They were a deep slate grey she saw now but there was a halo of gold around the pupil, a warm colour, though she had never seen warmth in his expression. She thought she saw a hint of it now, of the man he might have been if life had been kinder, and she had the sudden urge to see more, to reach past the impenetrable façade.

"Life's a vindictive bitch, Lady Georgina. Sooner you recognise that fact the easier it is to bear."

He raised his eyebrows at her, his arm still awaiting her hand.

Georgina slid her hand over his sleeve, too aware of the power of the man beneath the material. Even though she wore gloves, and there was his coat and shirt between them, she was viscerally aware of his skin, of heavy muscle and bone shifting under her fingertips. Her heart gave an erratic thud and a strange, liquid warmth pooled deep in her core.

"You're blushing," he said, and drat the man for noticing. "If being seen with me is too dreadful a fate, I'm happy to leave. I never wanted to come in the first place."

Georgie's gaze snapped to his. The words had not held a trace of condemnation, only offered her a way out.

"I don't want you to leave," she said crossly.

He frowned down at her. Did the man *have* another expression? "Why are you blushing, then?"

Georgie flushed harder. "Stop asking me that, you're making it worse."

"How am I making it worse? I don't know why you're blushing."

"Oh, shut up, will you!" she pleaded, aware that everyone was staring at them.

He obliged her by shutting up, which was a blessing, and they did a circuit of the room in silence as Georgie endured the stares and the whispers. It was horrible. The poor man. How did he stand it? Well, he didn't, did he? Which was why he never socialised and had all the patience of an angry bear.

Georgie glimpsed swirling skirts and movement through the open doors of the ballroom and realised the dancing had begun.

"Do you dance?" she asked him, before she could think better of it.

He stared at her liked she'd asked if he spoke Swahili.

"I never dance," he said coldly.

"Yes, I know that, but do you know *how* to?" she replied, striving for patience.

Another contemptuous glare. "I'm a duke."

"Excellent," she said, assuming that meant yes, and began steering him towards the ballroom. Naturally, he planted his feet, which meant tugging at his arm would have about as much effect as trying to move a twenty-foot block of marble. "Oh, do come along," she pleaded.

"I'm not dancing. I never dance."

Georgie sighed and released his arm. She turned and looked up at him, keeping her voice soothing. "Well, why don't you try something different? You never come to parties either, do you, and look how well that's turned out."

He quirked an eyebrow at her, imperious devil.

She tsked at him, impatient now. "Stop waggling your eyebrows and trying to look all ducal. It won't work. I'm immune."

"I am not *trying*. I *am* ducal. And what in the name of God makes you think this has turned out well? Everyone is whispering about us—about you. Do you want to be at the centre of their tittle-tattle?"

"No," she said frankly. "But I do want to dance and I'm not about to let their wagging tongues stop me."

He stood watching her, his expression unreadable. Georgie waited.

After what seemed an age, he made his usual harrumphing sound and took her hand, placing it back on his sleeve and strode towards the ballroom, muttering as he went. Naturally, the whispering behind fans increased tenfold as Rochford appeared in the ballroom. It was as if he were some dangerous beast who'd strayed into their territory.

Georgie felt a sudden swell of protectiveness rise inside her, which clearly proved she was utterly deranged. Of all the men who needed protecting here, the duke was the least likely candidate, surely? Yet that was only on the surface. Yes, he was big and fearsome if you took him at face value, and admittedly, getting on the wrong side of his tongue was akin to being lashed with glass paper. Still, she couldn't help herself. Something in her nature told her he needed looking after even if he didn't want it.

"Are you quite sure about this?" he asked, his voice even, giving nothing away.

"I am," Georgie said, though her heart was careening about behind her ribs. "Quite sure."

"It's your funeral," he muttered, and reached for her.

Oh. Oh, this was a bad idea. The worst. Oh, Georgie, you nitwit.

But there was no backing out now.

He danced superbly. Perhaps not with the finesse of some, but for a man of his size to move as he did, and to hold her so carefully… Georgie was melting. Though she enjoyed dancing, Georgie did not enjoy being paired with a man over whose head she could see, which was far too many of them. Not that she minded the men being short—it was no more their fault than that she was tall—only that it made her feel such an elephant in a room full of fairies. It wasn't a problem with Rochford. His powerful physique made her feel almost delicate by comparison. He certainly held her as though she was, as though he might break her if he wasn't careful. And then she made the mistake of looking up into his eyes. She didn't see the scar, nor anything that seemed the least bit out of place. It was simply Rochford, and his dark grey eyes were on her, for once unguarded. He looked like a man stripped bare, like someone seeing the ocean for the first time.

Georgie wanted to reach up and stroke his face, to show him she wasn't like the others, that she wasn't afraid of him.

Thankfully, some fraying shred of sanity remained, and she kept her hand glued to his shoulder, but she could not tear her eyes from his.

The dance ended, and Georgie was uncertain if it was too soon or if that had been an eternity. Her head was spinning, and her heart was pounding and….

"Well. You've had your dance. I'm off. Goodnight."

Rochford stalked away, leaving her in the middle of the ballroom by herself.

Chapter 7

The dress is ready for a fitting.

Tonight.

—Excerpt of a note to Miss Evie Knight (daughter of Mr Gabriel and Lady Helena Knight) from Louis César de Montluc, Comte de Villen – slipped under her door.

12th December 1840, Beverwyck, London.

Georgie didn't care. No. Not at all. Four days of being ignored didn't bother her one little bit. She simply did not give a fig. She didn't. So what if Rochford hadn't spoken a word to her since the night of the rout? That was his loss. Not hers. Especially not when she was sitting next to the Comte de Villen at dinner this evening.

Goodness, but he was breath-taking. If she wasn't careful, she'd just spend the entire evening gazing at him like an idiot. It took her a moment to realise she was doing just that and that Evie, sat on her other side, was speaking to her.

"You've not heard a word I've said, have you?" Evie smiled, her eyes twinkling mischievously.

Georgie returned a rueful expression. "Sorry."

"It's understandable. I know women find him dreadfully distracting."

"Don't you?" Georgie asked, bending closer to Evie and lowering her voice. How Evie could be around Louis and not just sit sighing over him she couldn't fathom.

Evie shook her head. "No. I mean, I can see he's beautiful, obviously. I'm not blind, but he was my friend first. Perhaps when we met, I was just too young to see him in a romantic light and it stuck. Or perhaps he's just not my type," she added, laughing at Georgie's sceptical expression.

"You're an odd duck, Evie," Georgie replied, shaking her head.

"Lady Georgina," Georgie turned her head and was immediately struck dumb by Louis' brilliant blue eyes. "Your napkin."

He held the folded square out to her, which must have slid off the silky skirts of her dress.

Georgie swallowed. She didn't seem able to speak. Or move.

Louis smiled gently, took her hand and placed the napkin in it, and returned his attention to his dinner. Georgie felt the blush all the way to her toes. Hurriedly, she stuffed the napkin back in her lap and elbowed Evie, who was sniggering uncontrollably.

"Shut up," she muttered, mortified.

Glancing up at the table, her gaze collided with the Duke of Rochford. His sneer seemed more pronounced than ever, perhaps because of the rigid set to his jaw. Appalled that the duke might have seen her behaving like such a prize ninny, Georgie put her head down and concentrated on eating.

After dinner, everyone retired to the parlour for tea or brandy. Aunt Prue had banished the tradition of the men sitting over their port by themselves as soon as she'd become duchess, but as it was an informal gathering, the port was available in the parlour for those who wished, or tea for those abstaining. Thankfully, there were no parlour games this evening, for which Georgie was grateful. She wondered if her aunt had done that deliberately, to ensure it did not make Rochford uncomfortable.

Everyone seemed relaxed and in good spirits. The scent of Christmas lingered in the air, the warmth of the fire fluttering the red silk ribbons of the decorations, and stirring the thick arrangement of holly and fir and evergreen studded with cinnamon sticks on the mantelpiece. For a moment, Georgie acknowledged a pang of homesickness. Christmas at Wildsyde was always a jolly affair. Mama had such a knack for decorating the castle and making everything seem magical. Even her brothers were tolerable during the festive season and made time to go sleighing with her, even if their snowball fights became rather violent. She decided she must write to them tomorrow and tell them everything that had happened since she'd arrived. Well, perhaps not everything. She could certainly leave the duke out of any correspondence. The great, overbearing—

"Lady Georgina."

Georgie let out a yelp as the deep voice rumbled in her ear.

Well, speak of the great, overbearing lout and he shall appear.

"Your grace," she said, pleased with herself for sounding so cool and detached when her heart had begun a riot behind her ribs.

"Did you enjoy dinner?"

"Of course. Dinner at Beverwyck is always a work of art."

"The company helps, of course."

There was no sarcasm, not a hint of mockery in his words, but Georgie's cheeks burned all the same. "Of course," she returned with a tight smile.

"Do you think he appreciates his good fortune?"

Georgie forced herself to look at the duke then, wondering if he smirking again, but no. Although the scar tugged at his lip as always, his expression was curious.

"I'm not certain," Georgie replied. "Perhaps his beauty is as much a burden as your scar."

Rochford snorted at that, clearly unconvinced. "Yes, it must be terrible, having women fall at your feet without lifting a finger."

He levelled what she could only describe as an accusing gaze at her, and Georgie stared back at him, refusing to be further embarrassed. So, she found the comte beautiful. Who didn't? Well, apart from Evie, apparently.

"Perhaps it becomes tedious, never knowing if people truly like you, but only want to be with you for your pretty face?" she suggested. "At least if someone spends time with you, your grace, you know it is because they wish to. Oh, wait… no. I forgot. You think everyone is after your money and your title. If you'll excuse me…."

Georgie turned away, appalled at herself. She must put some distance between them before she said anything truly reprehensible.

Strong fingers grasped hers, tugging her to a halt. Georgie glanced around, wondering if anyone had seen, but her skirts hid their hands from view, and he hadn't let go. She couldn't breathe. Her heart simply could not keep up this demented speed. It would explode.

"Did I not apologise for insulting you so?" he asked sounding a little impatient.

"It's so hard to remember. There have been so many things to apologise for," she replied tartly, though her mind was consumed with the fact he was still holding her hand and showed no sign of releasing her.

"Only two, surely."

"There was only one apology," she said, glaring at him, though she still hadn't pulled her hand free. Why hadn't she done that?

Why haven't you done that, Georgie? You are furious with him. He's an obnoxious arse.

Remember?

"Two apologies," he corrected, and her breath hitched as his thumb caressed her palm.

"T-Two?" she stammered, finding it harder and harder to concentrate on the thread of the conversation.

"I came to the party for you, didn't I?"

She blinked up at him. "That wasn't an apology."

"Yes. It was."

Oh.

"Goodnight, Lady Georgina."

He released her hand and left her standing by herself. Georgie stared at her palm, half expecting to see a mark, a burn, as if his touch had scalded her. Good heavens. What on earth had that been about? Had that been an apology, too? Or had he simply not liked the idea she might have been thinking about the Comte de Villen and not him? Oh, good Lord! Did he *know* she'd been thinking about him? How ghastly. Georgie put her hands to her cheeks, wishing she did not blush quite so easily. She had her mother to thank for that.

"Whatever did he say to you?" Georgie looked up to see Rosamund staring at her with wide eyes.

"Who?" Georgie replied defensively, which was clearly an idiotic thing to say in the circumstances. A fact reinforced by the look Ozzie send her in reply.

"I-I hardly know," Georgie said apologetically, unable to dissemble with her friend and too bewildered to try.

"Oooh, was he flirting with you? He looked awfully intense."

"Of course not. He always looks that way," Georgie said absently… or had he been flirting with her? The touch of his thumb stroking her palm reverberated in her memory, making her flush. That *had* to be flirtatious, but… but surely….

Ozzie gave her an odd look but said nothing, only taking her arm and leading her on a walk about the room. Georgie followed like a lamb, too focused on unravelling the conversation with the duke to object.

"I think he's taken a fancy to you," Ozzie whispered.

Georgie snorted. "He said I was a graceless, mannerless baggage," she said dryly. "Obviously he's head over ears in love."

Ozzie laughed but refused to give up on the subject. "Everyone but you is terrified of him, I think. I admit I find him dreadfully daunting. I've not spoken a word to him yet, which vexes me, for I do not wish to be the kind of woman who judges by appearance. Indeed, I never thought I was, but every time I try to gather the nerve to attempt a conversation, I get all tongue-tied. I'm sure he thinks me a horrid creature."

"I shouldn't worry, he thinks that of everyone," Georgie reassured her, and then considered that. Why oughtn't he think that, if even kind-hearted people like Ozzie wouldn't speak to him. Perhaps he did not realise how intimidating he was. Or perhaps he did it on purpose, to keep everyone away, like a dog with a thorn in its paw, snarling at anyone who tried to help it.

"You're awfully quiet, Georgie."

Georgie looked up, startled to discover they'd done several turns of the room in complete silence.

"I beg your pardon, Ozzie," she said with an apologetic smile. "I shall try to do better."

Georgie woke early the next morning after an uneasy night's sleep. Her head felt muzzy and no clearer than the previous evening, so she dressed in her riding habit and went to the stables. A good hard ride ought to clear the cobwebs and give her an appetite for breakfast.

The grooms knew her by now and didn't quibble over her choice of mount, a big sturdy gelding who would not ordinarily be thought suitable for a woman. She had learned to ride with her brothers, though, and she had always been too stubborn to be left behind by them. It had taken her a lot of falls and bruises, and even a broken wrist, but she had learned to keep up and eventually even outride them. She could manage the same horses that they could, but was far lighter in the saddle, and she was also an excellent markswoman. Though she did not enjoy hunting, she could hit a target in a bullseye with far more accuracy than most men. Her brothers respected her abilities and treated her little differently than they did each other. She'd enjoyed that fact as a girl. As she had grown, though… not so much.

She wondered what they were doing now and imagined them getting under Mrs MacLeod's feet and stealing Bannocks in the deliciously steamy fug of the kitchens at Wildsyde.

Georgie rode hard, enjoying the chill bite of the wintry morning air upon her skin and her hair whipping about her face. The grounds at Beverwyck were so extensive it was easy to forget you were in London. The noise and the bustle seemed far away from her here and calmed her uneven spirits. The horse, a fine beast named Apollo, was eager for more and so Georgie let him have his head, exhilarated by the speed and power. This had to be the closest thing there was to flying.

Out of the corner of her eye, Georgie noticed a dark shape looming behind her and turned her head. Impossibly, Rochford was gaining on her, his huge black Percheron charger eating up the ground. Her heart did an odd little flutter in her chest, which she tried hard to ignore.

"Oh, no," she said aloud. "We can't have that. Come on, my lad."

Rochford watched in consternation as Lady Georgina put on another burst of speed. He had only wanted to speak to her, hoping to slow her down, for surely she'd break her neck galloping upon that enormous horse. It was full of juice still and far too powerful for her to handle.

Helplessly, he called after her, trying to get her to slow, but she either did not hear or ignored him. Not that he could blame her for trying to give him the slip. He'd acted like a damned lunatic since the moment he met her. She had turned everything upside down, and he hated her for it. Yet he could not stay away. Dancing with her had been a mistake. She had felt so right in his arms that the rest of the world had fallen away. He'd forgotten the judging eyes of the *ton* were upon them, had forgotten everything for that brief space of time. He'd even forgotten he was hideous, for she had looked at him, truly looked at him, not with horror or pity or forbearance, but as if he were a man, just a man.

You're still just a man, and an ill-tempered, rude one at that.

Whenever he remembered her words, it made him smile. She'd said he was pompous. She'd called him an obnoxious arse. Why such insults should please him so, he couldn't fathom, but there it was. He was a lunatic.

Rochford hung back, afraid it would only spur her on to greater folly if he tried to catch her. So, he was too far away to shout at her, to tell her to have a care when he saw her galloping towards a thick, high hedge.

"Georgina!" Her name left his lips anyway, fear a cold sensation gripping his heart as he watched the horse gather itself for the jump.

Please, please, please, don't break your pretty neck.

He watched, helpless with terror, as she sailed perfectly over the hedge. Rochford followed her, wild with fury, which only grew as he landed safely and discovered her waiting for him, a smug grin on her impossibly beautiful face. Damn her.

"You irresponsible bloody halfwit!" he thundered. His heart was still skittering in his chest and wasn't certain if he'd be able to catch a proper breath for the rest of the day. "What the devil were you thinking? You could have broken your stupid neck."

She stiffened, glowering at him. "Thank you for your concern, your grace, but I was in no danger."

"You can't go around throwing an unfamiliar horse at unknown obstacles. He's far too powerful for you. Christ, you were lucky he followed through. If he'd refused, we'd be picking your broken bones up off the floor as we speak."

Her expression grew colder. "You forget, your grace, that this is my godmother's property. I have been riding here since I was a little girl, and Apollo and I are well acquainted. I am an excellent horsewoman, and need no advice from you. I most certainly do not need a scolding. You saw me take that jump, and you know very well I did it to perfection. I am a proficient sportswoman and can outride and out-shoot most men, so I'll thank you to keep your blasted opinions to yourself."

Rochford heard her words and knew in some rational part of his brain that she was likely spot on, and he owed her an apology. Another apology. The jump had been impressive, and executed perfectly, just as she said. But his heart was still careening about; terror had infected his blood and he was very far from rational.

He leaped down from his horse and grabbed hold of her mount's bridle.

"Get down," he said through gritted teeth.

"No! And take your hands off my horse."

"Get down, damn you, or I'll get you down."

She narrowed her eyes at him, her fingers tightening on her crop. "Try it."

He snorted. "Ah, going to stripe the other side to match, are you? That would be fitting."

All at once, the anger he'd seen flashing in her tawny eyes diminished. "Of course not. I would never hit you. I admit I might have fantasised about it, though," she added with a sigh. "And I can see I scared you witless, so I suppose it ought not surprise me at your becoming an overbearing arse. It is your usual response to most situations after all."

Rochford blinked up at her, too startled by her rapid change in temperament to respond.

"I suppose you weren't to know I can handle a horse like Apollo, and it would be a tricky jump for most people, but I am not *most* people, Rochford. I have three large and annoying brothers whom I could never resist beating at everything. I had to be better than them, don't you see? Or at least as good. To lose would have been too awful to endure."

"By God, you are a stubborn piece of work," he said, staring at her in wonder. He wasn't certain if that had been admiration or irritation in his voice. Perhaps both. She was an infuriating woman but… But. Damnation, that *but* was going to land him in a world of trouble if he wasn't careful.

"I am, and don't look so appalled. My godfather would have scolded me too, I don't doubt. He doesn't like me riding alone."

Rochford frowned, stroking the horse's silky nose, and trying to catch his breath.

"Do you feel less like murdering me now?" she asked conversationally.

"I'm not sure," he admitted. "My heart is still crashing about like disaster is imminent."

Her lips quirked into a wry smile of understanding. "Well, it does seem imminent any time we are in each other's vicinity, so… so perhaps we should stay away from each other. It might be safer. Best for both of us."

Alarmed by the vehement disagreement that burst to life in his chest at her suggestion, Rochford answered quickly, before he could change his mind, and so perhaps with more force than he had intended.

"Yes," he said. "An excellent idea. Good morning to you, my lady."

Chapter 8

Dear Mama, Papa — and I suppose, Lyall, Muir, and Hamilton,

I am having a marvellous time at Beverwyck. It is so lovely to see Evie and Rosamund again and we have talked and laughed so much it's a wonder we've not lost our voices. Eliza's husband Monsieur Demarteau is here, and he is very charming, though he looks like a wicked rogue. Eliza is obviously besotted with him. Lottie and Cass are as funny and entertaining as ever and it is lovely to see them again. All the Adolphus clan sends their love. The children are growing like weeds and are adorable. Oh, and the mysterious Comte de Villen, I cannot leave him out, can I? Everything they say about him is true. He looks like a fallen angel, and I become a babbling idiot whenever he turns his gaze in my direction. Thankfully, it isn't often, or I should look a dreadful ninny. He seems charming, but remote, the only people who truly make him smile being his young ward, Agatha, and Evie. Evie seems completely immune to his charms, and I cannot help but wonder if that is why he seeks her company so often.

*—Excerpt of a letter to the Right Hon'ble
Ruth and Gordon Anderson, The Earl and
Countess of Morven, from their daughter,
Lady Georgina Anderson.*

12th December 1840, Beverwyck, London.

Georgie's plan to avoid the duke was scuppered almost at once as she discovered she'd been placed next to him at dinner again that evening. Though being ignored by him had been infuriating, she supposed she understood his impulse. They brought out the worst in each other and so it was best they stayed far apart. Except fate did not seem to agree with this sensible decision.

They got through almost the entire meal without speaking to each other, until the dessert course. The footmen presented everyone with a crystal dish containing the most glorious individual trifle. Georgina devoured hers far too quickly, ahead of everyone else, and with far too much enjoyment for good manners, before noticing Rochford hadn't touched his. Of course, he'd said he didn't like sweet things.

She told herself not to mention it, but she had a dreadful fondness for trifle and the dratted thing was calling to her. Every time she convinced herself she would not mention it, for he'd only think her ill-mannered *and* greedy, temptation drew her gaze back to the pretty arrangement of raspberries and sponge and cream and….

"Aren't you going to eat that?" she blurted out, instantly regretting the impulse as Rochford turned to look at her.

"I don't like sweets," he reminded her.

"What kind of person doesn't like sweets?" she demanded crossly, though why the fact should irritate her so, she did not know. "It seems an inherently untrustworthy trait in a person not to find pleasure in dessert."

"Well, you already know I am unreasonable, pompous, overbearing—"

"An arse, yes, I remember," she said, surprised by the glint of satisfaction in his eyes, as if he'd been waiting for her to interrupt him and was pleased about it. "So now I must add untrustworthy to the list, too, must I?"

He frowned at her, though she wasn't certain she believed it. She wasn't certain he was cross at all, or irritated. How odd. "I am many things, but never untrustworthy," he said, holding her gaze.

Georgie turned away from him, unsettled, but the dratted trifle was still there, uneaten, tempting her. She dared a glance back at the duke to find him watching her. He quirked one eyebrow as her gaze settled on the pudding. Drat it, he knew she wanted it. Well, he wouldn't have the satisfaction of hearing her ask for it.

She sat like a proper, well-mannered young woman and admired the table, which was beautifully decorated. Candlelight glinted upon crystal and silverware and table decorations of holly studded with berries, and Christmas roses.

"It's killing you, isn't it?"

Georgie looked back at the duke, keeping her expression bland. "I have no idea what you mean."

"You want my trifle."

"No, I don't."

"Liar."

"Well, I ought to have known you'd resort to insulting me," she said with a sniff, turning her head resolutely away from him.

"Why not? You insult me all the time."

"*You* deserve it," she retorted, goaded into turning back to look at him.

He grinned at her, and it was a remarkably boyish expression that ought to have sat ill upon his harsh features, but it made a strange sensation flutter in her chest. *Lud.* This was why she ought not talk to him.

He leaned down, so close that if she turned her head, she was certain to feel his beard tickle her cheek. "What's it worth?"

Georgie gave him a suspicious glance. "What do you want?"

He shrugged. "Nothing, but you're the one who covets my trifle. It's got to be worth something."

"Oh, honestly. Why did you even take the dratted thing if—" She broke off, realising suddenly that he'd taken it on purpose. "You horrid creature! You did it to provoke me."

"How on earth could I have known taking a trifle I have no intention of eating would provoke you?" he asked, which from any other man might have been a reasonable question.

"You *lied.* You know I adore dessert. Oh, you're not the least bit trustworthy," she accused him.

He shrugged. "But I still have the trifle. Perhaps I'll give it to Jules, he has a sweet tooth." He reached for it and Georgie's hand shot out before the thought connected with her brain, snatching the little crystal dish from him. Deftly, she picked up her spoon and scooped up a large helping, stuffing it in her mouth.

"Mm-mm," she said, glaring defiantly at him. She licked her lips. "Delicious."

His gaze darkened, his eyes falling to her lips. "You are a bad girl, Lady Georgina."

"A graceless, mannerless baggage," she agreed equitably, taking another spoonful with undisguised glee.

"And happy about it."

"Aye," she retorted, trying not to snort as he shook his head in despair.

Rather to her annoyance, Georgina's attention was taken from the duke, as a discussion about the Bedwin's annual Christmas ball the night after next had everyone else chattering excitedly.

"Do you remember last year's, Georgie? It was marvellous, wasn't it?" Rosamund asked her, eyes alight with anticipation.

Georgie replied with a smile, but grimaced inwardly. She remembered it well. Mostly she remembered hardly dancing at all with anyone who wasn't a friend or a blood relation. Gentlemen simply did not wish to dance with an Amazon. Jules had been kind and taken pity, and her family had been here that year. Her father, and even her brothers, had danced with her. It had been too humiliating for words, because her brothers had been unusually kind to her, which only proved how obvious it was that she was being left with the wallflowers.

For a moment she considered persuading Rochford to go, for no doubt he wouldn't unless someone blackmailed him into it. Their dance had been wonderful. She sighed as a peculiarly warm and wistful sensation unfurled in her belly… which was why that was a dreadful idea. It was fine bantering with a man like Rochford, but she must not give him ideas. He might accuse her of trying to seduce him again, or worse still, he might actually take a fancy to her and propose. Good heavens! Being married to a devil like that would be a nightmare. They'd murder each other before the year was out. Something horribly like regret whispered through her mind and she pushed it away. Rochford obviously strongly disliked the idea of her as a duchess, he'd made that clear, and she had absolutely no desire to be one. So that was that. Georgie looked up and the comte's beautiful face caught her eye. Wistfully, she considered dancing with him at the ball. The comte was tall enough not to make her feel she was so wretchedly big and clumsy compared to the other young ladies. Not so heavily built as Rochford, so she wouldn't have the extraordinary sensation of feeling dainty in his arms, but at least she'd not see people laughing at her for looking foolish. She wondered if she could get Evie to persuade him to ask her. He caught her gaze then and smiled at her and Georgie turned away with a blush, embarrassed at being caught staring again.

"Lady Georgina."

Georgie forced herself to look back at him, suppressing a shiver of pleasure at the way her name sounded with the soft 'g's his French accent gave it.

"Yes," she replied, relieved to have managed a response this time.

"I hope you will reserve a dance for me."

"Oh." Georgie's colour rose dramatically, so hot she was certain Rochford must be able to feel it scald him. Oh, he would mock her for this. "I-I should be pleased to do so. *Merci, monsieur.*"

The comte nodded politely and returned his attention to Lottie, who was sitting beside him.

Georgie sighed and set down her spoon, pushing the empty trifle glass away from her. Turning back to the duke, she considered trying to gain his attention again, but he was conversing with Evie, and it was so rare to see him talking to anyone else but her or Jules, Georgie thought she'd best let him be. It was good to see him relaxing and becoming a fraction more amiable, but she regretted missing the opportunity to provoke him again. Perhaps when they retired to the parlour after dinner.

Yet, as soon as the party rose from the table, Rochford excused himself.

Georgie tried to catch his attention as he left the room, wondering why he was leaving so early in the evening.

"Has my diabolical company scared you off at last?" she asked him as he passed her on his way towards the stairs.

He barely paused, his manner brisk and terse. "No, my lady, but I find I am not in the mood for further inanity. Besides, I am certain you have more agreeable company than mine to enjoy. Goodnight."

Georgie stared at him, taken aback by both his words and the coldness of his tone. He'd not even looked at her.

Inanity? The wretched man. He had been as big a part of that silly conversation as she had. It was him who'd taken a trifle he'd no intention of eating. How dare he mock her so? Her temper sparked to life, and she felt utterly furious that he had denied her the opportunity to give him a proper set down, stalking off like that, the horrid creature. Oh! Now she remembered why she hated him. She sat simmering for the best part of half an hour before she realised she was in too dreadful a temper to be good company and excused herself.

Georgie stalked up the stairs, muttering under her breath and turned towards her room, which was in the family wing of the immense house. As she went, she saw Rochford's valet, a delicate, almost pretty young man who gave her a polite nod as he passed her. That was Rochford's suite, she realised, turning to see the valet hurrying towards the servants' staircase. And he was alone.

Too provoked for good sense to prevail, Georgie hammered on his door.

He wrenched it open a moment later, the action swiftly accompanied by an irritated exclamation as the duke's gaze fell upon her.

"What the devil do you want?" he demanded.

For a moment, Georgie was diverted at the sight of him in his shirtsleeves, with his cravat abandoned. She could see wiry black hair curling upon his chest where the shirt fell open. *Goodness.* Wrenching her gaze up to his face, she reminded herself she was furious with him, ignored the heat blooming in places it had no business being, and launched into an attack.

"Why were you so horrid to me?"

"I'm an obnoxious arse, remember?" he retorted.

Either the scar at his mouth was twisting his lip into a furious sneer, or perhaps he really wanted to look so angry and fearsome, though what she'd done to make him so furious she did not know.

"Yes, you are," she retorted, deciding too late that this had been the most appalling mistake.

She turned to leave and then squealed in alarm, the sound smothered by his large hand as he tugged her into his room and slammed the door.

Georgie went very still, vibratingly aware of the massive, hard body behind her, the muscular arm banded about her waist, and his hand still clamped over her mouth. He was breathing as erratically as she, his heartbeat hammering against her back, though what he had to be alarmed about she couldn't fathom. She was the one who'd just been accosted. *Kidnapped!* She made a muffled sound behind his hand, and he released her.

Georgie spun around to glare at him.

"What did you do that for?" she demanded, annoyed to discover her voice had turned high-pitched and squeaky.

"The comte's blasted valet was walking straight towards us! A fine juicy bit of gossip that would have been in the servants' hall, or did you come here with the express intention of ruining yourself?"

"Oh! Don't you start that again," she retorted furiously. "If you are so utterly deranged as to think I would wish to be married to a surly curmudgeon like you... *Argh!* Why do I bother?"

"Yes, why?" he demanded, equally angry. "Why the bloody hell do you bother tormenting me when you've the likes of Louis César to cast your lures at?"

Georgie glowered at him and folded her arms. "Oh, I see. We're back to lures again, are we? Like I'm trying to trap some poor fellow into marrying me, because that would obviously be a fate worse than death!"

"It might well be," he thundered, and in some better behaved part of her brain she wondered why on earth she wasn't terrified of him. He was big and annoyed and bellowing, and yet she did not for one second feel as if she was in any danger. How odd. Or perhaps she was merely unhinged.

"You're just a dog in a manger," she said, a little startled by the look in his eyes at her accusation, but she ploughed on. Too late to turn back now. "You don't like me or want me, but you don't want anyone else to like me or want me, either!"

"That's a damned lie!"

"It isn't!"

"Is too!"

"God in heaven, you'll drive me insane, you ridiculous creature."

"I am not ridiculous!"

"You're bloody absurd if you can't see how much I bloody want you, you little nitwit!"

Before she could understand the meaning of his words, he'd pushed her up against the wall, his hands pressing her wrists above her head. Georgie gasped, staring up at him in shock. Her heart thudded unevenly. In a distant—very distant—part of her brain, she registered that, as a well-behaved young lady, she ought to be anxious about this. He was far bigger and stronger, and she was alone in his room, but all she felt was desperate excitement uncoiling and an insistent if unnerving throb between her thighs. His grip on her wrists was firm but gentle, his thumb caressing the place where her pulse beat an erratic tattoo until she shivered. She knew he would release her if she struggled or told him to let her go. Why wasn't she struggling? Why wasn't she demanding he let her go? Georgie tried to consider the question, but her rational mind—what remained of it—had turned to pudding. Must result from too much trifle.

Rochford was staring down at her, his grey eyes intent, his massive chest rising and falling too fast.

"You shouldn't have come," he groaned, the words low and breathless.

"I know," she admitted, wondering what he intended. She could only describe his expression as hungry. Perhaps he should have eaten the blasted trifle, she thought wildly. Anticipation was fizzing beneath her skin like champagne flowed in her veins, and her nerves were all on end. Was he going to kiss her?

Kiss me.

Don't kiss me.

Kiss me!

A panicked voice in her head kept repeating the same two phrases over again, but one was certainly louder than the other. Yet, he made no move, just stared down at her with that ravenous look in his eyes.

"You should go," he said, gritting the words out as if it hurt to speak them.

Georgie nodded automatically before thinking better of it. "No."

"You nodded. You mean yes," he said irritably.

"No. I mean no."

"But you nodded."

"I know. I was confused."

He rolled his eyes to the heavens. "You are deranged."

"Yes, that too. It's your fault, you know. You make me act like a madwoman."

"You make me act like a blasted lunatic."

"We should stay away from each other," they said in unison.

Georgie laughed.

He sighed and released his hold on her, but did not move away. "You should go," he said again, softer this time.

"Should I?" she asked, staring at him.

He swallowed, his Adam's apple bobbing, before he gave a resolute nod. "My valet will be back soon. You mustn't be seen here."

"Ah yes. Ruination followed by marriage. A fate worse than death," she said, unable to tear her gaze from him.

"Exactly. A fate worse than death indeed." There was humour in his eyes, and something else. Was that regret? She hoped so.

"For you or for me?" she asked, trying to recapture some of her earlier good humour.

"Perhaps both of us, but certainly for you, love," he said, before stepping away and walking to the door. He opened it, checked the corridor was empty, and gestured for her to leave.

"Good night, Rochford."

"Good night, my lady."

Chapter 9

Dear Prue,

Lucian and I are so looking forward to your Christmas ball. It holds fond memories for us, as I think you know.

Philip and Thomas will be there, of course, and have been given strict instructions to dance with the wallflowers. Feel free to enforce my directives if you see them shirking their duties.

—Excerpt of a letter to Her Grace, Prunella Adolphus, The Duchess of Bedwin from her friend, The Most Hon'ble Matilda Barrington, The Marchioness of Montagu.

Night of the 12th of December 1840, Beverwyck, London.

Once again, Evie found herself hurrying through the darkened corridors of Beverwyck en route to an illicit rendezvous with the Comte de Villen, this time in her nightrail and wrap. She snorted with amusement. Well, that made it sound dreadfully scandalous, when it wasn't really at all. It would be far too difficult to try on the dress quickly if she had to take one off first, though, so this seemed the best solution. She hoped Louis wouldn't be dreadfully scandalised. He could be very sensitive about such things, which, considering his behaviour, was rather amusing. But he was a man, and she was a woman, so they lived by utterly different rules. It was idiotic, but she couldn't fight society, so there it was.

She got to the library without incident and crept inside to discover Louis already waiting for her. He frowned as he saw her state of undress, and though he was standing in the shadows, she was quite certain his expression darkened.

"I thought it would be quicker this way," she said defensively.

"Quicker for what, to ruin yourself utterly?" he asked mildly.

"Well, being alone with you would ruin me, so whether or not I'm dressed hardly seems relevant."

"Does it not? *Alors,* how remarkably sophisticated you have become. I feel positively gauche by comparison."

The sarcasm in his voice was unmistakable, and she flushed as his gaze skimmed over her. No doubt she appeared dreadfully immature and silly in her white cotton wrap and nightgown, with her hair all undone. Very far from sophisticated. However, she did not take his words to heart; he was only cross because he worried for her. Louis was never cruel. He would certainly be used to worldly ladies in silks and satin, the sorts of pretty bits of nothing she'd seen among her mother's things, but Mama was a beauty too, even now. It was hardly suitable for a young woman like Evie. And besides, why was she even thinking about this? What she wore was of no consequence to Louis. This whole ridiculous endeavour was only because she'd made a fuss over the blasted dress, and he wanted to make her feel better. She shouldn't have complained so bitterly. It was only a stupid dress.

Evie wrapped her arms about herself. "You said the gown was ready."

Louis sighed and nodded, gesturing to a large box. Another, smaller, sat beside it and he opened the lid of this one. "You'll need to put these on first."

He handed her a shift. It was of the finest muslin, so thin it was almost sheer, and embroidered about the neck and hem with rosebuds.

"How exquisite," Evie said in wonder, taking the article from him. It felt like gossamer, it was so fine.

"And this," he added curtly. He held a corset out to her.

Evie took one look at it and gasped in shock. "I-I can't wear that!" she exclaimed.

"Why not? It is made precisely to the sizes you gave me, and you will find it fits far better than that monstrosity Madame Blanchet made for you, which flattened everything you have."

"B-But it's pink and lacey, and it… it has bows. *Pink* bows and… and I can't accept this from *you*!"

He made a brusque sound of annoyance. *"Tiens,* who will know?"

"My maid?" she suggested.

"Tell her your sister sent it to you. She is a married lady now."

Evie considered this and looked again at the corset. It was beautiful, and far prettier than any underwear she'd had before. All her wardrobe was of the finest quality, but it was quite inappropriate for a young, unmarried woman to buy such wickedly pretty things before she married. But as a gift from her sister….

Temptation won.

"Very well," she said, blushing hard. She took it from him, very relieved to discover it did up in the front or the evening could have become awkward indeed.

Evie scurried behind a section of bookshelves, out of sight, and stripped off her night things. It was a most peculiar sensation, being naked in the library at night and knowing Louis was only a few feet away, but she tried to ignore the way her skin prickled with gooseflesh. She slipped the shift quickly over her head and then put on the corset. It took a little while to get it quite right, but Evie saw at once what a difference it made. This corset shaped her generous bust and lifted it, as well as highlighting the curve of her waist and hips. There was no mirror here, but she could certainly see the effect. She looked like an hourglass, but the bust was surely rather immodest.

"Louis?"

"Oui?"

"It's… Isn't it a little… well, actually, isn't it a lot…?"

"Non," he replied curtly, and then a hand reached past the bookshelf, holding out her dress.

Evie sighed and took it, studying the remade gown. It was far simpler than before, with no frills or flounces. The cut was almost severe, the lowered shoulders angling diagonally down towards her décolletage, and the line echoed on both sides by tiny, pintucked seams that arrowed down to her stomach. It was beautiful work. As fast as she could, Evie tugged it over her head and wriggled until it was in place. Reaching back, she tried to fasten it, but after a deal of muttering and cursing, she gave up. Drat it. Hesitating she bit her lip. There was no other choice.

"Louis? It's on, but I can't do it up."

"Come here, then."

Evie emerged, pink-cheeked, as Louis moved behind her. He carefully brushed aside the thick curtain of her hair, draping it over her shoulder, and went to work on the fastenings. She supposed it ought not surprise her he was as accomplished at getting women into clothes as he was at getting them out of them.

"You're awfully good at this, quicker than my maid," she said conversationally, for there was a strange prickling atmosphere between them this evening which seemed odd to her, and she wished to disperse it. Usually, they were so at ease with each other, but then this was a bit of a peculiar thing to do, even for Evie. No doubt Louis was embarrassed for her.

He got to the top, just above her corset, and his knuckles grazed her bare skin, making her gasp in shock. How strange it was. Only her mother, her sisters or her maid had ever touched her skin before and the sensation was oddly electrifying. The warmth of his breath fluttered over the back of her neck, and she shivered. Louis' hands had stilled, but now he carried on and finished the intricate little fasteners. Louis stepped back.

"Turn around."

Evie turned, feeling foolish to be dressed in a ballgown with her hair down and her feet bare.

"Is it better?" she asked, unable to tell from his intent expression. "Well?"

Louis cleared his throat. *"Oui.* Better," he said curtly. He moved closer, eyeing each seam critically before tugging at the bodice where it curved to her waist. "A bit more here, I think. You've not been starving yourself again?" he demanded.

"No, Louis," she replied, sighing. "Did you not see me devour that trifle at dinner?"

He was silent for a moment, his blue eyes lifting to hers and then away. "I did."

"Then you should be happy, so there's no need to scold me again."

He muttered something under his breath in French, which she didn't catch.

"Oh, don't go speaking French at me," she complained. "You know I cannot bear it when I don't understand what you're saying."

"Well, you ought to learn the language better."

"I *am* trying," she objected. "But the lessons are so dull when anyone but you teaches me, and you never come and see me anymore…."

Evie trailed off, realising too late that there had been a distinctly whiny quality to her voice, which she immediately regretted. He was a grown man with a life of his own. No doubt her friendship was not as important to him as it was to her, but she had missed him terribly.

"I am sorry, *chérie*," he said, his voice quiet. "But I cannot come too often. People would talk. As it is, we ought not take such risks, but I could not have you go to the ball feeling anything less than beautiful, for that would be a crime."

"I hate people. Why can't they mind their own business?" she muttered.

Louis pulled a small tin box from his waistcoat pocket and gave a wry smile. "Why indeed? Now hold still, I do not wish to stab you with the pins."

Evie watched in surprise as he crouched before her, his long, elegant fingers pinning the waist in tighter. "Louis, can you sew?" she asked in astonishment.

He glanced up, a wicked glint in his eyes. "I can do many things, *ma puce,*" he said, a note to his voice that made her shiver.

"Yes, you're full of secrets, aren't you?" she murmured, frowning at him.

"Peut-être, et toi ma chérie, tu en connais déjà trop."

Evie considered his words, translating.

Perhaps, and you know too many of them already, my darling.

"You mean I don't know nearly enough," she retorted. "You don't tell me anything anymore."

"I ought never to have told you a damned thing in the first place," he said darkly. "I am not a good friend to you, Evie."

Evie reached out and took his hand. "Don't say that. You are the best friend, Louis. *My* best friend. Please… don't stop being my friend. I could not bear it."

Louis didn't look at her, but squeezed her fingers before he withdrew his hand. *"Non.* I won't stop, though I ought." He returned to his work and then straightened, standing back to look at her. "Lovely."

Evie smiled, knowing he was being kind, but confident that it must look a good deal better than the horror she had given him. "Thank you so much. I don't know how you did it, but I won't feel such a fright now stood beside all the beauties."

"Merde, stop speaking of yourself so, Evie!" he said, his voice hard and his eyes flashing with irritation. "You are forever doing that. It is *they* who should compare themselves to you, and don't you forget it."

Evie looked at him in surprise, taken aback by the vehemence of his anger. "Yes, Louis," she said meekly, uncertain once again of his mood and deciding it was best simply to agree with him. "Would you undo me, please?" she asked, turning her back on him.

She waited, but he didn't move. Evie glanced over her shoulder at him. "Well, I can't do it by myself, so unless you want me to sleep in it—"

"Dieu ait pitié," he grumbled, but began deftly undoing the dress.

Evie held her breath until the bodice sagged and then scurried behind the bookshelves again. She had just unlaced the corset and put it aside when he spoke.

"You can manage now, I think. I had better go."

"Oh, no, wait!" Forgetting herself entirely, she went to stop him and then realised she wore only her shift as Louis swore violently and turned his back on her. *"Putain!* Evie, for the love of God!"

Evie gave a little shriek and disappeared again. "Sorry, I forgot!" she said, mortified as she stripped off the shift and dressed again in her nightclothes.

"I think you forget a great deal, Evie," he said, and he sounded really cross now. "You forget just who and what I am. I'm not another damned debutante, you do realise that? I'm a man, and an unmarried one. I think sometimes you want us to be caught so you'll be ruined!"

"I do *not*!" she retorted, for really, that was dreadfully unfair. "I would never do that to you, Louis. You know I wouldn't. I know you don't wish to be married, and it would spoil everything and make us both wretched."

"Yes," he said, his voice tight. "It would. So have a care."

"Yes, Louis." She peeked around the bookshelves at him. He still had his back to her, his shoulders set. "I'm sorry if I embarrassed you," she added contritely, though as an inexperienced virgin she could not help but find his outrage somewhat entertaining in the circumstances.

Louis snorted and let out a breath. *"Oui,* I know. Now give me the wretched gown. I'll have it sent to you once it is finished, but you must take the shift and corset now."

Evie nodded and gathered up her things, hugging the box to her chest. She gave him an awkward smile, unsure if he was still angry with her. "Thank you for everything, and I am sorry for being such a trial to you."

He smiled then, and she thought he looked tired, though his expression was warm, the first proper smile she'd had from him all evening, she realised. "You are not a trial, *ma puce*, but a joy, and I am unworthy of your friendship. Forgive me for being so cross and unkind."

"You're never unkind, Louis," she said honestly.

"Ah, but I am," he said, and though she did not understand his words, some sixth sense told her she had better not question him. Instead, she bade him goodnight, and hurried back to her room.

Chapter 10

Jules,

I'll be in town for a couple of days after your mother's ball. We should go out. It's been an age. I seem to remember you still owe me for our last little adventure.

—Excerpt of a letter to The Most Hon'ble Jules Adolphus, Marquess of Blackstone (Eldest son of Prunella and Robert Adolphus, Duke and Duchess of Bedwin) from his friend, The Right Hon'ble Philip Barrington, Earl of Ashburton (Son of Lucian and Matilda Barrington, The Marquess and Marchioness of Montagu).

13th December 1840, Beverwyck, London.

Georgie woke early once again. She had not slept well. Forcing herself out of bed, she washed, splashing her face several times with cold water to rid herself of the gritty eyed feeling from lack of sleep. Despite her tiredness, she felt restless and irritable.

"You're in a bad skin this morning, aye?" Meg observed as she brushed out Georgie's hair. "Yer lookin' a bit peely-wally."

"Aye," Georgie muttered absently. She simply could not stop thinking about last night. What was wrong with her? Of all men to get herself all in a dither over, it had to be Rochford. Honestly, why could she not get herself in a lather over a nice, even-tempered fellow?

Because you'd find a nice, even-tempered fellow as dull as ditch water and you'd far rather have a challenge on your hands, echoed back a little voice in her head.

"Best get yourself out for a walk in the fresh air, hen. Put some colour in your cheeks and wear yourself out. Ye might sleep better tonight. That or find the big fella and get him to tumble ye about a bit."

"Meg!" Georgie exclaimed, wide-eyed.

Meg smirked. "Well, it's plain as a pikestaff that's what ye're getting yourself all het up about. Yer blood's runnin' hot, ye numpty. Get the devil to kiss ye and ye'll feel a deal better for it."

Georgie glared at her outrageous maid. "Not helping, Meg!"

Meg chuckled unrepentantly. She stabbed Georgie with a couple more hairpins and went about her work, humming merrily to herself and leaving Georgie in more of a stew than ever. The wretched woman. Now, there was no hope of ridding herself of the heated waking dreams that had disturbed her last night. Dreams where Rochford had not let her go but held her fast against the wall whilst he kissed her thoroughly, his big body pressed firmly against hers and his hard—

"Stop it!" she scolded herself.

Well, at least that had put some colour in her cheeks, she thought, catching sight of herself in the mirror. Thoroughly frustrated, she took Meg's advice—not the bit about letting Rochford have his way with her—and took herself off for a walk.

An hour later, the colour in her cheeks was most definitely from exertion and the cold. A few tentative flakes of snow had even made an appearance, leaving a fine scattering of white like a giant hand dusting a cake with sugar. In a far better temper than when she'd left the house, Georgie returned via the stables to visit Apollo.

The stables at Beverwyck were just as impressive as the house. Two storeys high, with four ranges set around a spacious courtyard, she'd seen mansion houses which were less imposing. There was a large entrance bay with clock and bell tower in the form of a domed lantern, and the horses entered each of the luxurious stable blocks via grand arched walkways.

After a pleasant half hour spent with Apollo and chatting to the grooms, many of whom she'd known since she was a little girl, Georgie meandered back through the stables, towards the house, pausing when she heard a familiar deep voice. Ducking back behind one of the stable arches, she peered around to see that Rochford had sat down upon a low wall to remove one of his boots and shake out a small stone. He was now trying to put it back on and hampered by three mewling kittens, who seemed to think he was a very fine playground.

"Get off me, you ridiculous creature," he grumbled, picking a kitten off his shoulder and placing it gently on the ground. He turned his attention to another that was chewing the buttons on his waistcoat as the first climbed up his leg again. "Ow, you little blighter. You've sharp claws."

Georgie bit back a giggle. As fast as he unhooked one, another climbed back up his leg. An intrepid ginger kitten made a heroic leap from the floor to his foot and sank its tiny needle claws into his big toe.

"Ouch! Stop that, no… Argh!"

He released it from his foot and put it down, thrusting his foot into his boot quickly before he was attacked again. Then he reached for the kitten which had made a triumphant climb up to his shoulder where it clung on precariously. This time, instead of putting it on the floor, he put it in his lap, where it immediately made itself comfortable and settled down.

"No, don't go to sleep, you can't stay there," he warned it, unhooking another kitten from his thigh and putting it with the first. There was a little mewl of displeasure at the third kitten lost its grip on his calf and fell back to the ground where it sat, crying piteously. Rochford glared at it before she heard his usual harrumphing sound, at which point he picked it up by the scruff of its neck and deposited it with its siblings. "Only for a minute, you hear?" he instructed them as they purred and kneaded at their comfy new bed.

A little like last night's trifle, the opportunity was simply too delicious to resist.

Georgie crept out from behind the arch and gave a sigh. "Well, if that isn't the most adorable thing I have ever seen in my life. The curmudgeonly duke who's kind to kittens."

"I'm not," he objected at once. "I'm only—"

Georgie's eyebrows went up as he cast about for another explanation for having a lapful of kittens.

"Only?"

"I want a fur lining for my hat," he said, scowling at her.

Georgie snorted and went to sit beside him. "Oh, give over, Rochford. Admit it, they're adorable and you're not half so scary as you'd like everyone to believe."

"They're a blasted nuisance, and not the only one around here, I might add. Take them away."

He gestured for her to remove the kittens, but Georgie shook her head.

"Oh, no. I'm enjoying the sight far too much. I love cats, and there's something about a big man holding kittens that makes my insides go all squirmy."

"Must be that second helping of trifle coming back to haunt you," he said darkly.

Georgie snorted.

"You're supposed to be staying away from me," he remarked, absently stroking a soft, fluffy head.

Georgie watched his large hands caressing the tiny furball with such care and gave a despondent sigh. "I know."

"Have you no willpower, woman?"

"No. Not a scrap of it," she admitted. "Will you come to the ball tomorrow night?"

He returned an uncompromising look, and she grimaced.

"Oh, don't make out like you'll be pining away for the lack of me," he muttered, gently prising tiny claws from his thigh and the material of his trousers. The kitten yawned and stretched, revealing soft, pink paws. "You'll be danced off your feet, no doubt."

"Oh, yes. Jules and my godfather, and my friends, and their fathers." She pulled a face.

"What do you mean by that?" he demanded.

Georgie rolled her eyes at him. She stood up and swept an impatient hand up and down to indicate her person. "Look at me, Rochford."

"I am," he said, obviously missing the point.

"I'm taller than most men, which makes them uncomfortable, and dancing awkward. No one who isn't a friend or a relation will ask me. Not unless you come, anyway," she added crossly, sitting down again with a flounce of skirts and petticoats.

"What's wrong with them?" he demanded.

"Nothing," she said, throwing up her hands. "They just want some delicate little flower to protect, and that's not me, not by a long chalk. I'm robust, not fragile. I've never swooned in my life. If I did, I'd likely knock down any man standing close enough if he even tried to catch me."

"Don't talk nonsense."

"It isn't nonsense! Oh, come to the ball, Rochford, at least for long enough to dance with me."

Her cheeks burned. That had been perilously close to begging. Not that it mattered.

Rochford shook his head. "If I danced with you again, tongues would truly wag, and that won't do you a bit of good."

Irritation burned in her. The pig-headed lummox. "Oh, so what? I'll never find a match here. One of my brother's friends back home has always had a fondness for me. I suppose I'll end up with him, eventually."

Her lack of enthusiasm for this idea was not hard to discern.

"Well, there you are, then." Rochford folded his arms.

"There I am then," she agreed with a sigh. It was clearly hopeless. He wouldn't come. "It just would have been nice to dance again. It's not like I'm expecting a proposal. I'm *not,"* she added hastily.

"Stop trying to work upon my tender sensibilities," he warned her. "I have none."

"This from a man with a lap full of kittens," she said, quirking an eyebrow at him.

"Hat lining," he growled.

"Oh, yes. I forgot."

They sat in silence for a while, the kittens' contented purring the only sound between them. A groom appeared, leading a pretty bay mare. Georgie waved at him.

"Good morning, John. How is Martha?"

"Ready to drop, I reckon, my lady," the man said cheerily. "She's certain it will be a boy this time. Though she's said it the last three times an' all. Not that I care, long as it's healthy."

"I shall keep fingers and toes crossed for that," she promised. "Keep me posted."

"I will do, and thank you kindly for that recipe for tea you sent. Worked a treat, she said."

"Oh, don't thank me, thank my mother's housekeeper, Mrs MacLeod. It was her recipe."

The fellow waved goodbye and walked away. Georgie turned her head, unsurprised to see Rochford with a face like thunder.

"Go on, then," she said, aware that her frustration with him was simmering beneath her skin.

Why couldn't the wretched man just dance with her once? *Because you're supposed to stay away from each other*, returned the voice of reason. She told it to shut up. Rochford was going to have something to say about being too familiar with the staff and she was spoiling for a fight.

"None of my business," he said, the words spoken through gritted teeth.

"No, it isn't. Nothing I do is your business. You don't give a damn, and that's fine. Well, I shall go to the ball and find someone else to dance with. I suppose there's the Comte de Villen to look forward to. Perhaps he'll deign to dance with me more than once."

"Stay away from him," Rochford said, his voice hard.

"None of your business," she replied in a singsong tone. She got to her feet and smoothed down her skirts.

He glowered at her, folding his arms. "It isn't, but if you've a lick of sense, which I'm well aware you haven't, you'll stay away from him."

"Why should I? He's charming, unlike some people," she retorted, aware only of the desire to prick at his temper because it was better than being ignored, damn him.

"He is, and as cool as the North Sea. You'll never know what he's thinking, for he gives nothing away, and you'll never reach his heart. He's not the type. He's no husband for you."

His grey eyes were impassive. She wanted to strike him.

Fists clenched, Georgie glared at him. "You can't judge people that way, Rochford. You don't know him at all."

His voice was low and even, emotionless, and yet she sensed the tumult of feeling boiling beneath the surface as he spoke. "I can and I will. I know human nature well enough to judge it. I've seen enough to know what's likely, and I recognise damage when I see it."

"Damage?"

"Yes, damage. I've watched him, the way he holds himself apart. Not all scars are visible, Lady Georgina. That man's got a past, I tell you. A dark one. The kind that will haunt him and make him a wretched partner in life. Believe me, I know the type. He'll make you miserable. If he has a grain of decency, he'll never marry at all."

"Why must you always expect the worse?" she demanded, shocked by his words, by what it revealed about him as much as the comte. "So what if you're right? Perhaps he has a dreadful past to overcome. Perhaps he needs someone to love him, to heal him. Maybe if you gave people a chance for once in your life, you'd be pleasantly surprised."

"I've given chances enough and had every one of them thrown back in my face," he retorted, and there was something raw and unguarded in the words that gave her pause. The kittens stirred, unsettled by the noise and Rochford picked them up, carrying them carefully inside to where their mother had been snoozing with one eye open, watching proceedings. Rochford put them down beside her and stalked back outside.

"Rochford," Georgie said, hurrying after him.

"Go away."

"Rochford, I'm sorry. I didn't mean to—"

"No, you never mean to," he muttered, not slowing a whit.

"Oh, please stop," she begged, picking up her skirts to run after him. "Rochford, don't be cross."

"I'll be cross if I choose to be, you irritating baggage, and you may follow me about all day if you wish, but it won't change my temperament. I'm a devil right enough and you'd do well to stay away like we agreed."

Georgie knew she ought to stay away, and not because of his words. She had a growing suspicion he wasn't half so awful as he made out, and she knew that gaining that knowledge of him would be dangerous. But surely, if someone attempted to please him occasionally, he'd not be so cross? Of course, she was not a likely candidate for that position, as she'd put him in the devil's own temper in the first place.

Instead of returning to the house, he diverted to the gardens, obviously hoping to lose her if he walked long and fast enough. Georgie was used to walking miles over rough terrain, though, and in all weathers. After a good half hour of military style marching, he relented. They'd come to a large lake that cut through the landscape in a narrow sickle shape, giving the impression of a river as it disappeared into thick woodland. Large rocks jutted out of the hillside and Rochford sat upon one, staring out at the water.

Georgie glanced at him, noting the uncompromising line of his jaw. He was still furious. She swallowed, wishing she knew what to say, but how could she know? He'd said he recognised damage when he saw it. Well, the reason for that was obvious, and perhaps the answer was the same as the one she'd given for the comte.

She bit her lip, trying to gather her nerve, uncertain whether she would make him angrier still, but it was all she could think of, and it had to be worth the risk. Tentatively, she reached out and took his hand, pulling it into her lap and holding it within her own.

He stiffened for a moment, and she could almost hear the words brewing on his tongue, angry words that would flay her and leave her smarting. They never came. He let out an uneven breath but didn't move, just stared out at the view. She left him to his thoughts for a while, just holding his hand, hoping perhaps it gave him some comfort, for surely that was what this man so desperately needed, even if he didn't want it.

"This is one of my favourite places on the estate," she said eventually. "It's so peaceful."

He returned a wry look that made her smile.

"Well, if you don't come with someone whose tongue runs like a fiddle. I tried for as long as I could. Give me some credit," she said.

He huffed out a laugh, shaking his head. "I do. Believe me. You're a brave girl."

"No, just stubborn," she replied with a sigh.

"That too."

She turned to look at him. Despite the scars, he had a noble profile, a strong Roman nose. He looked like a man out of time. Beauty and refinement, manners, and the perfect outward appearance counted now, far too much. In centuries past, Rochford would have been revered for his size, for his strength in battle, and his uncompromising character. Or else, she could easily imagine him as a warrior king of the ancient Britons, and she had a sudden vision of his powerful body clad in animal skins and painted with blue woad, as described by Caesar in *De bello gallico*. Heat swept over her, and she blurted out a question to cover her confusion. "What's Cumbria like? That's where Mulcaster Castle is, I think?"

He nodded. "It's wild. Remote and harsh and beautiful. You'd recognise it, perhaps."

"Like Scotland?"

"Somewhat. It was Scottish once upon a time, remember."

She nodded, and then dared to voice the question she really wanted to ask. "Who—"

"Don't," he said, cutting her off. Some instinct must have told him this enquiry was more personal, but Georgie had not been exaggerating her stubborn streak. She waited a moment and tried a different tack.

"Is your mother alive still? I know you said your father died when you were seven."

He narrowed his eyes at her, but answered reluctantly. "She is."

Georgie chewed at her lip, trying to sit quietly in the hope he might speak to her. He gave a heavy sigh and muttered an oath.

"My father was a madman. Is that what you wished to hear?" he demanded. "It's not like there isn't gossip enough if you care to find it."

She turned to stare at him, wide-eyed. "Rochford, I-I do not wish to pry secrets from you for my own entertainment, I—"

He waved this away irritably, but his left hand remained in her lap still. She stroked his thumb with her own, hoping he might carry on.

"I know you're not prying for its own sake," he said grudgingly. "You've a kind heart. Anyone can see that. You see a problem and wish to fix it, or to mend something broken, which is why you must have a care. Someone will take advantage of you if you don't, and there are some things you can't fix with a recipe for tea or kind words."

"That's not fair," she objected, stung. "You make me sound like a simpleton."

She withdrew her hand, but Rochford's grip tightened. He laced their fingers together, and Georgie's breath caught.

"It was my father did this," he said, his right hand tracing the ragged scar on his cheek. "He attacked me with a whip. Knocked me out cold after the second blow, which was a blessing. He had syphilis and by the end he was a fright to look at, with his nose all gone, and quite insane. I was afraid of him, but he was my father and I loved him anyway, or tried to. The staff did their best to keep me from him, but I always found a way to be near him. That was a mistake, for he was paranoid, and he'd have violent episodes, thinking everyone was trying to murder him. Even his six-year-old son."

Georgie watched in appalled silence as he shrugged his big shoulders.

"Oh, Rochford," she said, feeling a tear slip down her cheek.

He glanced at her and scowled. "Save your tears, Georgina. Some monsters can't be saved. Don't you see? You can care all you like, and it won't make a scrap of difference. You'll only get hurt trying."

She stared at him in horror. "You cannot think—Rochford, he was *mad* and… Oh, you idiot man. You're not a monster. You're just a man with scars."

He released her hand abruptly and got to his feet. "We'd best go back before we're missed."

Georgie couldn't bear it. His tone was emotionless, perfectly cool, and she was in pieces, wanting to weep for him and everything he'd been through. In Georgie's family, there was an abundance of hugging and affection. Just as the boys rough and tumbled like puppies, they were easy with themselves and each other, quick to give a hug if they'd caused offence or noticed she was sad. The way Rochford held himself so stiffly, so apart from everyone else, she wondered when the last time was anyone had touched him with affection. Suddenly, she could not bear it for another moment. She ran to him and flung her arms about his waist, laying her head on his chest and holding on tight.

"What—" He jolted in shock, his arms outstretched as if he didn't know what to do with her. Perhaps he'd try to unhook her like he had the kittens. "What are you doing?" he demanded in outrage.

"Hugging you," she said, snivelling a little. "I'm sorry. Please don't tell me to stop."

"Why, for the love of God?" He sounded sincerely bewildered, which only made her hug him tighter.

"Because I've met no one in all my life who needs a hug more than you do."

He groaned, but his tone softened. "Stop acting like a damned mad woman, you daft creature."

"I already told you I can't. You bring out the worst in me."

"Hell and damnation, Georgina. Don't get yourself all upset about something that happened years ago. This is—"

"Nice, Rochford. This is nice. Isn't it?" She glanced up at him uncertainly. Comforting him was one thing, but if he really didn't want her affection....

"Yes," he admitted cautiously, relieving her mind. "But—"

"Just shut up, will you?" She interrupted him, satisfied there was no real objection beyond the usual muttering about her reputation and the fact they were like oil and water and ought to be kept apart.

He subsided with a huff.

She glared up at him. "Are you going to stand there like an idiot or are you going to hug me back?"

"You never said I had to play an active part in this nonsense," he said, looking revolted.

"Well, I'm saying it now. *Please*," she added, finding she wished for the feel of his arms about her more than anything.

Looking like she'd asked him to kiss a three-day-old fish, Rochford reluctantly put his hands on her back, his arms not touching her.

She rolled her eyes. "Rochford. That's not a hug. Do it properly."

His lips twitched, amusement glinting in his dark eyes. "Maybe I don't want to hug such a bossy little madam?"

"Or maybe you want to a great deal and don't wish to admit it," she retorted.

"Fine."

Georgie let out a little *oof* as he pulled her against his chest, holding her close. She sighed, content, and quieted, hoping that perhaps this soothed him as much as it did her. Uncertain, she glanced up again, wondering if he was merely humouring her still, to find him watching her. There was certainly warmth there now, and the desire to kiss her shone starkly from his face. She held her breath, her gaze falling to his lips, and he turned away at once. His scar, she realised. He thought she was staring at the scar, when she was only desperate for the feel of his lips against her own. She reached up, her fingers caressing the damaged skin gently, turning his face back to her. She touched the place where his beard became patchy as the scar cut through the hair and stroked, surprised by how soft it was. Then she touched her finger to his lips, gently tracing the outline of his mouth, over the scar, over a surprisingly delicate cupid's bow and a full lower lip.

His breath caught.

"Don't back out this time," she whispered, and lifted on her toes, sliding her hand into his hair and tugging him down.

Mistake! Mistake! Retreat! screamed an agitated voice in her head, but it was already far too late. The moment his lips touched hers, she was burning as if she was fuel, and he was the spark that lit her.

Although most of the local lads around Wildsyde dared not touch her for fear of her father's or brothers' wrath, Georgie had managed a few stolen kisses over the years. Only innocent pecks, but she'd thought she'd experienced enough to have a basic idea of how to go about it. Yet nothing had ever felt like this. Rochford was gentle, touching his lips to hers with so many soft presses of his mouth she was uncertain if it was still one kiss or a hundred. His large hand cupped her face, his thumb caressing her cheek as he tilted her head back. The warmth of his tongue tracing the seam of her mouth made her gasp at the intimacy of it, and he swept inside, tasting her. A groan of pleasure rumbled through his chest, so raw that a strange longing sensation jolted through Georgie. She wanted to hear him make that sound again; she wanted to be closer to him.

Thought became deed, and she clung to him, arching her hips against his, equally shocked and delighted by the feel of his arousal. He wanted her, and the knowledge rocked her to her core, the pleasure of it dizzying as she realised she wanted him too, far more than she'd realised. Oh, Lord. This was why he'd warned her to stay away, but she didn't care in this moment. She only wanted....

The sound of a throat clearing had Rochford dropping his hold on her as if she'd turned into a venomous snake.

Georgie gave a squeal, startled and unbalanced by the sudden removal of the large body that had been holding her up. Without him, her knees, which had been feeling strangely unsteady, gave up.

Strong arms clasped her before she landed on her backside on the icy ground, but they weren't Rochford's. Georgie turned to see that Jules had caught her. He was staring at Rochford, his expression not exactly threatening, but not entirely friendly either. Jules tore his gaze from his friend to look at her.

"You well, Georgie?" he asked softly.

Georgie nodded, rather mortified but relieved at least that it was only Jules, who could be relied upon to keep his mouth shut. She flushed and glanced at Rochford, intending to give him a rueful smile, but the expression died on her lips as she saw the furious glint in his eyes.

"So, this was why you were so eager for me to come for Christmas. Cooked this little scheme up between you, I suppose?" he said to Jules, and though she heard the rage in his voice, she saw too the colour on the crests of his cheeks. Georgie stared at him for a moment, not comprehending his words. Then they sank in.

"You… You think we planned this? *Together?* Oh, my God," she exclaimed, surprised by how much the accusation hurt her. By the look in Jules' eyes, he wasn't best pleased either. The bloody imbecile. Oh, how she hated him!

"Rochford!" Jules snapped, his face white with anger, but Rochford didn't heed the warning.

"Well, it's convenient, isn't it? That he just happens along at the correct moment?" he said to her, and the sneer at his lips was most certainly deliberate now.

Georgie's temper lit. "And how *exactly* did he know we'd be here? You were the one that led me on a merry dance about the gardens. I only followed you—you obnoxious arse—because I wanted to make amends, and I wish to God I hadn't now!"

"Really? Because Jules looks like he's ready to demand satisfaction," he remarked, folding his arms.

Those arms had held her against him just minutes ago. What a fool she was for believing he'd understood she'd been trying to comfort him, to soothe something raw and broken and—and perhaps he'd been right. Some things could not be fixed. Not by her, at least.

"Jules, there's no need to get all upset about my honour," she said to him stiffly, her cheeks blazing with mortification. "I kissed Rochford. He took no liberties, I assure you."

"No, they were handed me on a plate," he said darkly.

Jules took an angry step forward, his expression murderous, but Georgie put out a hand, staying the motion.

She turned back to the duke, praying she could disguise how much his words hurt her and hold back the tears burning behind her eyes. "Just so we're clear, Rochford, I wouldn't marry you if you were the last man on earth, and it's nothing to do with your scars, but because you're a coward. You'd rather believe the worst of everyone than put yourself at risk of getting hurt. Well, you were right. We ought to stay away from each other. You can rest assured that I will do so from now on."

Georgie stalked away with her head held high, and managed to get out of sight before the tears began. She paused for a moment, leaning back against a tree as she fought for calm. *Fool. You stupid, stupid fool, Georgie.* She wept and berated herself until she was calm again.

Then she found her handkerchief, wiped her eyes and blew her nose, and hurried back to the house.

Chapter 11

Dearest Georgina,

I expect you have already written, but the post is so dreadfully slow I suppose I must be patient a while yet to receive it.

I do hope your journey to Beverwyck was uneventful. We miss you terribly, darling, especially your father, who sends his fondest wishes, but with luck you are enjoying all the diversions London can offer you and having a marvellous time. We long to hear everything you have been up to, so write often or your Papa will be on the next carriage south with your brothers. They miss you too, which is evident by the increase of bickering between them.

We have dressed the castle up in its finery for Christmas, and this morning had a thick snowfall. The children have been out making snowmen and having snowball fights, which naturally all the men at Wildsyde felt obliged to join in. A fierce battle was waged here, and I must confess to having done my part to defend our castle.

*Papa bids me tell you now that I am a
dreadful turncoat and hit him in the back of
the head on purpose despite being on his side.
(The temptation was too great to deny.)*

**—Excerpt of a letter to Lady Georgina
Anderson from her mother, The Right
Hon'ble Ruth Anderson, The Countess of
Morven.**

13th December 1840, Beverwyck, London.

Rochford watched Jules warily. He might be a deal taller and wider than the young man, but he wasn't about to underestimate him. He'd seen the devil fight, and he looked as if he wanted Rochford's head on a platter.

"You bloody bastard," Jules said, his voice low and unmistakably angry. "It's bad enough you insult me, but to hurt Georgie like that! How could you, Rochford? Can't you see the girl likes you, though God alone knows why! Come to that, I'm not sure why I like you, either."

Rochford snorted. "Perhaps you don't. Hardly a bloody surprise, that. I got you out of a difficult situation, that was all. It doesn't make us friends."

He turned away, intending to leave. He'd leave Jules standing here, the only man who'd ever troubled to be a friend to him. He'd leave Beverwyck, leave Lady bloody Georgina Anderson, and go back to Cumbria, to that monstrosity of a castle that so befitted his wretched title.

Something inside him was bleeding, though. He could feel it. A wound so profound there would be no burying it this time, but he didn't know what else to do. He made people angry. He made people hate him. It was easier that way. Easier than seeing disgust or distaste or worst of all, pity.

"Oh, no you don't!" Jules grabbed hold of his arm and stopped him. "You're not turning your back on me."

"Want satisfaction, do you?" Rochford said coldly. "Fine. Give me a place and a time."

"Don't be an unspeakable arse, Rochford. I will not put a bullet in you, though I'll admit the idea is growing on me." Jules glared at him.

"What, then?" Rochford demanded wildly, just wanting this over with. He needed to get away from here, from all of them and their happy, bloody families, before he did or said something truly reprehensible. Oh, wait—too late.

Jules took a deep breath and Rochford got the distinct impression he was praying for patience. Well, he could hardly blame him. When Jules turned back to look at him, the fury in his eyes had dimmed a little.

"You're right about one thing. I hoped you might make a match with Georgina."

Rochford's jaw tightened at the admission.

"Do you know why?" Jules asked him conversationally.

"Because your friend has a fancy to be a duchess, I don't doubt," he said irritably, unable to think of any other reason.

Jules rubbed a hand over his face and muttered something that sounded less than complimentary. "No, Rochford. That is not the reason."

"Why, then?" he demanded.

Rochford stiffened, unsettled by the sympathy in Jules' expression. "Because, you great ox, you're my friend, and underneath crabby exterior is a good fellow with a kind heart. I knew you'd need a formidable female to stand you and, having known Georgie since infancy, I thought perhaps she might be the one. By some miracle, it seems she likes you too, or at least, I assume she was kissing you for a reason? She doesn't go about doing such things as a matter of course, you know. As for her wanting to be a duchess, well, I'm sorry, old man, but she doesn't give a brass farthing for such titles, so you may as well stop dangling it in front of her because you'll have the devil's own job getting her to take it. If ever you're lucky enough to persuade her to marry you, which you've just made about a thousand times more difficult, it will be in spite of the bloody dukedom, not because of it."

Jules folded his arms regarding Rochford with an enquiring expression. He seemed to require some sort of response, in which case he'd have a long wait, as Rochford didn't have a damned clue what he was supposed to say to that.

"I thought you liked the girl?" he said in bewilderment and after an interminable wait. It was all he could come up with.

"I do," Jules replied. "She's a good friend, almost a sister really."

"What in God's name are you doing throwing her at me, then? I'd think you might have a care for her happiness."

"I do," Jules said again, frowning. "Didn't I already say all this?"

Rochford stared at him, utterly baffled. "If you care for her, for her happiness, why would you put her in my care?"

Jules rubbed a hand over his face and took a deep breath. "If—and right now this is a very large if—but if Georgie was your wife, would you beat her?"

"God, no!" Rochford exclaimed, taking a step backwards.

The idea of laying a hand on any woman in anger revolted him, but Georgie…. He'd rather die.

Jules nodded. "And if someone insulted or hurt her?"

"I'd bloody kill him," he said at once.

"And if she were ill?"

"She'd have the best doctors, the best care, of course. What the hell are you driving at?"

"I'm just trying to figure out why being married to you would be such a dreadful fate," Jules replied gently.

Rochford snorted. "I think she might look higher than a man who'd not beat her and would fetch a doctor if she were ill."

"So do I. Is that all you can offer her, then?"

Jules watched him, his expression too intent, and Rochford wished once again that he'd never come here. He'd been content enough with the way things had been, until this family had gone and stirred things up, had shown him what a family was supposed to look like. Except he'd not been content, had he? Which was why he'd come, rather than return to Mulcaster, to his only kin: a woman who could not look upon him without revulsion.

Rochford tried to consider the question with detachment. What could he offer a woman like Georgie? Well, she'd be his duchess. It was the only thing he had going for him, but Jules seemed to think that would be reason enough for her to turn him down.

"Don't say the title," Jules warned him, confirming his thoughts.

He shrugged. "Damned if I know then," he said, exasperated. "A bad-tempered husband who hates society and is liable to terrify any children we'd have."

Jules muttered under his breath. "Has it never occurred to you that your temper might be a deal sweeter if you woke up to discover a woman like Georgie beside you?"

Rochford started in shock. His fists curled, as he realised he was furious with Jules for speaking of Georgina so intimately, for even suggesting such a thing, and yet… and yet, now he could not get the image from his mind. He could see her at Mulcaster, in his bedroom, in his bed, her dark curling hair spilling over the pillow.

Christ, what would it feel like to wake beside that beautiful face every morning? There was an odd stabbing sensation in the vicinity of his heart. He imagined watching her dress, perhaps even brushing out her hair for her, sharing breakfast with her. His breath caught.

"She'd be lonely," he said, reminding himself of all the reasons he'd be a terrible choice for her, when all he truly wanted was for Jules to find an argument to counter each reason.

"She lives in the backend of beyond in Scotland, Rochford," Jules said, shaking his head. "She's used to such a life. Of course, she'll want to see her friends and family, but you could bear that now and then for her sake, couldn't you?"

Privately, Rochford thought he could stand being slow roasted on a spit for her sake, but he held his tongue. There was something horribly like hope flickering in his heart and he was bloody terrified it would snuff out at any moment.

"I'd embarrass her," he said, frowning at Jules. "People would mock her."

Jules' expression hardened. "Well, I'm sad to say she's used to that, too. Her grandfather was a cit, and a vulgar one at that. She's no shrinking violet. Georgie is strong and loyal, and fiercely protective of those she cares for. If a woman like that loved you, she'd stand up to anyone and anything and be proud to do it."

"It sounds like you ought to marry her yourself," Rochford remarked carelessly, though his heart thudded too hard in his chest with wondering why on earth Jules hadn't done so, if he could see all her fine qualities so clearly.

"I told you already. She's like a sister to me," Jules said, rolling his eyes. "Besides, we'd never suit."

"And you think I would? You're soft in the head." Rochford stalked away. He was being a fool to even consider it. He'd be setting his foot on the path to misery and humiliation if he even dared consider courting her. "You heard the lady. I'm the last man on earth she'd ever marry."

Jules hurried after him. "She was angry with you, you bloody half-wit, and with good reason. You insulted her—and me, I might add."

Rochford frowned but slowed his steps, glancing back at Jules. "I… I apologise," he said awkwardly. "Though it appears I wasn't entirely wrong about your intentions."

Jules gave a bark of laughter. "Well, that's a half-arsed apology, but I suppose it will have to do. I suggest you do a better job with Georgie, though. In fact, I'd strongly suggest getting on your knees and grovelling."

Rochford stopped and swung around to face his friend. "You're not serious?" he asked, whilst something raw and vulnerable trembled in his chest. "You don't really think that… that she'd ever consent…?"

"She kissed you, Rochford," Jules said with a smile. "And I'd wager that's the first proper kiss she's ever had. You're a bright fellow—well, some of the time—you'll figure it out."

And with that, Jules clapped him on the shoulder and walked away.

Aggie looked up from the paper dress she was cutting out. Monsieur Le Comte had bought the beautiful set to appease her for not being able to attend the ball tomorrow night, telling her it was an early Christmas gift. Beautifully printed with lavish colours, the little paper doll that went with it had a comprehensive wardrobe that any girl would covet. She was not so disappointed about missing the ball now, for Fred and Victoria would be with her and the duchess had promised they may watch the dancing from a hidden balcony for a while if they were good. Instinctively, she felt Monsieur was not so happy about the ball himself, or about being here at all. Since he had rescued her from the streets, she had come to idolise her guardian, though not so much that she did not see his faults. She was too much a realist for that, having lived a harsh life for too long.

She knew her guardian's closely kept secret too, that his life had been equally hard, and that he understood the difficulty of always feeling an outsider, even if one was welcomed with open arms. He seemed more unsettled of late, though, unhappy, and she did not know why. Aggie had become attuned to his moods and could tell when he was truly happy and when he was putting on a show to be polite. Usually, Miss Knight's company was enough to make him relax and smile, but even that did not seem to be working. She wasn't quite certain, but she thought perhaps it was only making matters worse, which she did not understand at all. Miss Knight was such a lovely, warm young woman who made everyone laugh and feel at home, even Aggie.

It was a talent few people had, but everyone who knew her loved her and sought out her company, not that she seemed to realise the fact.

Monsieur was watching Miss Knight now as she poured the tea, his expression pensive.

"Do you think the yellow or the green?" Aggie asked, raising two carefully cut out carriage dresses up to show him.

Her guardian's astonishing blue eyes moved to study the paper gowns. "The green."

Aggie nodded. "Yes, that is what I thought."

"You have excellent taste, child."

Preening a little, Aggie grinned, and then gave into the impulse to jump up and hug him, pressing a kiss to his cheek. *"Mille mercis pour mon cadeau, monsieur.* It is a splendid present."

He regarded her with surprise, clearly taken aback by the show of affection. Aggie blushed, feeling foolish now, but he smiled at her, a proper smile, and she was glad for having done so.

"It was my pleasure, Agatha, and both your French and your English are coming on wonderfully well. I am proud of you."

The praise was enough to have Aggie walking on air, and she beamed at him. She settled down at his feet, returning her attention to the paper dresses, though she watched him covertly from under her eyelashes. "Are you looking forward to the ball, monsieur?"

If she had not been studying him, she might not have noticed how his face shuttered up, but she saw.

"Of course," he said lightly, though she knew he did not mean it. His attention drifted to the other side of the room where his brother, Nic, was laughing with Eliza and her mama.

Something like pain flickered in his eyes and Aggie's heart ached. He would never say so—he'd do nothing to spoil his brother's happiness, but he missed Nic dreadfully. She wished he was truly her Papa, so she could live with him and keep him company, for he hated being alone, but that was not allowed. Monsieur had explained why, and she'd said she understood, but it seemed a stupid rule. But rules were rules and Aggie realised she must obey them, for the consequences could be very bad indeed.

She sighed. If only he would marry, then perhaps she could go and live with him and his wife, but then his wife might not like her. A wife might make him leave Aggie alone. The idea made her heart squeeze with fear.

"You won't ever leave me, will you, monsieur?"

He looked at her, startled by the anxiety in her tone. *"Dieu,* Aggie! Whatever would make you say such a thing?"

Aggie shrugged miserably, wishing she'd never thought such a horrid thing, for she couldn't shake the idea now. "If… If you got married, your wife might not like me. You know people s-say I'm your bastard."

His face hardened, his eyes glittering, and he reached out and took her hand, squeezing her fingers. "I will never abandon you, Aggie. Never. You have my word."

"Oh," she said, the breath leaving her in a rush. "Oh, thank you, but—"

"But?" he asked gently, a smile in his eyes.

"But if you married and—"

He shook his head, the smile vanishing. "Never, Aggie. You may be easy on that point."

Aggie nodded, reassured.

"I need some fresh air," he said, though the weather outside was cold and grey. "Would you like to come for a walk before tea?"

Aggie nodded, leaping up to take his hand. "Yes, I'll come, but may we have crumpets when we come back?"

He chucked her under the chin and winked at her. "You may eat crumpets and jam until you burst."

Aggie grinned and followed him out of the room.

Chapter 12

Dearest Aisling,

I hope you are having a marvellous time at Rowsley Hall. It is a shame I won't see you this Christmas.

I would be having a lovely time here at Beverwyck if not for the presence of the most vexing man who ever lived. If you didn't know already, that title belongs to the Duke of Rochford. Oh, how I hate him!

Except I don't hate him half as much as I should, which is horribly frustrating. Why must men be so difficult? It's like they are an entirely difference species. If only I could talk myself out of liking a man I dislike so much and please do not write back to tell me that doesn't make the slightest bit of sense, for I am very well aware of the fact.

Oh, I shall run mad!

—Excerpt of a letter to Lady Aisling Baxter (daughter of Luke and Kitty Baxter, The Earl and Countess of Trevick) from Lady Georgina Anderson (daughter of Gordon and Ruth Anderson, The Earl and Countess of Morven).

14ᵗʰ December 1840, Beverwyck, London.

Rochford glowered as his valet laid out evening clothes on the bed.

"I never said I was going to the bloody bedamned ball!" he barked at the young man, who didn't bat an eyelid. But then Joe Browning didn't bat an eyelash at much at all, which was the reason he'd got and kept his job for almost a full year, unlike every valet who had come before him. At best, they usually lasted around six months before they decided enough was enough.

"No, you just stomped about all day with a face like a slapped arse," Joe remarked, a comment which would have earned him instant dismissal from most employers, if not the nearest heavy object flung at his head.

Rochford, however, wasn't most employers.

Joe hadn't even wanted the position as valet, protesting he didn't know the first thing about it. But he'd spent much of his life working on making costumes for a big London theatre and he knew clothes. Rochford had been desperate, and at the time Joe had no better options. He'd warned Rochford that he'd speak his mind and if he didn't like it, he could lump it. Strangely, Rochford had discovered he preferred someone who wasn't merely polite because he was paid to be so and told him when he was being a bastard—which was most of the time.

"Now," Joe said, clearly striving for patience. "Why don't you sit your bottom down in that chair and let me trim your beard. You're looking more like an angry bear with each day that passes."

"To the devil with you!" Rochford muttered crossly, feeling increasingly like an angry bear.

Joe sighed and folded his arms. "You're being a big baby. She asked you to go, didn't she? She wants you dance with her."

"Asked. Wanted. Past tense," Rochford bit back.

Joe's lips took on a pinched expression as he made a little moue of displeasure. "Well, so you cocked things up. Don't we all? Now, get yourself prettied up and go and apologise to the lady."

"Prettied up?" Rochford repeated, incensed.

Joe rolled his eyes and waved a delicate hand. "Yes, yes, you're a big strong fellow who could snap me in two and you're not the least bit pretty. A great, ugly devil you are. There, better now? You still want to look your best, don't you?"

Rochford snorted and folded his arms.

"Oh, I swear I don't know why I bother," Joe threw up his hands and flung himself down in the nearest chair. "Why I gave up my work at the theatre for this, I truly don't know."

"Because after your last tantrum you burnt your boats and didn't have any other options, and neither did I," Rochford said dryly. "We're not exactly well behaved, either of us."

Joe sighed. "True enough. It doesn't make you any less of an idiot where the fairer sex is concerned. Truly, Rochford, Blackstone is right. It's high time you married and got that witch of a mother off your back. It would certainly make my life easier."

"And that's my job, is it? To make your life easier?" Rochford shot back, knowing he was being an obnoxious arse, but doing it anyway. He was a duke, after all. If he wanted to be insufferable, he could be.

He sighed, despondent. He wanted Georgie to call him an obnoxious arse again, and a pompous fool, and a horrid creature, and whatever the hell else she wished to call him. So long as she did it to his face, he didn't care.

He glanced back at Joe, who was watching him with a knowing expression. Grumbling furiously under his breath, he went and sat his backside down and had his beard trimmed.

"Good heavens, Evie!" Georgie said, staring at her friend in wonder.

"Oh, dear. It's too much, isn't it?" Evie fretted, covering her cleavage with her gloved hands. "I knew I ought not to have listened to… to my sister." She flushed and bit her lip.

Georgie shook her head vigorously. "No! No, that's not what I meant at all. I mean… you look beautiful. Splendid. My word, that gown. Wherever did you get it?"

Evie mumbled something Georgie didn't hear, but took her arm, hurrying down the corridor to the stairs. "You're sure? I don't want to make a spectacle of myself."

"I'm quite sure. You've never looked better. Truly."

Evie returned a pleased smile. "Thank you, Georgie. I think I needed to hear that tonight. You look stunning too, you know, but then you always do."

Georgie smiled, but her stomach was in knots. She didn't know why it bothered her so much, for tonight she would be with her friends and that was enough for her to enjoy herself. So what if no eligible men ever asked her to dance? Well, not any with the slightest interest of finding a prospective bride, anyway. So what if people sniggered at her and called her a giantess? It was only words. She had people who loved her. Just no man who wasn't a friend or relation who wanted to dance with her. It was nothing new and there was no point lamenting it all over again. Yet, that one dance she shared with Rochford had opened her eyes to how it could be, to dance with a man who didn't feel awkward to be with you, or made you feel awkward in return.

She'd felt at home in her own skin, which only ever happened when she was at home with her family. That was it, she realised then. That was the reason he drew her to him. She could be entirely herself, without trying to shrink or watching her tongue. Well, it was one of the reasons, the others being a physique that made her mouth go dry, and the suspicion that something soft and lovable lurked under that uncompromising exterior. Except, if it did, it was dashed well hidden. *The big lout.*

Georgie and Evie made a circuit of the ballroom, greeting friends and accepting invitations to dance. These they noted on pretty mother-of-pearl fans which served as dance cards. So far, Georgie had invitations from the Duke of Bedwin, Jules, Nicolas Alexandre Demarteau, and the one she'd already gained from his half-brother, the comte. She'd not seen the Comte de Villen yet, though he must be here somewhere. You could hide a herd of elephants in this crush. The Duchess of Bedwin's annual Christmas ball was *the* event of the festive season and anyone who was anyone was here.

The sound of sniggering and the sensation of Evie stiffening beside her gained Georgie's attention, and she turned to see a group of five pretty debutantes, giggling and whispering behind their fans. That she and Evie were at the centre of their amusement, she did not doubt. She supposed they made an odd pair, with her towering over diminutive Evie.

"No, no, Goliath and his fat pony," said the nearest girl, not bothering to lower her voice as the others went off into peals of laughter.

"Oh, I know," said another, bouncing on her toes. "Lofty and Dumpling."

"Just ignore them," Evie said with a sigh, cheeks blazing.

Suddenly, the whispering and giggling subsided, and an awed hush fell over the girls. Georgie looked to see what had taken their attention and saw the Comte de Villen moving purposely through the crowd. Though—and despite scolding herself soundly for it— she'd been hoping to see the less elegant figure of the Duke of Rochford heading towards her, Georgie's breath still caught. Heavens, but he was beautiful. He looked like a young god moving among mere mortals. Everyone turned to look at him as he passed, their gazes drawn to him whether or not they wanted to be.

The debutantes sighed and batted their eyelashes as well as their fans, trying to gain his notice, and he ignored them utterly. The comte's gaze seemed fixed on Evie, his expression intent.

"Lady Georgina, Miss Knight. May I say how lovely you both look this evening," he said, giving them a very formal bow. He barely glanced at Georgie, his gaze lingering on Evie a touch longer than it ought, apparently taking in every detail of the gown she wore.

They curtsied, and Georgie returned a wry smile. "Thank you, monsieur. I'm afraid the young ladies did not agree with you. What was it, Evie? Lofty and Dumpling?"

The comte's face darkened, and he turned to regard the young women, his expression cool. "Silly children," he remarked, a comment nicely designed to set them down a peg whilst doing no harm to their reputations. "I hope you will heed my opinion over theirs. You are both exceptionally lovely."

The cluster of young women gasped, flushing with embarrassment, and one let out a sob of mortification as they all hurried away.

"Thank you, Louis," Evie whispered.

His gaze shot back to hers. "Monsieur le Comte," he reminded her, his voice hard.

Evie flushed at the reprimand, and his expression softened. "Will you dance with me, Miss Knight?"

Evie relaxed, smiling up at him. "Oh, of course. I'd love to."

Georgie gave Evie a little wave as she walked off on the comte's arm. Sighing a little, she stood back to watch the dancing, and nearly leapt out of her skin as someone spoke directly into her ear.

"Lady Georgina."

She turned, sent reeling off balance to find Rochford standing close behind her. He grasped her arm, steadying her, and she yanked it from his hold.

"Oh!" she said crossly, her hand pressing against her thundering heart. What on earth was he doing here? "Oh, you made me jump."

His dark eyebrows drew together. "Well, I didn't creep up on you, if that's what you're implying. I'm not exactly built for stealth."

Georgie huffed out a sigh. Clearly he'd come with the express intention of irritating her. "No, apparently you're built for annoying me. I thought we agreed to stay away from each other."

He shook his head. "No, you said you'd stay away from me."

"Well, you told me to stay away from you too, did you not?" she retorted, folding her arms. Georgie glared at him and wished his nearness didn't have her nerves leaping with excitement. Honestly, she was an idiot to be besotted with him just because he was so big and strong and… and had the temperament of a baited badger with a naturally dyspeptic disposition, and a toothache.

"I did," he agreed, looking strangely awkward. He rubbed the back of his neck and she studied him, realising he looked very smart indeed. His beard and hair had been trimmed and everything about him was immaculate.

"You look very nice," she said grudgingly, partly because she suspected he didn't get many compliments, and partly because it was true.

To her astonishment, colour tinged the crests of his cheeks. "My valet insisted I trim my beard," he said, rubbing at it self-consciously.

Georgie clenched her fists, before the desire to reach up and stroke it herself got the better of her.

"You look very smart, very… ducal," she added stiffly, resisting the urge to tell him he was handsome because he'd think she was mocking him. She wasn't. Oh, she knew he wasn't handsome, not at all, at least, not in the conventional sense. Yet there was something about him that appealed to her so deeply that it seemed to overcome his scars and his damaged skin. All she saw was his physique, his grey eyes, the thick dark hair, and that tantalising suspicion he was nothing but a big fraud underneath his angry exterior. Damnation, she was a fool.

"I'm sorry," he said, though his words were muffled as the music swelled around them.

Georgie sighed, assuming he'd not heard her. It was very noisy with the orchestra and everyone chattering. "I said, you look very *ducal*," she repeated, raising her voice to be heard over the din.

He looked perplexed. "And I said, I'm sorry."

"What?"

"Oh, for the love of God," he muttered. "It didn't ought to be this hard."

"What didn't?"

"Will you dance with me?" he demanded.

Georgie stared at him in shock. "You made it very clear you wouldn't dance with me. I even begged, and you still refused. You clearly have no desire to do so," she said, waving her fan vigorously. It was hot in here, wasn't it?

"I do. I just asked you."

"Well, don't," she snapped, waving her fan harder still. "I don't need your charity, I thank you."

"Oh, for heaven's sake. You wanted to dance with me."

"Yes. *Wanted* to. Now I don't," she retorted, which was a big fat lie, but she'd die rather than let him know that. The great ox.

"Please, Lady Georgina. Will you dance with me?"

The desire to say yes was burning on her tongue, but then she remembered how he'd hurt her with his accusations. He'd accused her of being the worst kind of manipulative female and… she couldn't trust him. He was too difficult, too suspicious, too broken, and it wasn't her job to fix him. She shook her head, not trusting her tongue to say what it needed to.

His expression was so grim she thought perhaps he truly regretted her refusal, but that was just her wishful thinking.

"I'm sorry for what I said to you. I know it wasn't true. You were right, it was all me, my… *cowardice*. That's… it's why I came, to apologise, I mean. It's just…."

He let out a sigh of frustration and Georgie looked up at him, stunned by his words and wanting to hear more, even though instinct told her she would be an idiot to let him any closer. She was too susceptible to him. He appealed to her on a visceral level she did not understand, and it would be so easy to be drawn in, too easy, and she did not wish to end her days married to a man who didn't know how to let anyone close and would make her wretched.

"It's just…?" she prompted, her desire to hear him explain overriding good sense.

His grey eyes met hers, warm and surprisingly vulnerable. "It's hard," he said softly. "To believe someone as beautiful as you would want to give me the time of day for any other reason than my title. I can assure you, no one has before."

She smiled, profoundly touched by his words. "You mean you didn't think it was your winning personality that drew me in?"

He snorted, returning a crooked grin which made him look almost boyish. "I did not." His expression sobered, and he gazed at her. "You are the most beautiful woman here tonight, Lady Georgina, and I do not know why you might want to, but I would be honoured if you would dance with me."

Oh.

Well. What choice did she have after a speech like that?

"Oh, Rochford," she said with a sigh of resignation. "I should like that very much."

Rochford let out a breath of relief, which made her smile. He held out his hand to her, and she took it, too aware of his touch even with gloves between them.

Georgie followed him out onto the dance floor, conscious of curious gazes watching them together. This was the second time they'd danced together, and Rochford never danced. Tongues would wag, but she didn't care. Let them talk. All she had wanted was to dance with him again and she had her wish. After Christmas, she'd return to Scotland and their silly chattering would die out quickly enough.

Rochford swept her into the dance, and Georgie relished every moment. Though she doubted either of them would win any prizes for style or elegance, he moved very well, and it was a joy to be close to him again. His powerful arms seemed the safest place in the world to be, as he guided her effortlessly about the floor. Goodness, but this was heaven. She never wanted the dance to end.

"Do you like living in Scotland?"

The question caught her off guard, and it took a moment for her attention to return to reality.

"Yes, very much," she said, a little surprised that he would try to make polite conversation.

"You don't find it too dull, too remote, lacking in entertainment?" he pressed, studying her face intently, concern in his eyes.

Georgie watched him in return, puzzled by his sudden interest. "No. Not at all. I love the countryside. I walk for miles, and ride too, though I confess I enjoy coming to town as well. I have been so looking forward to this visit with Aunt Prue and everyone, but I would not wish to spend too much time here."

He nodded. "You would hope to settle in the country when you marry, then?"

"I suppose so," she said cautiously.

Her answer seemed to reassure him, his expression clearing, though he wasn't done. "But what if your family were far away? Wouldn't you miss them?"

"Of course," she said at once, wondering where this was going. "But that is the fate of many brides, and I hope they would visit often, and that I would visit them."

"I suppose you'd want a place in town, too, and to arrange balls and parties and the like?" he added, sounding far too casual.

She frowned at him suspiciously. "Why on earth would you suppose that? I'm hardly angling to be a society darling. Of course, if I married a man whose position demanded a great deal of entertaining, I would have to adapt, but I'm certainly not searching for the role. As I said, I like coming to town from time to time, but I prefer a quiet life."

"You do?" he asked, a pleased glint in his eyes.

"Yes, I do. Rochford, why all the questions?"

"No reason," he asked, and then swept her into a dizzying series of turns until she could hardly remember her name, never mind what they'd been discussing.

Chapter 13

Dearest Georgie,

I must correct you, I'm afraid. The title of most vexing man who ever lived has already been taken. Mr Sylvester Cootes has certainly earned the title. His brothers are both charming, though the elder Lord de Ligne is a dreadful rogue. I think Greer is smitten with him, however. I should not be surprised if there is an announcement in that quarter very soon.

Do have a care with your duke, Georgie. Just think how dreadful it would be to end your days married to a man who makes you cross every time you speak to him.

—Excerpt of a letter to Lady Georgina Anderson (daughter of Gordon and Ruth Anderson, The Earl and Countess of Morven) from Lady Aisling Baxter (daughter of Luke and Kitty Baxter, The Earl and Countess of Trevick).

14th December 1840, Beverwyck, London.

"Thank you for the dance, Monsieur Le Comte," Evie said, grinning at Louis César. She adored dancing with Louis, for he was a marvellous partner and always made her feel light as a feather. She suspected he could make anyone feel like they floated on air.

He smiled at her, tucking her hand into the crook of his arm as he guided her from the dance floor.

"It was my pleasure, I assure you." His expression grew serious. "I hope you will not allow those vacuous creatures to spoil your evening. They are the kind to criticise everyone, even each other, for their own amusement. You must not heed them."

Evie laughed and shook her head. "Of course not. My self-esteem is not so fragile as that. Actually, Lofty and Dumpling are quite accurate, I suppose, and I rather adore dumplings. I'd take it as a compliment, only they meant to taunt, of course, which is never pleasant. They may think what they like, though. Georgie looks quite stunning, and I adore parties. I've decided you were quite right about the silly diet, too. I was foolish to let Madame Blanchet overset me. I don't know what I was thinking. The food tonight is too delicious not to enjoy. Plus, my gown is the prettiest I have ever seen. Nothing will spoil this evening for me, I assure you."

"I am glad, *ma petite*. I cannot stand to see you unhappy."

She looked up at him, touched by his obvious concern. "How could one be unhappy at such a marvellous party and in such good company?"

She felt his hand cover hers, his expression warm and approving. "You look stunning, Miss Knight, and that gown is a triumph. I do not know whether to congratulate myself or wish I'd been a deal less clever."

She gave him a curious glance, not taking his meaning.

He sighed. "There's not a man here who hasn't noticed you," he said, not looking entirely pleased by the fact.

Evie laughed, startled. "Don't be silly."

"I am not *being silly,*" he said curtly, but they were obliged to halt the conversation as a young man she knew hurried up to her.

"Miss Knight," he said, smiling broadly at her. "Might you jot me down upon your dance card? If it's not full, that is," he added.

Evie smiled at him. "Of course, Mr Greaves. I shall save you a country dance."

"Oh, jolly good. Until then." He executed a neat bow and took himself off.

"See?" Louis said darkly as she jotted his name on her fan.

Evie snorted, amused. "I always dance with Mr Greaves. He's very nice."

Louis muttered something she didn't catch, but guided them back to where his brother and Eliza were standing. He fell into conversation with Nic as Eliza tugged her aside.

"Oh, Evie, do let me introduce you," she said, smiling at her. "This is Mr Humphrey Price and Mr Jeffrey Hadley-Smythe. Gentlemen, this is my dear friend, Miss Evie Knight."

A lively conversation ensued as Mr Price and Mr Hadley-Smythe were easy-going gentlemen and it appeared they had several acquaintances in common.

"Ashburton is here, isn't he?" Evie said, finding they all knew the Marquess and Marchioness of Montagu's eldest son, the Earl of Ashburton. Ashburton had told Jules he was coming, so he must be among the throng. She suspected his parents must have forced him to attend, for he was not one for society, unlike his younger brother, Thomas.

"Yes. So's his pa. Caused a stir as usual, with ladies swooning all around. The two of them together are more than some women can take," Mr Price said dryly, before adding. "Though that fellow seems to cause as much stir all by himself. Who is he?"

His sour expression spoke volumes and Evie suspected more than a touch of the green-eyed monster. She did not need to turn her head to know he spoke of Louis César.

"The Comte de Villen," she said with a smile, feeling a burst of pride in her friend.

"Oh, a Frenchie," Mr Price said, somewhat disparagingly.

Evie scowled, irritated, and struggled to bite back an angry comment.

Mr Hadley-Smythe hurried to fill the gap, aware of Evie's indignation. "Might you do me the honour of a dance, Miss Knight?" he asked. "There's a waltz beginning if you've not already a partner?"

Evie looked up into his eager brown eyes. He had a friendly face and looked to be the kind of man who was willing to be pleased by everything. She decided she liked Mr Hadley-Smythe far more than his friend.

"I don't, and I should like that very much," she said, and took his arm.

Rochford watched Georgie dancing with the comte's brother, Nic, relieved the man was married. He felt like a cat on hot bricks, certain that some nicer, handsomer fellow would spot the treasure that was right in front of them and sweep her away before he got the chance. Of course, that was hardly his only problem. He didn't have the least idea how one went about courting a woman, but he needed to discover the trick of it, and quickly. Though if courting relied solely upon charm and romantic gestures, he was in deep trouble. He hadn't even managed to apologise without causing a row. Still, he'd got there in the end, and she *had* danced with him, which still seemed something of a miracle. She'd even appeared to enjoy it.

Remembering how very right it had felt to hold her in his arms stirred something anxious and panicky in his chest and he battered it down with difficulty. He told himself this was ridiculous. He barely knew the girl and he must stop getting himself in such a lather. The likelihood was she wouldn't want to marry him. She *didn't* want to marry him, she'd told him twice at least. The idea of being a duchess clearly didn't appeal, and he was hardly a catch if you put that attraction to one side. Jules was a fool, and Rochford himself was a bigger one for getting his hopes up, and yet—he was going to try. He had to try, even if his chances were slim at best. So what if he made a horse's arse of himself? It would hardly be the first time. Besides, how hard could it be? He could ask her to dance again. That would be a start, and then… perhaps tomorrow he could take her out riding with him. That was what courting couples did, wasn't it? He chewed at his lip and decided he'd best ask Joe what he thought. The devil was always full of advice, whether or not it was wanted. He'd been right about the beard.

"Good evening, your grace."

Rochford looked around to see Miss Knight at his elbow. Of everyone at this house party—except for Georgie—she was the easiest person to be around. He did not intimidate her, and she didn't seem to expect anything of him. She was quite content to sit in silence, but she didn't look horrified if he spoke to her either.

"Miss Knight," he said, nodding politely. She followed his gaze to Georgina and smiled.

"She looks stunning this evening, doesn't she?"

"She does," he agreed.

The young woman beamed at him. "You looked very well dancing together. It's tricky for her to find a suitable dance partner. Well, for me too," she added with a laugh. "If I don't want to end the evening with a crick in my neck."

"I think I might cause you a permanent injury in that case," he replied, rather surprised to be enjoying a conversation at a ball.

Her laugh was merry, the kind that invited others to join in, and drew the gazes of several people around them. "Oh, not permanent, I think. I'll risk it if you will," she added with a mischievous glint in her eyes.

Rochford stared at her in surprise. Had she just invited him to ask her to dance?

She laughed again at his obvious astonishment. "I'm sorry, your grace, but the cat is out of the bag. Jules has just told me I'm not to believe you are as fierce as everyone says because you're not half so scary as you make out."

"Yes, he is," retorted a familiar voice. His favourite voice.

Rochford turned to see Monsieur Demarteau guiding Georgina back towards them. She was giving Evie a mock serious glare. "Don't you believe a word of it. Jules said the same to me, but he's wrong. His grace is quite dreadful and very scary. I should run if I were you."

"Well, duke? Who has the right of it?" Miss Knight demanded. "Should I run or demand my dance?"

Rochford looked between them, uncertain of what to do or say. He was unused to being teased. Mocked, yes, but not this friendly banter and… and he did not know how to reply. Perhaps sensing his predicament, Georgie answered for him.

"I think perhaps we are both right, but you should judge for yourself, Evie. Will you dance with her, Rochford?"

"It would be my honour," he replied gravely, and gave Miss Knight a formal bow before offering her his arm. He hesitated before leading her off. "And you, Lady Georgina, will you dance with me again?"

"Again?" she replied. Colour touched her cheeks, a glorious flush of pink that made his breath catch. Was that pleasure or embarrassment? Did she want to dance again, or was she scrabbling about for a reason to refuse him? He waited, embarrassment growing as she dithered.

"Yes. Yes, I will dance with you again." She stared down at the delicate sticks of her fan to find one that had not been written upon. "The last waltz is yours, then."

Rochford let out a breath. "It is," he agreed, and escorted Miss Knight out to dance.

Georgie watched Rochford and Evie walk out onto the floor and smiled. Evie was in high spirits this evening, though she seemed oblivious to the effect she had on people. Wherever she went, she left people laughing and in a far better mood than when she'd arrived. Even Rochford seemed to unravel under the warmth of that smile. Georgie hugged her arms about herself, pleased to see him enjoying himself. She wondered just how rare that was for him and hoped perhaps this evening would show him the world was not such an unfriendly place if he gave it a chance.

"My dance, I believe, Lady Georgina."

Georgie turned to find herself face to face with the Comte de Villen. "Oh," she said, immediately sent into a dither. "Oh, yes, it is. Of course."

Georgie bit back a smile as she noticed the covetous looks on the faces of women around her, enjoying the moment. Unsurprisingly, the comte danced like a dream and Georgie relaxed, wondering at her good fortune in having danced with two such remarkable men, neither of whom made her feel like a family obligation.

"You have set tongues wagging, my lady," he remarked, guiding her into an effortless turn.

"Have I?" she asked, daring to meet those extraordinary blue eyes.

"The Duke of Rochford never attends balls, is never seen in society, and he certainly never dances, yet this is the second event at which he has appeared, and he has danced with you at both."

"He's dancing with Evie now," she pointed out, suddenly grateful for that fact.

The comte's expression darkened. "So he is. He's looking for a wife."

"Who says so?" she demanded, startled.

He looked back at her. "I say so. It's obvious."

Georgie watched Evie and the duke, watched Evie say something and then laugh, throwing her head back. The duke's lips twitched, and he smiled too. Something hot and unpleasant that felt horribly like jealousy squirmed in Georgie's chest. *Stop it*, she scolded herself. Everyone loved Evie. He was not looking for a wife. *Well, he might be,* said a little voice in her head. Just because the idea of Georgie being his duchess made him furious, it didn't mean he wasn't looking for someone to do the job. Someone gentle and easy-going, who always smiled and never said hateful things to people.

Oh. Oh, no.

Georgie stepped on the comte's toe.

"Oh, I beg your pardon," she said, mortified.

"My fault," he said easily, though his expression was tense.

He too was watching Evie and Rochford, Georgie realised. Well, Evie was his friend. No doubt he worried for her. Everyone knew Rochford for his difficult personality and for being an ill-tempered wretch. Though Georgie was certain much of this was not only untrue, but unfair, he hardly did anything to mitigate the situation.

The dance could not end quickly enough, and Georgie was grateful to discover the comte guiding her back towards Evie and Rochford.

"Good evening, your grace." The comte smiled and bowed to Rochford politely, though there was something unmistakeably cool and brittle in his gaze. Rochford hardly looked any friendlier, glowering at the comte. The atmosphere between them prickled. Evie looked at Georgie in alarm, clearly not having a clue what the problem was.

"Thank you so much for the dance, your grace," Evie said, smiling as she addressed the duke. "You will be pleased to know my neck has survived without incident."

Rochford took her hand and kissed her fingers, and Georgie was certain he'd done it with the sole intention of riling the comte. Sadly, it made her stomach squirm too.

"I am relieved to hear it, Miss Knight, though the pleasure was mine. Perhaps you might brave the ordeal again, in that case?"

"I might indeed," Evie said with a laugh, only to give a little squeal as the comte took her arm and pulled her away.

"My dance, I believe, Miss Knight," he muttered.

Evie, with little choice in the matter, hurried after him. "No, it isn't," she hissed. *"Louis!* Louis, I'm supposed to be dancing with—"

The rest of the conversation was lost as they disappeared into the crowd.

Georgie looked back at Rochford to discover him watching her. She blushed.

"Did you enjoy your dance with the handsome Comte de Villen, then?" he asked, studying her. "Was he as charming as you hoped?"

"I enjoyed it very much, and yes, he is very charming," Georgie replied, perplexed by the obvious animosity between the comte and Rochford. Perhaps they were just too different to get along, though she knew Rochford's opinion of the comte already.

"Hmmm," he replied. A comment which she did not know how to interpret.

"You looked to be enjoying dancing with Miss Knight," she said, wishing she hadn't sounded quite so prickly.

Rochford studied her, his expression unreadable. "I did. She is a very kind-hearted young lady and takes no one at face value. A refreshing change among this crowd."

"Yes," Georgie replied, unhappily realising she was suffering another unpleasant attack of envy. It made her feel quite revolted with herself, especially as every word was true. "Yes, she is a darling creature."

Rather to her surprise, he offered her his arm. Georgie hesitated and then took it, and they strolled about the ballroom with Georgie stopping here and there to speak to friends. She smiled as she saw a face she was especially happy to see.

"Matilda!" she exclaimed, releasing Rochford to run and embrace one of her mother's dearest friends.

"Georgie, darling. How beautiful you look this evening. Are you having fun?"

Georgie dared a glance at Rochford before replying. "I am," she said, smiling at Matilda.

"Lucian, look who I found." Matilda tugged at her husband's arm, and Montagu turned.

He was still an exceptionally handsome man and, though Georgie knew his reserved demeanour had seen many accuse him of being cold and high in the instep, that was certainly not true for the people he cared about. His cool silver eyes lit with warmth as he saw her. "Georgie. How good to see you. It's been too long."

His gaze strayed then to Rochford, a calculating glint in his eyes as he glanced between them. "Rochford. This is a surprise."

"Not too dreadful a surprise, I hope," Rochford returned dryly.

Montagu's eyes lit with amusement. "Not *too* dreadful," he agreed.

"Have you danced with Philip yet?" Matilda asked her.

Georgie laughed. "No. I've not seen him yet, though Jules tells me you ordered him and Tommy to dance with all the wallflowers, so I suppose he'll get to me."

"I did not mean that you were a wallflower," Matilda said with a tut. "You ought to be fighting the invitations off with a stick. Still, it seems you have an… agreeable partner," she added after a moment's hesitation, giving Rochford an assessing gaze and glancing at her husband to gauge his reaction.

Montagu was watching Matilda, though, a soft look in his eyes. "You find the most interesting creatures hiding among the wallflowers. If those boys have a lick of sense, it's the first place they'll go."

Matilda laughed, taking her husband's arm. "Well, it worked out nicely for me, I'll admit."

"Are you in town long?" Montagu asked Rochford.

Georgie found her attention was far too riveted on the answer, though she was returning to Scotland after Christmas, so she supposed it did not much matter what the duke's plans were.

"I return to Mulcaster on the twenty-seventh," Rochford replied.

Montagu nodded. "If you have time before then, look me up. We'll go to my club."

Rochford looked taken aback by the invitation, but nodded. "Thank you."

The orchestra struck up for the next dance, and Matilda looked at her husband expectantly.

"I find… I am not in the mood to dance," Montagu murmured, but offered his arm to her.

To Georgie's surprise, Matilda blushed. "Me either," she said, taking his arm.

"If you will excuse us," Montagu said, and guided his wife out of the ballroom.

Georgie smothered a chuckle.

"What?" Rochford asked.

She turned back to him and shook her head. "Don't tell me you never read their story? I thought the entire world had." He still looked blank. Georgie rolled her eyes. "The one Aunt Prue wrote about them. The Eagle and the Lamb? They had an interesting encounter at this very ball some years ago. Not that she detailed everything that happened, far too scandalous."

Rochford shook his head. "Of course. I had forgotten the duchess was a celebrated novelist. She writes romance, I collect," he said, looking vaguely nauseated.

Georgie sighed. "Yes, Rochford, romance. Have you never read one?"

He shook his head, watching her. "Ought I?"

She gave an indelicate snort. "I never knew a man who ought to more," she said, and then hesitated, wondering how he would react to her teasing. To her delight, his eyes sparkled with amusement.

"Is that so? And what would I learn, were I to read one?"

Georgie took his arm again, trying not to let the play of heavy muscle beneath her fingertips distract her. "Perhaps that we all deserve a happy ending."

"Even the villains?" he asked, arching an eyebrow at her.

"That depends on the villain," she said, staring up at him. "Not if he is truly wicked, but if there is goodness in him, if perhaps his actions were driven by circumstance, then yes, even the villain. In fact, those stories are often the best of all."

Rochford shook his head at her. "You've a soft heart. I keep warning you, you must guard it more carefully."

"Why?" she asked, laughing, though her laughter caught in her throat as she saw the look in his eyes.

"Because some villain might try to steal it from you," he said, his voice low.

Georgie stared at him, entranced by the softness of his expression, so at odds with his fierce appearance.

"You're no villain," she said.

He smiled. "Perhaps not, but my intentions might be the same."

"Rochford?" she said, feeling panic fluttering in her chest as something far hotter and more demanding flared to life inside her.

"Would you care to go for a ride tomorrow, Lady Georgina?"

What was happening? Georgie gave herself a mental shake, trying to force her wits out of the stupor they'd fallen into. He was asking her to go for a ride with him, like… like he might if he were courting her. *Oh. Oh, Lord. Danger! Run!* shrieked the sensible voice in her head. *Yes, yes, yes!* squealed another which heeded nothing but pleasure. Georgie swallowed, too unnerved to reply.

"Is it such a revolting prospect?" he asked after a long moment, during which she only starred at him like a brainless twit. His voice held an edge to it, which she did not underestimate. She did not wish to hurt him, to reject him, but she did not wish to be hurt either.

"W-What happened to staying away from each other?" she managed breathlessly.

He shrugged, his gaze never leaving hers. "We're neither of us up to that challenge, it seems, and besides which, I have changed my mind. I've changed my mind about a lot of things. About you."

"Oh," Georgie said faintly.

"It's only a ride about the park," he said, his deep voice resonating through her, inviting her to give in. "No strings attached."

Ha! That's what you think, she retorted inwardly. If she spent too much time with him, she might find herself tangled up in a Gordian knot that she could not undo.

"With a chaperone?" she said in a rush, because if she took the correct chaperone, there would be far less danger.

"Naturally," he replied at once.

Georgie knew there was no choice, for she could not bear for him to feel rejected. She was too aware that he let no one close and that this was something rare and extraordinary. It was not in her to be cruel, especially to him, and so there was no other answer she could give. "Very well, Rochford. I will ride with you tomorrow."

Evie kicked off her shoes and tucked her feet up on the settee, balancing a plate of food on her knee and holding a glass of wine in one hand. It was her third glass, which was very bad of her when she ought to stick to lemonade, but she was thirsty, and the server had been close at hand. She gave a little sigh of relief and sipped at the cold white wine with pleasure, her muscles relaxing as the alcohol entered her blood. The glow of an oil lamp plus the flickering firelight warmed the room, the flames leaping back to life since she'd stirred the coals and got it blazing again. It had been a long night. Not that it was quite over. People were still dancing and making merry, but Evie had danced until her feet hurt and she was worn out. It had been a marvellous evening, though, and she had enjoyed it very much, except… she was vexed and puzzled over Louis' odd behaviour. What the devil had got into him tonight? Sighing, she considered the plate of food before her and picked up a delicate mushroom tart. She was about to devour it when the door opened, and she stiffened in alarm.

This was one of the family's small, private parlours, well away from the ballroom. She'd thought she could hide here safely enough.

"Oh," she said with relief as Louis appeared in the doorway. "It's only you. What a relief."

He sighed. "You devastate me, *ma petite.* Only you could set me down and shatter my confidence with so few words."

"Don't be silly," she said crossly. "I only meant I was glad it wasn't someone come to cause me trouble."

"Like I said," Louis muttered dryly, closing the door behind him.

He stayed where he was, leaning against the door, watching her.

"How did you know I'd be here?" she asked, regarding him warily. He was in an odd mood tonight. Was he foxed?

"I looked everywhere else."

"Oh."

"I believe Mr Hadley-Smythe is searching too, hoping you'll grant him the last dance."

"Is he?" Evie said, brightening. She had liked the young man very much, for he was rather sweet. He'd also seemed very taken with her, which was flattering.

"Ah, this pleases you," he said, and she frowned, unnerved by his tone. How could she know this man so very well for so long and yet suddenly not understand him at all? "He's not the only one, you know. I was right about that gown, was I not? You'll have besotted suitors queuing up to call on you in the coming days."

"You were right about the gown, but there's no need to exaggerate. Besides, I've always had suitors," she retorted, a little stung. "It's just they've always been lured by my enormous dowry before, not my…."

She paused, deciding she'd best not be indelicate and refer to the amount of cleavage on display, even with Louis.

He snorted, amused. "Well, I can assure you they're now lured by all the other delicious temptations you have previously hidden so well."

Evie frowned but put the tart in her mouth and chewed rather than comment.

"I see you're still cross with me."

He pushed off the wall, moving about the room, inspecting the pictures, and picking up a small china shepherdess to study it. She watched him set it down and move to a large bookcase, selecting a title and running an elegant finger along the spine. For some reason, she shivered.

Evie sighed. "No. I can never stay cross with you, you know that. Only you did vex me rather. You've been acting very strangely tonight."

His eyes glinted at her from the darkened corner of the room. "Have I?"

"You know you have," she said impatiently. "Oh, do stop prowling about and come and sit down." She patted the space beside her on the settee.

He didn't move for a long moment and then crossed the room to her. Evie shifted, meaning to put her feet on the floor again to make room for him, but he took them in his hands, setting them in his lap.

"Louis," she began, startled, meaning to pull away, except his long, strong fingers began to massage her sore feet. "Oh," she gave a blissful sigh, relaxing and stretching her legs out to let him continue.

Evie closed her eyes, biting back a moan as he kneaded and caressed her aching feet through her stockings.

"Oh, Louis, that feels so good. Divine," she murmured. His warm, clever hands stilled for a moment before continuing once more.

"You ought not be here, Evie, alone with me."

"Don't start that again," she said, smothering a yawn. "No one knows we're here. Besides, you found me this time."

"So I did."

Evie stretched, feeling like a cat in the sun. She reached one arm up behind her and laid her head back, the plate balanced on her thighs. Though she wanted to eat the delicacies she'd selected, she was too sleepy and content to move a muscle. Her eyelids grew heavy, and she relaxed into the cushions.

"You look like a pampered goddess, waiting for someone to feed you," Louis observed, his voice soft.

Evie chuckled, but didn't open her eyes.

"It seems I must oblige then."

She murmured a complaint as he set her feet down on the cushions, moving to kneel beside her. Evie forced her eyes to open before sleep overcame her to see Louis holding a small pastry to her lips.

"An offering from a lowly supplicant," he said, his eyes bright blue, even in the dim light. The scent of him reached her, shaving soap and clean linen, some expensive cologne that teased at her senses, and the warmth of brandy on his breath. He *had* been drinking.

"You're foxed," she observed sleepily.

"I think perhaps you are too," he remarked.

"Not really. Only a little tipsy, but you are a lot foxed." She opened her mouth to take the morsel he held out.

"Enough, and not nearly enough," he said cryptically, placing the pasty between her lips. His fingers brushed her mouth, and she saw his gaze fix there, watching her.

Evie chewed, studying him curiously. "Enough for what? Not enough for what?"

His eyelashes lowered, and the colours in the room seemed to dim without that extraordinary blue in sight. "Enough to be dangerous, not enough to entirely lose my mind."

"Dangerous to wh—"

Louis jolted as the door opened, moving to shield her from view.

Evie gasped, suddenly wide awake and panicked, knowing this would not look good, only to let out a sigh of relief as she saw Louis' brother in the doorway.

"What the devil do you want?" Louis demanded irritably.

Nic's gaze drifted from Louis to Evie, reclining on the settee with his brother knelt beside her. His expression darkened. "Evie. You're well?"

Evie frowned at him. "Of course. Just a bit worn out. I came for some peace and quiet and Louis was keeping me company."

Louis stood up, glowering at Nic. "What did you expect her to say, brother?"

"Just that," Nic said easily, walking into the room. "But you're missed, Evie. I was sent to find you. It won't be for long. Everyone is leaving now."

"Oh, very well," Evie said with a sigh. Wearily, she got to her feet and smoothed out her skirts, pushing her shoes back on with regret. She paused to smile at Louis and give him a peck on the cheek. "Good night, *Monsieur*," she said with a grin, and hurried out of the door.

Chapter 14

Dearest Viv,

I was so sorry you missed the Christmas ball. How wretched for you to come down with a cold at such a time. It seemed very strange to see Ash without his twin sister. I hope he has told you all about it at least and look forward to seeing you as soon as you feel better.

Get well soon.

—Excerpt of a letter to Miss Vivien Ashton (daughter of Silas and Aashini Anson, The Viscount and Viscountess Cavendish) from Miss Evie Knight (daughter of Lady Helena and Mr Gabriel Knight).

15th December 1840, Beverwyck, London.

Georgie did not come down for breakfast the next morning until gone eleven, though she was not the only one. Everyone appeared to be feeling somewhat left over after the excesses of the night before, and the breakfast table was remarkably quiet.

Evie gave her a bleary smile and smothered a yawn. "Morning, Georgie. Must you look so bright-eyed and bushy tailed? You put the rest of us to shame."

Jules grimaced, glowering over the top of his coffee cup. "Yes, do stop it, Georgie. It's giving me a headache."

Georgie grinned at them and accepted a cup of chocolate from a footman. "I slept like a log and it's hardly the crack of dawn. I can imagine Jules was up to no good, but what were you doing that has you so pale and lethargic, you naughty creature?" she asked Evie.

Evie gave a husky laugh. "Nothing at all! Well, I did drink rather more wine than was good for me. I knew I ought not for it always makes me sleepy."

"She was flirting with Mr Hadley-Smythe last I saw," Jules cut in, winking at her.

Evie blushed. "I was not," she retorted.

"If you say so," he murmured.

Georgie chuckled, amused. "Well, well. Mr Hadley-Smythe. I think I met him."

"You did," Jules agreed. "Third son of a baron. Good family, dreadful mother. They're very plump in the pocket, I understand. The father is in politics. He's a decent sort. So is the son, if a bit brainless. Nice but dim."

They both stared at Jules, taken aback by his neat summary. "What? I pay attention to people."

"He's not dim," Evie countered, looking annoyed.

"What did you talk about?" Jules asked, waving away a footman offering him a plate of sirloin with a pained expression.

"Umm, mutual acquaintances, dancing, his dogs…."

"Yes, that's about the limit of his repertoire. For heaven's sake, don't ask him about art or books. He'll run a mile. Well, unless you want him to run a mile," he added judiciously.

"That's not very kind, Jules," Evie said, frowning.

"Who said I was kind?" Jules countered.

"Not me," Georgie added with a smirk.

Jules smirked right back at her. "Touché."

The conversation drew to a halt as Nic and Eliza entered the breakfast parlour, followed closely by the Duke of Rochford. Georgie's skin seemed to come alive the moment he entered the room, every particle of her attention aware of his proximity. Lord, but he was big. The breakfast parlour was a family room and hardly the grandest room at Beverwyck, but it was by no means a broom cupboard either, yet it seemed so when he entered. Georgie tried to concentrate on sipping her chocolate, but her heart was tripping about making it hard to breathe and she feared she would choke. She set down the cup and told herself not to be such a ninny.

"Good morning, Lady Georgina."

Georgie looked up, surprised to discover he had seated himself directly beside her.

"Your grace," she replied politely, feeling ridiculously shy.

"I am looking forward to our ride out this afternoon. The weather looks set to hold fine. Cold but sunny."

"Yes, umm… yes. It does. Me too," Georgie managed, cursing herself for sounding like a nitwit. She looked up to see Evie watching them, her expression alight with mischief.

Georgie widened her eyes at her in a *what are you smiling about* expression.

Evie batted her lashes, trying to look innocent and failing. Georgie snorted.

"Pardon?" said the duke.

"Oh, nothing, just… nothing," Georgie said as Evie choked on her chocolate.

"Evie," Georgie said, her voice firm. "Would you care to accompany us this afternoon? Rochford has suggested we go for a ride together.

Evie dimpled, looking smug and pleased and as if butter wouldn't melt. "Oh, Georgie, how lovely. I would be delighted to."

They managed to get through the rest of breakfast without incident, at least, and Georgie watched in astonished awe as Rochford put away a vast plate of food in a remarkably short space of time. She supposed a man that size must need feeding a proportionate amount, but was still a little staggered. Jules just groaned and cursed him, demanding he take his sausages and bacon elsewhere. Rochford ignored him. Once he'd finished his coffee, he turned back to Georgie.

"I shall be waiting at one thirty. Does that suit you, ladies?" Rochford asked them.

"Perfect," Evie said, nodding.

"Thank you, yes," Georgie agreed.

Rochford nodded and got up, promising to see them later, his gaze lingering on Georgie for long enough to make her colour rise.

"Georgie!" Evie whispered across the table, but Georgie hushed her, aware Nic, Eliza, and Jules were still present.

"I think I shall have a lie down," Jules said, massaging his temples. "If you don't see me at dinner, don't worry. I've probably died."

"Right you are," Eliza said, with all the cheerful unconcern of a sibling.

"Everybody is so cruel to me," Jules grumbled and levered himself to his feet.

"I suppose no one has seen my brother?" Nic asked, grim-faced.

"Not since I woke, but he was in a worse state than me when I gave up. That was about five o'clock this morning, so he's probably dead in a ditch. Devil's got a stronger constitution than I have if he isn't," Jules added with a sigh, dragging himself out of the room.

"Sounds about right," Nic muttered before kissing Eliza's cheek. "I'd best go check on him."

Evie frowned, her expression concerned as she watched Nic go.

"He'll find him, don't fret," Eliza said kindly, noting Evie's anxiety. "He'll just be nursing a hangover no doubt."

Evie nodded with relief and now the men had gone, both women turned their attention to Georgie.

"Well, then?" Eliza said, picking up her cup and saucer and coming to sit beside Georgie.

"Yes, spit it out," Evie urged her, suddenly looking a lot more animated.

"What?" Georgie protested, though she knew very well what they were getting at.

"Oh, come on. Rochford! Is he courting you?" Evie demanded.

"No! Oh, no, nothing like that. No. Of course not." Georgie flushed as both their eyebrows went up. "It's just a drive. It's not… it isn't…." She subsided, too flustered to continue.

"He *is!*" Eliza squealed, clapping her hands together. "Oh, Georgie. Isn't he terribly intimidating? He always seems so cross."

"Y-Yes," Georgie stammered. "And no. No, he's not, but… oh, Lord. I don't know what I'm doing. I think I ought not to go, only I can't bear to hurt his feelings, and I do like him. Well, when I don't hate him."

Evie snorted. "You like him *and* hate him?"

"Yes," Georgie wailed, throwing up her hands. "One minute I want to throttle him and the next…."

"The next?" Evie pressed, looking intrigued.

Georgie flushed and turned to Eliza in panic. "Oh! What shall I do? Eliza, you're a married lady. Advise me, for heaven's sake."

"I don't think I can, dear," Eliza said. "You must listen to your heart on this one, I think."

"Yes but…" Georgie lowered her voice. "How do I tell the difference between my heart and, well, other parts of me?"

Evie laughed, clapping a hand over her mouth. "Georgie!" she exclaimed, scandalised.

"I can't help it!" Georgie blushed. "He's just so big and strong and—"

"Big," Eliza echoed.

"And strong," Evie snickered.

They all burst out laughing.

"I think there's a kind man lurking under that growly exterior," Evie said with a smile, once their laughter had abated.

"That's what worries me," Georgie admitted. "But what if he only ever lurks? What if he never lets that side of him show?"

"You'll never know if you don't give him a chance," Eliza said. "Nic was horrid to me, you know. Really quite cruel, but I felt certain there was something between us, something special, so I persevered. It turned out he was trying to keep me at a distance because he thought his brother should marry me, that he wasn't good enough."

"He would have let his brother court you when he wanted you himself?" Georgie said, shocked.

Eliza gave a rueful smile. "No, but for a while he fooled himself into thinking he could let it happen."

"Louis helped him see the error of his ways, didn't he, Eliza?" Evie said.

"He did."

Evie's expression darkened. "Except now Louis is all by himself. He's dreadfully lonely."

"I know," Eliza said, concern in her eyes. "We've asked and asked him to come and stay with us, but he won't. I don't think we'd see him at all if Nic didn't track him down occasionally."

"He's been avoiding me too until this holiday and now.... Well, he's acting very strangely. I'm worried about him," Evie admitted.

Eliza nodded. "So are we. Christmas is a difficult time for him though, so perhaps it will pass. Nic won't say much about it, and what I do know I cannot speak of, but... Louis is a very troubled man, I think."

🎩 🎩 🎩

"Very smart," Joe said approvingly. "Those breeches and those muscular thighs... a match made in heaven, it is. She'll swoon into your arms, providing you don't open your mouth and ruin things."

"How am I supposed to court her if I don't speak to her?" Rochford retorted irritably.

"How are you supposed to court her if you do, more like," Joe said, attacking Rochford's shoulders with a clothes brush.

"Very comforting. You're supposed to be helping." Rochford glowered at his reflection in the looking glass, but he had to admit, from the neck down, he was quite smart. His mother always remarked that he looked like a barbarian whatever he wore, but he could hardly help his build.

"I am helping," Joe said with an indignant sniff. "You look your best, don't you?"

Rochford snorted. "I do, but that's not saying much."

"Oh, give over. So what if your face isn't the prettiest? It's a damn sight better when you're not scowling at everyone, and you're a fine figure of a man, Rochford. Use the assets you've got, that's what I say."

"If I do that, I'll have a horde of angry Scotsmen baying for my blood," Rochford replied, though he wondered if the idea had merit. If he could seduce her, she'd have to marry him. He pondered this, wondering just how big her male relations were.

Joe rolled his eyes. "I didn't mean you had to bed her! Blimey, you're hard work. I only mean that you've a strong pair of arms to hold her with. Lady Georgina is a statuesque young woman and there's few men who will make her feel delicate and fragile, but you can. Use that to your advantage. Take care of her. You're good at that despite what people think, and she liked it when you kissed her before, didn't she?"

"I think so."

Joe made an exasperated sound.

"Yes!" Rochford said hurriedly. "Yes, she did, until I accused her of scheming to get the title."

"Not your finest hour," Joe said dryly. "Do try not to accuse the poor girl of any other diabolical crimes. Not everyone is as cynical as you are."

"I know, I know. I apologised, didn't I?"

"Well, she's a kinder-hearted creature than I am. I'd have made you grovel for days. You need to marry that girl, Rochford, for you'll not find another like her. For heaven's sake, don't cock it up."

Rochford's anxiety level rocketed to a new high, as Joe confirmed what he'd known all along. "I'm trying not to! Why do you think I'm enduring your advice and all this damn primping? For the pleasure of hearing you nag me to death?"

"You don't pay me enough," Joe said, smacking Rochford's hands away as he tugged at his cravat. He pointed a threatening finger. "Leave it!"

"It's choking me," Rochford protested.

"Good."

"Why do I put up with you?"

"Because I'm the only daft beggar who'll put up with you," Joe shot back. "Now hold out your hands."

"What's that?" Rochford asked, eyeing the small glass bottle suspiciously. "I'm not wearing bloody perfume!"

Joe took a deep breath. "Give me strength. It isn't perfume, it's cologne, which most elegant gentlemen wear, the ones who care a fig for their appearance and style, anyway. For your information, it's the same cologne the Comte de Villen uses, and I had to leap through a great many hoops to get my hands on it, you ungrateful sod. I need to get it back to his valet quick sharp, though, so stop getting hysterical and put it on."

"I'm not hysterical," Rochford said indignantly. "I only said...."

"Oh, come here." Too impatient to wait, Joe poured a small amount onto his fingers and applied it to Rochford's gloves, cravat, and handkerchief. Rochford gave a sceptical sniff, but his expression eased as the sophisticated scent teased his senses. Something citrusy, lime perhaps, and.... "Tobacco?" Joe sniffed too and gave an appreciative sigh. "Yes, and sandalwood, I think. Very masculine. You smell good enough to eat."

With a harrumph, Rochford accepted his hat from Joe and strode to the door.

"Oh, and your grace?"

"What?" Rochford demanded, hesitating at the door.

"Don't bollocks it up."

"Thank you so much for your sage advice, Joe. I don't know what I would do without you," the duke grumbled, closing the door on his smug valet.

"Stop fiddling with your hair. It will all come loose if you keep on," Evie scolded, her breath clouding on the frosty air. Though the sun attempted to shine down on them, there was little warmth to be had. The ground was still white in places and an occasional snowflake drifted silently to earth.

Georgie stuffed her hands under her armpits, hoping to still them as they walked around to the stables. "I'm trying," Georgie muttered. "But I always fidget when I'm nervous. Is this a bad idea? It is, isn't it? It's a bad idea, Evie. Perhaps I should pretend I've hurt my ankle."

"Don't be a dimwit. Then you'll have to sit about with your foot up for days and miss out on all the fun, and you won't be able to escape him if you really want to either."

"I hadn't thought of that," Georgie admitted. "See, my brain turns to pudding when I'm anxious."

Evie shrugged. "My brain is always pudding or thinking about pudding. Especially ones with custard. Mmm. Drat it, now you've made me hungry."

Georgie stared at her. "How is that my fault?"

"You were the one that mentioned pudding."

They both laughed, and Evie took Georgie's arm. "Stop fretting. It's just a ride about the grounds. If you don't want to be alone with him, you have me to chaperone, and if you do, you need only ride in your usual manner, and you'll leave me miles behind. I'm not as brave as you, remember, and if you go over any big jumps, you are most certainly on your own."

"I do want to be alone with him, Evie. That's the trouble. I just don't think I ought to. What if he really does wish to court me?"

"Would that be so bad?" Evie asked. "If you like him?"

Georgie chewed at her lip, thoroughly agitated; "But his reputation is so…."

"Daunting," Evie agreed. "And there's no smoke without fire, I know. But what if all the talk is unfair? Remember how our parents told us they disliked Montagu at first. He was vilified by everyone when all along it was his horrid uncle telling everyone lies about him and saying he was wicked."

"Yes, of course. The duke *is* cross and difficult, though, and suspicious and cynical and distrustful. I've been on the receiving end often enough to know. It's only that there's another side to him, but what if the cross, difficult side, always overpowers it?"

"You can only get to know him better, Georgie. What's the rush? If he wishes to court you, let him. You don't have to marry tomorrow, do you?"

Georgie let out a sigh and smiled. "No. No, of course not. Thank you, Evie. You always give such good advice. I feel better now, only…."

"What?" Evie asked, sensing Georgie's uncertainty.

"Do you like him too?"

Evie blinked at her. "Like, Rochford? *No!*" she exclaimed, laughing. "I mean, yes, I like him well enough. He was very nice to me at the ball, but I have no interest in marrying him. Good Lord, what an idea. I'd have to stand on a ladder to kiss him. Well, I would for most men, to be fair, but especially Rochford."

Georgie snorted and let out a breath of relief.

"You weren't really worried, were you?" Evie demanded.

"No. Well, yes, a little bit jealous, I'm afraid. When I saw him dancing with you."

Evie went off into whoops of laughter. "Good heavens, you are in a bad way if you think I'm any competition."

"Why wouldn't you be? Evie, you were besieged last night if you didn't notice."

Evie waved this away. "Oh, yes, but only with gentlemen who enjoy my company. I am a lot of fun, after all," she added with a mischievous smile. "But none of them look at me in a romantic light. They were all goggling at Rosamund for one. She is turning into a beauty, isn't she?"

"Yes, she is, but are you sure *none* of them look at you in a romantic light?" Georgie pressed, amused.

Evie shrugged, blushing a little. "Oh, well, perhaps Mr Hadley-Smythe. His attentions were rather particular," she admitted.

Georgie shook her head, wondering if Evie was completely blind to her own appeal. It was true the prettiest, most glamorous young women took the gentlemen's attention, at least to begin with, but once people got to know Evie, everything changed. She might not be a beauty, but she had warmth and charm in abundance. Being with her just made the day better, for everyone.

"And do you like Mr Hadley-Smythe?"

Evie gave a nonchalant shrug. "Perhaps," she added, her eyes sparkling. "But never mind him now. Here's Rochford."

Chapter 15

Dearest Evie,

You were no sorrier than I was to miss the ball. The event of the season and I was stuck in bed with a red nose, looking like a three-day-old cadaver. And I had to endure Nani Maa scolding me for not wrapping up warmly enough and feeding me one of her disgusting concoctions. The devil of it is, I think it's working. I'm not admitting that to her, though, not for a thousand pounds. She's far too smug as it is.

Ash tells me it was a wonderful event, and that there was much talk about Rochford and Georgie. Tell me everything! And don't you dare leave out the bit where you danced twice with the Comte de Villen. Georgie won't be the only one setting the gossip mill alight if you don't have a care.

—Excerpt of a letter to Miss Evie Knight (daughter of Lady Helena and Mr Gabriel Knight) from Miss Vivien Ashton (daughter of Silas and Aashini Anson, The Viscount and Viscountess Cavendish).

15th December 1840, Beverwyck, London.

Nic rapped on door of his brother's room and waited for his valet, Elton, to answer.

"Monsieur Demarteau," the valet said, stepping back to let him in.

"Where is he?"

"Still abed, sir."

"I would like a word," Nic said, watching the valet's face tense. "That bad, eh?"

"I would rather not wake him, sir," the valet admitted sheepishly.

Nic snorted and clapped Elton on the shoulder. "Go on then, make yourself scarce. I shall beard the lion in his den."

"Yes, sir. Thank you, sir. There is a fresh pot of coffee on the table, just in case, sir," Elton said, making a dash for the door whilst the going was good.

Nic watched the valet go and then picked up the tray with the coffee on and went to his brother's room. It was dark and silent, the embers of the fire burning low. Setting down the tray, he tended the fire and then pulled back the curtains with a decisive tug. Bright daylight flooded the room, and a muffled groan came from the vicinity of the bed.

"Putain de merde!" Louis cursed, dragging a pillow over his head. "Elton, you bloody swine. Close the curtains."

"Elton has decided discretion is the better part of valour," Nic replied in French. His English was as good as Louis', but it was still a relief to use his mother tongue.

Louis' blue eyes glinted from beneath the pillow as he glared at Nic. "What do you want?"

"Is that any way to greet your dearest sibling? I come bearing coffee."

"You're my only sibling, and I don't want coffee. I want to sleep. *Va-t'en!*"

Nic sighed, understanding Louis was determined to be difficult. He poured out a cup of coffee. "I will not go away. I wish to talk to you."

Louis turned his back on Nic and pulled the covers over his head. *"Va te faire foutre."*

"My, we are vulgar this morning. You can curse me nine ways till Sunday, but I'm not going anywhere. You can try to throw me out if you like." Nic sat on the edge of the mattress and held the cup of coffee under Louis' nose. Louis sent him a look that would have shrivelled a lesser man, but sat up, muttering profanities all the while. He took the cup of coffee, sipping with his eyes shut.

"At least close the damned curtains."

Nic got up and obliged. He poured himself a cup of coffee before sitting down on the bed again.

"Well, and what was so damned urgent that you needed to disturb my sleep?"

"You're drinking too much," Nic said, cradling the coffee cup in his hands.

"Me and most of the *ton*. Go wake them up."

Nic smirked, shaking his head. "I don't give a damn about them. I care about you."

"How touching," Louis groused irritably. "Do you mind caring during hours when I'm awake?"

Nic stared at him, and Louis subsided with a huff.

"What's wrong, Louis?"

Louis frowned down into his coffee cup.

Nic sighed. "I know you're unhappy, but—"

He bit back the words at a murderous flash of blue eyes. Well, perhaps another tack.

"You're avoiding me."

Louis waved an impatient hand, dismissing the words. "I'm not. You're just busy with your beloved—and no, that wasn't a criticism," he added hastily. "I'm happy for you. You know that."

Nic said nothing, watching as his brother finished his coffee.

"I'm fine," Louis insisted, turning the empty cup in his hands.

Nic continued to watch him until Louis sighed and arranged his face into something placid and amenable.

"See? Perfectly fine."

"Yes, very convincing, to anyone who doesn't know you as I do," Nic said with a snort. He set down his coffee on the bedside table, steeling himself. "Louis, Christmas can be a difficult time for anyone if—"

"I will kill you if you continue this conversation," Louis murmured icily.

Nic threw up his hands, exasperated, and spoke before he really thought about what he was saying, driven by instinct. "Damnation. Is this about Evie?"

Louis went very still. "What the devil do you mean by that?"

"What the devil do you mean by last night's behaviour? Alone with her, Louis? And what the hell were you playing at?"

"We're always alone together," Louis snapped. "It never bothered you before."

"You never acted this way before."

His brother's face shut down, his eyes a glacial blue. "What exactly are you accusing me of? Do you think I'm intent on seducing her? Is that it?"

"Are you?" Nic demanded.

Louis erupted. He flung the coffee cup across the room where it shattered against the wall and scrambled across the bed, grabbing Nic by the cravat. "If any other man said that to me, I would kill him," he growled.

Nic held his breath, not moving an inch, taken aback by the fury in his brother's eyes. "And is this display of temper because it's something that could never, *ever* happen, or because you're terribly afraid it might?"

It was a risk, one that could have backfired badly, but Nic knew his brother better than he knew himself.

Louis released him and stalked from the bed, snatching up his dressing gown and pulling it on. The silence was so profound Nic felt it ringing in his ears. He had to admit he was shocked. Although he'd been shocked last night too, but to have his suspicions confirmed—*Putain! Louis and Evie?* Before yesterday, he would never have dreamed it possible. Louis was besieged by beautiful women and yet… and yet now he thought about it, it made an odd kind of sense. His brother might never admit it, but he did not want to be worshiped, he wanted—*needed*, love, security and kindness, things Evie offered in abundance and without hesitation. Did Louis realise that was what he wanted though? Did he comprehend the risks to both him and Evie?

"Louis," Nic pressed. "Talk to me, damn you. I know you care for her. I know you wouldn't deliberately hurt her."

Louis walked to the window, keeping his back to Nic. He pushed the curtain aside and stared out.

"I want her,' he said, the admission raw.

Nic blinked, startled by his brother's candour. He had not expected that. "Want to bed her, or…?"

Louis shot his brother a scathing look from over his shoulder. "My. You do have a high opinion of me."

Nic muttered a curse and ran a hand through his hair. "I didn't mean that you would, but… Truly, Louis? You're serious? You wish to marry her?"

"Yes. Yes, dammit, I do, but she is too young, Nic. Too young and far too innocent. She needs time yet."

Nic let out a breath of relief. He had wanted Louis to settle down for a long time. Admittedly he'd never considered Evie, but he understood her appeal for Louis. "She was eighteen in the summer. Many of her friends have married already," he pointed out.

"And I am almost ten years her senior in age, and a thousand in experience. I would feel like a damned predator taking a lamb. I do feel it. Believe me, you have no need to reprimand me for last night's performance. I have chastised myself quite thoroughly, I assure you."

"I believe you."

Louis put his head in his hands. "My God, help me, will you? What do I do?"

"You could court her. There is no need to rush."

Louis made a harsh, unhappy sound. "She does not see me, Nic. Not as a man, only as her friend and confidant. Is that not deliciously ironic?"

Nic's lips quirked at his predicament, despite Louis' obvious unhappiness. He could only imagine how galling it was for his beautiful brother not to be seen as a romantic prospect by the only woman he'd ever wanted for himself.

"Nic."

Nic looked up, aware of his brother's hard tone.

"If you tell anyone, even Eliza—*non, especially Eliza, I will* kill you," Louis said, his expression fierce.

Nic held up his hands in a peaceable gesture. "Not a word. Upon my honour."

Louis nodded, a little of the tension leaving his shoulders.

"So, what will you do?"

Louis shrugged. "I cannot seduce an innocent, and until she sees me as something other than her dear friend, I can do nothing but endure."

"You could tell her how you feel," Nic suggested.

"And have her run away from me?" Louis shook his head. "Out of the question. I could not bear it. Staying away from her this long has been agony. I cannot keep my distance as I ought to."

"She might not run…"

"She would."

Nic sighed, conceding the point. Louis knew the girl better than anyone, and he was an excellent judge of character. "Well then. You'll wait for her."

"Yes."

"You don't look very happy about it," Nic observed with sympathy.

Louis turned, leaning back against the windowsill. "Would you be?" he demanded.

Nic shook his head.

Louis hung his head, staring at the carpet, his expression taut. "I'm afraid I will lose her, Nic. She is everything good and true in this world. She makes me happy, and I know that for the rarity it is. I am at peace when she is near, and I want her so badly I'm sick with it, but I am afraid."

Nic stood, his heart aching as he heard the bleak note in his brother's voice.

"Why?"

"Because I am not the only one who sees her. I am only the one who saw her first, and I must stand back and watch her flirt with other men, allow her the little romances that all young women adore and need to experience before they commit themselves to a husband. I think it might kill me, Nic. And even if I endure all this, she may still never turn to me."

Nic crossed the room and grasped Louis' shoulders. *"Non.* She will come around. Like you said, you must tread gently, that's all. Be patient, Louis. You, of all men, know how to bide your time."

Louis let out a breath of laughter. *"Ah, oui.* So I do, but that does not mean I have to like it."

Georgie glanced across at Rochford, who must have felt the weight of her observation. He looked back at her, holding her gaze, and awareness prickled down her back.

"Do you miss your family, being away from them at Christmastime?" he asked.

Georgie nodded. "I do, very much. It's the first Christmas I've not spent with them, but when Aunt Prue invited me I was so excited to come, and Mama thought it would be a good opportunity for me to—"

She hesitated, wishing she'd not begun that sentence.

"To find a husband," he finished for her.

Blushing, Georgie nodded. "Yes."

"Do you look forward to being married?"

Georgie swallowed, glancing around to see Evie was riding close enough behind for propriety but far enough away to allow them a private conversation. The horses walked out, their breath puffing in clouds of billowing white as the tack jingled.

"I suppose so, though I'm in no hurry. I love my life in Scotland, especially at Wildsyde, and everyone there has known me since I was a baby. It's familiar and comforting. A new life with a husband… that's rather terrifying, to be honest. I'm not sure I'm ready for it. I suppose I would need to trust any potential husband a great deal to commit my future to him."

"I suppose you would, but any husband worth a damn would move heaven and earth to ensure your happiness."

"What about you, your grace?" Georgie said in a rush, his words creating a heady mix of pleasure and anxiety that made her heart skitter about in her chest. "Do you miss your family?"

His expression darkened. "No."

Georgie's mouth fell open at the firm remark. "Oh, well, of course you have no siblings, do you? And you told me of your father. But do you have no grandparents living? No aunts and uncles?"

"My line has a rather discouraging propensity for dying young and in ignoble circumstances," he said with a wry smile. "So, no. Only my mother lives, and she tolerates my company as one does a wasp in one's shoe, which is to say, not at all."

"I am sorry to hear you are estranged," Georgie said, meaning it. "My mother is the dearest creature, and I rely very much on her good sense and her comfort. I realise I am fortunate, though, not everyone is so lucky."

"Estranged?" Rochford mused with a rumbling laugh. "No, I do not believe we are estranged. That would imply there was once warmth between us when there has been nothing of the kind."

"Oh." Georgie stared at him, sympathy filling her chest. Coming from a large, boisterous, and loving family, it seemed incomprehensible that a mother could have no affectionate feelings for her only son.

"Don't look so stricken," Rochford said, his expression softening. "I've always been a difficult devil, as you know to your cost. I cannot pretend the blame is all hers."

"But she's your mother!" Georgie burst out, unable to keep silent. "And I do not believe you can have been born bad-tempered and cynical, no matter how flawed your character now."

His lips twitched at her words and the rather damning defence of his personality. "My word, Lady Georgina, do you mean to say you think there was a time when I wasn't *quite* so dreadful?"

Georgie flushed, aware he was teasing her. "I don't think you're dreadful at all," she said, sounding breathless. "You are too ready to think the worst of people and you sometimes say dreadful things, but that's not the same thing, you know."

Rochford's gaze on her was too intent, and she looked away.

"My father was a handsome man before disease ravaged him, and mother was a beauty—still is, for her years—and she is a perfectionist. She loves beautiful things, and for everything to be pretty and flawless. You can imagine how her hulking brute of a son fits into her immaculate world. I'm afraid I rather disturb her equilibrium."

"I can only imagine what she does for yours," Georgie shot back indignantly.

There was something bright and hopeful shining in his eyes as he stared at her now. "Would you defend me, love?"

His voice was warm, a note of wonder there that made her throat feel tight.

"Don't call me that," she said unsteadily, and urged her horse into a canter.

Chapter 16

Dearest Viv,

I am glad you are feeling better, your grandmother's foul potions aside. Having been once on the receiving end of one of her remedies myself, I heartily sympathise, though I too recognise their efficiency. I suppose it's better than enduring a head cold for days. Just.

So what if I danced with Monsieur Le Comte twice? I also danced with Mr Hadley-Smythe twice <u>and</u> the Duke of Rochford. So what do you make of that?

Shall I call on you next week?

—Excerpt of a letter to Miss Vivien Ashton (daughter of Silas and Aashini Anson, The Viscount and Viscountess Cavendish) from Miss Evie Knight (daughter of Lady Helena and Mr Gabriel Knight).

19th December 1840, Beverwyck, London.

"Oh, Vivien! We did not expect to see you so soon," Georgie exclaimed, greeting their friend as they gathered in the drawing room where the family were at home for morning callers.

There had been a steady stream of guests for the past few days, but this morning seemed especially busy. Most people came to thank the duchess for the marvellous party and to catch up with— or spread— the ensuing gossip.

"I am here too," Vivien's twin brother, Ashton, grumbled as everyone fussed about Viv and saw her comfortably settled with a cup of tea. "She only had a cold, you know."

"Ha! And if you'd have suffered the same ailment, you'd have ensured everyone knew you were at death's door," his sister retorted. "Whereas I suffered in stoical silence."

Ash stared at her in outrage. "Good God, was that what it was? I must look up the definition of the word *silence* when we return home, Viv, darling, for I believe we have wildly different ideas about its meaning."

"Oh, do hush, Ash, and stop putting on airs," Viv said tartly. "We all know you haven't the faintest idea how to use a dictionary."

Everyone laughed, amused as always by the twins' banter.

"Well, I like that," Ash said, tugging at one of his most eye-watering waistcoats. It was a vivid lime green with tiny oranges and lemons embroidered all over it. He grinned at Louis César, who was regarding it with a pained expression.

"Quite something, isn't it?" Ash said, regarding it with pleasure.

The comte quirked a dark eyebrow. "Quite," he agreed mildly.

"Quite revolting," Jules murmured, sotto voce. "You're giving the comte a headache, Ash. The French are sensitive to such displays of vulgarity, you know."

Ash pulled a face at Jules. "It is not vulgar, it is original, like me, and you wouldn't know style if it kicked you in the head."

"It is certainly one of a kind," Louis César replied, before adding with an anxious tone. "It is, isn't it?"

Evie laughed and took his arm. "Poor Monsieur," she said sympathetically. "Shall I seat you somewhere where you can't see it?"

"It might be best," the comte replied gravely. "I feel a megrim coming on."

"Oh, I see how it is," Ash said, giving Evie a reproachful glare. "It's everyone pick on Ash day. Well, if you don't want my company—"

"Oh, we do! Do stay!" cried the assembled company, which mollified him enough to sit and accept a cup of tea with a smug expression. Once everyone had been supplied with tea and a selection of delicious little cakes and biscuits, silence reigned for a few moments.

Georgie made herself comfortable next to Viv, who, she noticed, was covertly watching the Duke of Rochford. The duke was deep in conversation with Jules on the far side of the room.

"Shall I introduce you, Viv?" Georgie asked her.

Viv nodded, lowering her voice for privacy. "Yes, but not now. Tell me everything first. Everyone is talking about him and his interest in you. Ash tells me his appearance at two society events and his marked attention has the gossips all a-twitter. Is it true he's courting you?"

"I'm not sure, I think… perhaps he means to, but he's said nothing outright," Georgie whispered. "What do you think of him?"

Viv pulled a face at Georgie. "Oh, now. That's not fair. You know I'll have heard the gossip like everyone else. He's reclusive, ill-mannered, bad-tempered, and eats small children for breakfast.

If one was to judge him by appearance alone, I could well believe it, but from that besotted look in your eyes I'd say there's more to him than that."

"What besotted look?" Georgie retorted indignantly. "I haven't looked at him at all."

"No. Rather my point," Viv said dryly.

"Well, there's no point arguing if that's your logic," Georgie protested.

"None whatsoever," Viv agreed with a smirk.

"Mr August Lane-Fox," announced the butler as a tall, elegant man in his late twenties entered the room.

"Oh my, Georgie. Do you know him?" Viv whispered, elbowing Georgie.

Georgie looked up and nodded. She had met Mr Lane-Fox several times over the years and thought him a charming fellow, good natured and easy-going. He was handsome, too, with bright gold hair and light blue eyes.

"Mr Lane-Fox? Yes, I do. Though I've not seen him in an age. Entangled in some drama of his mother and sisters' making, as usual, no doubt."

"Introduce me," Viv demanded.

Georgie's eyebrows went up, and she stared at Vivien in surprise. Viv was quite simply the most beautiful woman Georgie had ever seen, but to her knowledge, she had never shown an interest in any man before.

"What?" Viv said, her golden skin glowing with sudden colour. "He looks nice," she said defensively.

"He is nice," Georgie said, grinning, though privately she suspected Viv would eat August Lane-Fox for breakfast. She had rather a forceful personality. Not that August was a pushover by any means, but she had never understood how someone who appeared to be such a sensible and well-behaved chap could have been best friends with Viscount Roxborough, Raphe de Ligne, *and* the Marquess of Bainbridge. He seemed very much the odd one out, but he had got into all the same scrapes they had, and the scandal sheets often connected his name to some brawl or misdemeanour. Somehow, his reputation had not suffered like the others, though, perhaps because he was so impeccably well-behaved in polite society, unlike his friends.

"August, old man. Good to see you," Jules said, waving him over. Georgie watched with interest as Jules introduced him to Rochford. The three men talked for a while, and then Jules guided August over to them. Georgie tried to suppress a surge of disappointment when Rochford didn't follow, but accepted an invitation from Aunt Prue to sit with her instead.

"Well, I suppose you don't look *too* disgusting," Jules said as he stood looking down at them, giving Vivien a critical once over. "Your nose is rather red, though."

"Jules. A pleasure as always," Vivien said, narrowing her eyes at him.

Jules returned a beatific grin. "August, may I introduce this dreadful creature, Miss Vivien Anson. Have a care, she bites. Viv, this gentleman is a friend and a jolly good fellow. Try not to upset him."

August gave Jules an uncertain glance, but smiled politely and bowed. "Miss Anson, a pleasure to make your acquaintance."

"I'm sure it must be, after such an introduction," Vivien remarked acidly.

"You must ignore Blackstone, Mr Lane-Fox," Georgie said with haste. "He is only funning, I assure you. He's rather—well, you've met him," she added apologetically.

"Ouch," Jules replied as August laughed.

"I take all of Blackstone's comments with a large pinch of salt, Lady Georgina, fear not, and anyone who can refer to Miss Anson as not looking *too disgusting* clearly needs urgent medical attention, if not a straitjacket," August said with an admiring smile.

"Thank you, Mr Lane-Fox," Vivien said, smirking at Jules. "There, you see, Jules? That is how a gentleman acts. It seems you need the instruction."

"You say that, but I wasn't the one who caused havoc at that balloon ascension at Green Park the year before last. Was I, August, old man? I believe they read the riot act?"

Jules smirked as August shifted uncomfortably and rubbed the back of his neck. "Ah," he said, grimacing. "Well, yes, but that was—"

"Bainbridge and Roxborough," Evie said, saving the poor man's blushes. "Arabella told Florence about it, and she told me. Mr Lane-Fox was likely just an innocent bystander."

Georgie noticed Viv watching August intently as he looked increasingly ill at ease. "Well, to be truthful, I *may* have played a part, but I can assure you, those days are behind me. Now Bainbridge and Dare have settled down, I hope my own life can follow suit. It is one thing for a young man to get up to mischief and into scrapes, but it looks rather undignified when your thirtieth year is almost behind you."

"Oh dear. You will not become a bore, will you, Mr Lane-Fox?" Vivien asked softly.

Georgie bit back a grin as Viv looked up at him from under thick, black lashes. It was a look that could turn a sensible chap into a blithering idiot. Georgie had seen her wield it before now and it appeared Mr Lane-Fox was not immune.

"I—er," he mumbled. "That is, no, I hope not. Only I intend to keep out of the print-shop windows from now on."

"Whatever for?" she asked, looking genuinely perplexed.

"Well, it's the sort of thing that puts the ladies off, you see," he explained.

"Oh. Are you looking for a wife, then?" she said, gazing up at him.

August cleared his throat. "I am," he said, a little too forcefully. There was the faintest touch of colour at his cheeks, but considering the way Viv was looking at him and her clearly flirtatious line of questioning, he was doing quite well, in Georgie's opinion. Some men could do nothing but stammer when Viv turned the full power of her dazzling attention directly upon them—which was rare.

Vivien's mouth curved in a slow smile. "How interesting," she said.

Once their guests had gone, Georgie surveyed what remained of the cakes, deciding which she would like. Only Jules, Rochford, Evie, and Louis César were in the parlour now, chatting amiably.

A footman was clearing away all the empty cups and saucers and Evie stood, approaching him. She was carrying a beautiful bouquet of pink hyacinths, the scent of which filled the room.

"Davies, would you see these are put in water and sent to my room, please?"

"Of course, Miss Knight," the footman said, placing the bouquet carefully on the tray.

"They're beautiful flowers, and such a glorious perfume. I think your Mr Hadley-Smythe is rather smitten," Georgie said.

Evie returned a pleased smile. "Yes, I think he is too."

"I notice he did not take part in our conversation about the French realist movement," Jules said mildly. "What was it you were chatting about?"

Evie scowled. "His new litter of pups, as you well know. Stop picking on him."

"I'm not picking on him. I am merely suggesting you might grow bored with a fellow who is not your intellectual equal."

"I do not believe Miss Knight is thinking of eloping with him," Louis César cut in, his voice mild.

"Thank you, Monsieur," Evie said, sending Jules an exasperated glare. "I am in no hurry to marry anyone at all, but Mr Hadley-Smythe is a nice man. He's genuine, and he likes me for me, not for my dowry. That is a rare enough quality to recommend him to me. Do you not think it preferable to marry someone kind and sweet and gentle, rather than someone who is clever and difficult, no matter how interesting?"

"No," Jules replied dryly. "It shows a lack of foresight. That's why villains are always the more interesting characters."

"Don't be ridiculous," Evie said impatiently.

"I'm not being ridiculous. Just look at that silly book that was all the rage a year or so ago, what was it? Something about ghosts."

"*The Ghosts of Castle Madruzzo*," Georgie cut in. "It was very good actually, though rather gruesome."

"And which character did you like best, Georgie?" Jules demanded.

Georgie sent Evie a guilty glance. "The villain," she mumbled, before adding hastily. "But that does not mean I should want to marry such a man."

Jules made a sound of disbelief. "Give over, Georgie. Every woman wants to see a wicked devil redeem himself for love. If the author had any sense whatsoever, they'd have changed the ending, shown the hero up for the spineless halfwit he was and had the villain get the girl."

"What nonsense," Evie said, sitting down with a flurry of skirts. "That's a romantic novel, Jules. What seems exciting and romantic in a book is not the least bit exciting in real life, but distressing and uncomfortable. I don't want a dramatic love affair, or duels of honour, or races to Gretna Green or anything of the sort, and neither do most people. You're being ridiculous."

"No, I'm not," Jules persisted.

"Jules," Rochford said. "Shut up."

Jules folded his arms looking mutinous but subsided, and Georgie sent Rochford a look of gratitude. A prickly silence filled the room and Georgie turned her attention back to the trays of cakes and biscuits hoping to distract everyone.

"I'm glad they didn't eat all these," she said, taking a small iced cherry cake from the few that remained. "I was too busy talking to try them."

"I had one," Evie said, grasping at the change of subject eagerly. "They're divine, so are the little lemon ones."

She gazed at the trays thoughtfully as Jules took one and put in his mouth whole, glowering at everyone.

"I suppose I ought not have a third," she mused regretfully.

Louis César immediately reached for the tray, offering it to her. "You should have whatever pleases you," he said.

She laughed, giving him a speculative look. "But there's only two left. Someone else might want one."

"Eh, alors? It's their loss. I've offered it to you now."

Her cheeks dimpled as she smiled at him. "Very well, but if I have one, you must, too. You ate nothing at all."

"As my lady commands," he said gravely, waiting until she had taken a cake before taking his own.

Evie took a bite and chewed, giving a little moan of pleasure. "Oh my, that is delicious," she said, licking icing from her fingers. She turned to look at Louis César, who was watching her, and laughed.

"Well, don't just sit there, eat it, or I might steal it from you."

Louis César looked at the cake in his hands as if he'd forgotten it was there, but obediently bit into it.

"Well?"

"Délicieux," he said softly.

Evie grinned.

The next morning, Georgie rose early to discover everything outside smothered in a soft layer of snow. With a little squeal of excitement, she dressed in her warmest clothes and hurried downstairs.

No one was about yet, and Georgie had the singular pleasure of being the first person to lay a footprint upon the pristine covering of white as she crossed the lawn. Yet as she made her way across the garden, movement to her right drew her attention to the fact that she was not the only one up and about. Rochford must have come out on the other side of the building, and was standing with his back to her, apparently lost in thought as he gazed out across the landscaped gardens.

Georgie bit her lip, indecision gnawing at her. The temptation was simply too great to resist though, and she gave in, bending to scoop up a compact handful of snow. Silently, she stood and crept closer, took aim, and threw the snowball.

It hit him in the back of the neck, knocking his hat to the ground and, from the violent oath that erupted from him, sent ice down the back of his shirt. He swung around, looking ready to do murder. Georgie quailed, wondering if she'd made an error of judgement. But then his expression changed, a very different light glinting in his grey eyes.

"Well," he said, his voice a soft murmur that made her shiver far more than the cold. "You started it."

Quicker than she would have credited from a man of his size, he grabbed a handful of snow and lobbed it at her.

Georgie squealed, trying to dodge out of the way, but too slowly. She turned at the last minute and the snowball hit her on the bottom.

"Oh!" she said, excitement surging through her blood. "This means war!"

"No quarter," he warned her.

"No quarter," she agreed, and ran up the hill to higher ground and the nearest tree.

Rochford hit her twice on the way. One glanced off her shoulder, but the next knocked her bonnet off so it dangled by its ribbons. Impatiently, Georgie tugged at the bow and cast it aside, quickly taking advantage of her sheltered position to gather snow enough for five balls before peeking out from behind the tree.

Rochford was advancing on her, walking up the hill with a snowball in each hand.

Georgie grinned and gathered up her prepared ammunition.

"Prepare to meet your maker, Rochford," she yelled, and then threw the snowballs one after the other.

He dodged the first, smacked the second aside with his hand, and the third missed altogether. The fourth hit his shoulder, but the fifth—the perfect fifth snowball—hit him square in the face.

"*Bweffh!*" came the muffled sound of Rochford eating snow.

"Huzzah!" she exclaimed, running about in a circle, crowing and doing a little victory dance.

"Never turn your back on the enemy," murmured a low voice from behind her, and Georgie shrieked as Rochford stuffed a handful of snow down the back of her dress.

"*Eeeek*!" she screamed, jigging about and tugging at the material to get the snow off her skin. She turned to see Rochford laughing himself silly, doubled over with mirth.

"Oh, you wretch! That's not fair," she complained, though she too was laughing as she ran at him and pushed with all her might. Rather to her surprise, he went down, but not before grabbing hold of her. He fell heavily and then gave another *oof* as Georgie landed on top of him.

They both stilled, their laughter dying as Georgie stared down at him.

"Sorry," she muttered, pushing at his chest to scramble away, but Rochford held onto her, his firm hands clasped about her waist.

"Don't go," he said, his voice quiet.

Georgie hesitated. His grey eyes were soft, and she could feel the heat emanating from his big body. The desire to burrow into his warmth was almost irresistible, but some measure of sanity kept her from moving. Sadly, there did not seem quite enough sanity left to climb off him. She swallowed as his icy hand moved to cup her cheek.

"I cannot stop thinking about you," he said. "You're in my mind every minute of the day. What do I do?"

Georgie's breath caught. "I'm going back to Scotland after Christmas," she said in a rush. "And you to Cumbria."

He nodded, his thumb tracing the line of her lower lip and sending thrills of sensation lancing down her spine.

"Out of sight, out of mind," she said, aware the words quavered, too aware of the powerful masculine body beneath hers. Everything feminine in her reacted to it, no matter how she told herself the provoking man would make a horrible husband.

"Is that right? If you leave here and return home, you'll not think of me again? Because I shall think of you. I shall think of you a great deal."

Georgie swallowed, uncertain of what she wanted to say.

"I shall take the lack of response as a positive sign, so if I've no hope, I beg you to speak now. For I mean to follow you to Scotland and ask your father's permission to court you."

She gasped, scrambling away from him, not having expected such a bold declaration.

He sat up, watching her intently. "Are you horrified? Do you wish me to the devil?"

Georgie could hardly breathe, let alone think of a suitable reply. "N-No," she managed. "But I—I do not think I wish to m-marry you."

He gave a dark chuckle. "I can hardly blame you for that. I've not been the most agreeable companion, have I?"

Unwilling to be unfair to him, Georgie shrugged. "You're nice sometimes, Rochford. It's the times when you're not that bother me. I don't want to marry a man who flies into rages and accuses me of wrongdoing for no reason."

He nodded, his expression grave. "I know, but it has been pointed out to me that I might find the world a happier place if I had a woman like you beside me. I think perhaps, with you, that might be true. Would you give me a chance?"

Georgie hesitated. "That's a lot of responsibility, duke, to be accountable for all of your happiness. I do not believe I am equal to the task."

"I disagree," he said, and the look in his eyes made her blush and drop her gaze from his. "But I understand your hesitation."

"I am aware of the honour you do me," she said carefully, needing him to know she did not dismiss his words lightly.

"But do you honour me enough to allow me the time to persuade you? Perhaps if I could prove to you I am not such a beast—"

"You are not a beast!" she exclaimed crossly. "I would never say or think it, Rochford, but you cannot deny the fact you are hardly an easy companion."

"So you are in accord with Miss Knight, then, that it would be better to marry someone nice and kind and gentle, who would bore you to tears in a matter of days."

"That is hardly what she said. That was only Jules being Jules and playing devil's advocate," Georgie retorted, irritated. "Why should a man who is sweet and kind and gentle be dull?"

"Because no one is always that way, love. We all have bad days; even the nicest of men can say hurtful things."

"And someone who is not nice and kind and gentle. What is *he* like on a bad day?" she demanded.

Rochford reached out and his cold fingers traced the line of her jaw. "I could be nothing but gentle with you, love. You need never fear me. I've never raised a hand to a woman in anger, and I do not mean to start now. I would be kind to you, too, and though I am not so blind to my own failings that I can promise I won't ever rant or give into a temper tantrum, you are at liberty to rant right back. Tell me I'm an obnoxious arse when you need to. I'll not punish you for it, God, I want to hear you scold me. I'd give anything to hear you telling me what a pompous idiot I am. Tell me every day. Please. I'll be the better for it, I swear."

Oh.

His words were beguiling, luring her in, and she wanted very much to believe them. She knew her own parents' marriage had got off to a shaky start because of her father's temper and lack of trust, but Mama had learned to manage him, and Papa had stopped being angry once he'd found someone to care for him. Could she really do that for Rochford? Georgie wished very much that her mother was here now so she could advise her.

"I don't love you," she said in a rush, because that was the crux of the matter.

He gave a little snort of amusement. "If you said otherwise, I'd question your sanity. I know nothing about love and would never expect that from you. Even if I hoped for it, we don't yet know each other well enough for more than liking, but I like you a good deal. Perhaps the rest will follow."

"Perhaps," she whispered, wondering if that could ever be enough to gamble away the rest of her life on him.

"Georgie," and she felt a flush of pleasure sweep up her neck at the intimate use of her nickname. "Tell me one thing, and be honest with me."

Georgie stared at him, panic rising in her chest. She didn't want to answer his questions, certainly not with any honesty, but he asked her all the same.

"Right at his moment, do you want me to kiss you?"

Her breath caught, and she gave him a reproachful glare. "Oh, Rochford, that's really not fair."

He grinned, a broad masculine grin, the smug devil. "That's what I thought," he said, and pulled her into his arms.

Georgie gasped as his mouth met hers. Despite the wintry day, his lips were warm, and her body reacted instinctively, with no thought or instruction from her. Her mouth opened to him, letting him in, and he took full advantage, his tongue sliding against hers in a sensuous assault that made her giddy. The feel of his muscular arms about her was everything she wanted, and she leaned into him. Her hands went to his face, and she stroked his beard, entranced by the soft warmth. His mouth left hers to press soft kisses to her cheek, and he nuzzled the tender place beneath her ear.

"Georgie," he groaned, and his weight bore her down, pressing her to the ground.

She knew it was a mistake, but she let it happen anyway. She did not have the will to fight him when everything about him made her blood heat on some primal level she did not entirely understand. The chill of the snowy blanket below her seeped into her clothes, a stark contrast to the fierce heat of him upon her. His body burned like a furnace, and she arched into him, seeking more, wanting his warmth and his weight, excited by the sheer power contained in his heavy frame.

His arousal pressed insistently against her, making her want to rock against him, to seek more contact. She tugged at him, pulling him down upon her, eager for him to crush his body to hers, wanting him to. Desire sang through her blood, with such force it made her afraid, afraid of what she might do or say if she allowed it to rule her.

"God, Georgie, you're so sweet, so beautiful. I've met no one like you in all my days. I want you badly."

His mouth trailed ardent kisses down her neck, returning to nip at her earlobe until she was panting and desperate. Something hot and demanding throbbed in her blood, pulsing in the private place between her thighs as his body fit snugly against hers, as if he'd been made for her, and she knew it would be far too easy to give in, to let this feeling rule her and take her choices away.

"I want you, love, so much, and it seems you're not entirely repulsed by my touch either," he added, something in his voice between amusement and wonder.

Georgie gazed up at him, staring into his eyes, seeing his hard features gentler than ever before, despite the harsh glare of daylight that did not treat him kindly, highlighting his flaws. Most might turn away, might call him ugly, but she could not. He was compelling, yes, but so much more than his scars and his damaged exterior. She did not see the scars anymore, not as flaws, at least. They were simply a part of him. He was Rochford, big and intimidating and bad-tempered and gentle, and thoroughly overwhelming. Georgie gasped as his hand cupped her breast and squeezed. Despite the layers of clothing under his hand, his touch sent a jolt of lust through her that made her moan with pleasure.

His breath caught, and he kissed her again, deeper and more insistent, and Georgie wrapped herself tighter about him, vibratingly aware of his arousal between them, of how it made her feel to know how badly he wanted her. As badly as she wanted him.

He stared down at her, his face intense, a desperate look in his eyes that made her heart jitter with agitation. "Ah, Georgie, marry me and have done with this. Why wait? You want me too, by some miracle. Be my duchess and I'll treat you like a queen. You'll have anything you want, anything at all. You need only name it. I'd give you the world if I could."

Panic rose like a hot tide, smothering desire. *No.* She couldn't. It was ridiculous, far too fast. This connection to him was too intense, too terrifying, and based on little more than physical lust. He was overwhelming her, with his hopes for what she would give him, with his desire for her and his domineering ways. She'd not let him rush her into a decision she'd have a lifetime to regret. She did not give a damn about the damage she could see. It was the damage inside him that made her shy away.

She pushed at his chest, shaking her head. "No. No, I can't. I'm sorry, Rochford… I can't."

He rolled aside, letting her up at once and loss of his heat made her shiver, the removal of his powerful body leaving her weak, and uncertain of everything but her need to get away from him.

"I'm sorry," she sobbed, and fled.

Chapter 17

Bainbridge,

Tell me what you know of Miss Vivien Ashton. I think your wife is friends with her. I met her today and cannot get the image of her beautiful face out of my mind. She is simply stunning, and I may be an arrogant devil, but I think she took a shine to me.

I only ask because she strikes me as the kind of woman who — well, who causes mayhem of the same variety as my mother and sisters. Lord help me, Laurie, but I do not need another female in my life that likes excitement and sets off explosions whenever her feet touch the ground. I want to put all the inappropriate behaviour and folly of the past behind me and live in a peaceful household where I can wake up each morning without being thrust into somebody else's drama.

Unless you can write back and tell me I have misjudged, I believe I must ensure our paths do not cross again.

—Excerpt of a letter to The Most Hon'ble, Lawrence Grenville, The Marquess of

*Bainbridge from his friend, Mr August
Lane-Fox.*

19th December 1840, Beverwyck, London.

Joe took one look at Rochford's face and thankfully refrained from making the obvious comment.

He'd cocked it up.

Not just a little either, but badly. He was so bloody furious with himself he wanted to hit something. Hard.

Joe sighed and went out of the room, returning not long after with a decanter of brandy and a glass. He poured a large measure and handed it over.

"Want to tell me about it?"

"Not really."

"Right you are."

Joe took himself off the adjoining room, where Rochford could hear him doing some aggressive tidying.

"I asked her to marry me," Rochford said miserably, before downing the brandy in one large swallow and setting the glass aside.

All movement ceased in the adjoining room. A moment later, Joe looked around the door. "You great pillock."

Rochford put his head in his hands and groaned.

"What on earth made you do such a thing?" his valet demanded.

"I don't know. She was there, in my arms, and it was so bloody perfect and… and I panicked. I knew in that moment there was not another woman alive who'd want me like that, who could put up with me and give as good as she got. I had to have her."

"So you proposed."

"Yes."

"What did she say?"

"She said *no,*" Rochford snapped testily, as if that wasn't bloody obvious.

Joe pursed his lips and folded his arms, repeating with excessive patience, "What *exactly* did she say?"

"She said, 'no, I'm sorry, I can't. I'm sorry,' or words to that effect. Then she burst into tears and ran as fast as she could. She's likely in Scotland by now, she moved so bloody quick."

Rochford watched as Joe stalked up and down the bedroom, muttering under his breath, no doubt cursing his employer's stupidity. Rochford didn't blame him. He wanted to go back in time and make it right, but he'd wanted that before now and nothing ever came right once it had gone wrong, so he might as well accept the fact he'd messed it up and lost her.

"Don't look like that," Joe said, scowling at him.

"Like what?" Rochford demanded, reaching for the brandy bottle and pouring a large measure.

"Well, if the next words out of your mouth are, 'pack my bags. We're going back to Cumbria.' I'll wash my hands of you for good."

Rochford snorted and shook his head. "I may as well. She'll avoid me now."

"And with good reason. You scared the poor girl off."

"Don't you think I know that?" he yelled.

Joe raised an eyebrow. Rochford huffed and reminded himself he was trying to behave in a more civilised manner. He reined in his temper… not that there was much bloody point now.

"Right, you cocked it up. Again," Joe said with a sigh. "But, on the positive side, she let you kiss her again. All is not lost. She likes you. You just overwhelmed her. Though, to be fair, it's hard to see how you could do otherwise," he muttered, eyeing Rochford up and down.

"Don't humour me, Joe," Rochford said. "If I get the chance, I'll apologise, but she'll keep her distance now."

"Don't you go falling into one of your black moods," Joe warned him, hands on hips, his expression mutinous. "I can't do a thing with you when you get yourself in a tizzy. It's like you dig a great hole and pull a big black cloud over your head."

"Probably to escape your nagging," Rochford muttered, pouring himself out another large drink. "Leave me be, will you?"

"Fine," Joe said, but he strode over and snatched up the bottle of brandy. "But you're not pickling yourself too. We'll find a way out of this. We just need to think. In the meantime, you're to go down to dinner tonight and make yourself agreeable, and find a quiet moment to tell her you're sorry you scared her."

"Right," Rochford said dully.

Not that he thought Joe could fix it. Joe had made a better job of his appearance than any of his other valets, so at least he did not look like a barbarian in a suit. He also talked to him as if he was a real person and didn't leap out of his skin in terror when Rochford stomped about like an enraged bull, but he couldn't mend the past. No one could. No matter how much they wanted to.

⌂ ⌂ ⌂

Meg stared at her, mouth agape. "Yer aff yer heid," she said, folding her arms and looking utterly disgusted. "Ye mean to tell me ye could have been a duchess, married to that great big hunk of a man, and you said *no*?"

"I am not fool enough to marry a man I barely know when I've spent half the time I have known him wanting to wring his blasted neck!" Georgie flung back, though in truth she was utterly wretched.

"You could have got to know him, ye great numpty. Just because you didn't want to marry him tomorrow, disnae mean you couldn't keep yer options open."

"It's not kind to give men false hope," Georgie said, but her throat was thick and the idea of going down to dinner made her nauseated. She'd eat in her room tonight. Might be safest.

"I could ha' been lady-in-waiting to the Duchess of Rochford," Meg groused, shaking her head sadly. "But nae, ye'll go back to Wildsyde and marry that gowk who's always mooning about after ye."

She picked up Georgie's discarded coat and muff, giving both items an angry shake.

"He's not a gowk," Georgie retorted, pulling the pins from her hair. They were stabbing at her skull and her head was pounding. "He's very well read. I'll have you know. He writes poetry," she added, as if that settled it.

Meg stared at her and made an expressive sound of disgust before stalking off and leaving her alone.

"Oh, Mama," Georgie said aloud. "Whatever ought I to do?"

She put her head in her hands, staring at the carpet beneath her feet where a tiny slip of paper caught her eye. Georgie bent down and reached for it, knowing already what it was.

Kiss a man under the mistletoe.

The words of her dare stared back at her reproachfully as her mother's voice echoed in her ears.

Trust in the dare, Georgie. It will lead you where you need to go.

Georgie groaned and wondered what on earth she ought to do now?

♖ ♖ ♖

24th December 1840, Beverwyck, London.

As Rochford had assumed, Georgie avoided him. Oh, not completely. If they were in company, she was scrupulously polite and included him in conversation. She did not look at him directly though, and if there was the slightest chance of being alone with him, she ran like a frightened rabbit with a hound at its heels.

Despite Joe's nagging and counsel, Rochford sank into despondency. He did not know how to fix what he had so clumsily broken. What did he expect, though?

You great clumsy brute. You ought not be around civilised people. Oh, why did your father have to die of disease and not you?

He pushed the hateful words away and told himself it didn't matter. So what? Yes, he was big and coarse and ugly, and people didn't like having him around. It wasn't as if he didn't know it. He'd been mad to think Georgie was different. No. She *was* different, kinder and more compassionate than most, but not fool enough to tie herself to him forever. Perhaps if he'd bothered to be the least bit patient, if he'd treated her with more care, he might have stood a chance, but that was the trouble with him. He did not know how to be careful. A memory surfaced of a smashed porcelain tea service and his mother's fury, but he buried that memory along with her accompanying words. Not the lesson though. He remembered the lesson. He broke things because fragile, pretty things did not belong in his world. He'd learned that a long time ago, or thought he had. This was just a reminder, that was all. One he had sorely needed.

Well, this wretched holiday would be over soon and his obligation to be a polite guest at an end. He'd go back to Mulcaster, where the great stone walls of the castle were better equipped to handle his particular brand of care.

It was late in the evening now, and everyone had gone to bed. Georgie among the first to leave, hurrying away in case he spoke to her alone. Rochford walked about the house as the servants gave him a wide berth, maids giving him anxious stares of alarm as he prowled about by himself. He would not sleep this night, though, and despite his dejection, he found pleasure in the way the grand house looked, even the way it smelled.

There was greenery everywhere: great boughs of holly and fir and mistletoe, kissing boughs and cleverly arranged wreaths studded with apples and pears and red berries. Christmas roses shone like stars in the glinting firelight, and the scents of cinnamon and exotic spices lingered in the air. This was what some people knew Christmas looked and smelled like. He had known that, but never experienced it first-hand. He wondered if Georgie would have made the big inhospitable castle he called home feel this way, cocooned in festive colours, the very walls of the building infused with the scent of a family at home with itself and its surroundings. You could almost touch the contentment in this place. The Bedwin family was large and powerful and yet, at the heart of it, was a household that loved and cared for each other and those around them.

Rochford moved to the fireplace, studying the beautiful arrangement of greenery, ribbons, and fir cones that adorned the mantle. One large candle burned at the centre, and he watched it flicker as his presence stirred the air, moving closer.

Movement behind him made him turn his head, but there was no one around. He stared at the flame for a moment longer, and then reached up his hand and snuffed it out.

Georgie took the stairs two at a time, reaching her room breathless and with her heart thudding wildly.

Stop it, she told herself, blinking back tears. *You cannot marry a man because you feel sorry for him.*

But her heart was aching.

She had waited until she was certain everyone must be abed before creeping downstairs to retrieve the book she'd left in her haste to escape the parlour earlier that day. It was the only way she had slept at all these past days, by reading until she was too tired to keep her eyes open. But then she'd seen him, walking about the house in the dark, all alone. She had watched him for a while, seen him touch a finger to the petal of a Christmas rose and stand admiring the decorations. At first she'd smiled at the sight, for he'd seemed like a boy, full of wonder on the most exciting night of the year, except then she'd caught sight of his expression in the firelight and known he was looking upon this as an outsider, curious to know about the world other people lived in.

He's not something you can mend, Georgie. This is your life. It isn't your job to fix him because he's broken. He might break you if you're fool enough to try.

Except something inside of her did not believe that and knotted up in her belly, tight and anxious. Georgie lay back on the bed, staring up at the ceiling, a small slip of paper clutched tight in her hand.

Chapter 18

August,

If you are looking for a quiet, biddable wife, I suggest you give Miss Anson a wide berth. She is a headstrong female with a mind of her own and 'opinions'. Your mama would adore her.

Frankly, if a creature as beautiful as that has given you anything resembling encouragement, I should say 'tally ho' and 'Godspeed'. Why on earth would you want to marry a milk and water female when you could have one like that? She'll lead you a merry dance, I grant you, but it will be a devilish lot of fun along the way.

—Excerpt of a letter to Mr August Lane-Fox from his friend, The Most Hon'ble, Lawrence Grenville, The Marquess of Bainbridge.

25th December 1840, Beverwyck, London.

Georgie surveyed the parlour. The hour was growing late, and everyone was too full to move after the most splendid Christmas dinner imaginable. Jules had given up on being sociable an hour ago and was stretched out in an armchair, snoring softly. His sister

Lottie had fallen asleep against her husband, Cass's shoulder, while he sketched Evie and the comte. They were both intent on a game of whist, their concentration absolute. The children had been allowed to stay up late, far too excited and full of sweetmeats to go to bed yet… except for one-year-old Octavia, who snuggled in the duchess's arms, blinking sleepily, determined not to miss anything. Her papa looked on fondly and reached out, stroking the baby's soft cheek and murmuring something that made Aunt Prue smile up at him with adoration shining in her eyes.

Rosamund was doing her best to keep the younger children's attention on a board game named enticingly, The Majestic Game of the Asiatic Ostrich. From what Georgie could gather, the game itself was less exciting, offering lessons in *Ranks and Dignities of the British Peerage, Clergy and Military*. Fred and Aggie were most vocal in their demands to play spillikins or another round of charades. Little Harry was sitting on the rug by his mother's feet in front of the fire, lining up his new toy soldiers in neat ranks.

Octavia finally gave into sleep after being given into her father's care. The duchess regarded her sleeping daughter with a smile and then reached out, ruffling her small son's hair affectionately. Harry glanced up from his soldiers and grinned at her before turning back to the war in progress. Georgie looked up to see Rochford watching the boy too, watching the way the duchess's hand lingered in her son's soft curls. As if sensing her gaze, Rochford turned towards Georgie, and then looked away. He moved to stand by the window and pulled the curtain back. Large flakes of snow fell outside, soft as down. The perfect Christmas scene.

Rochford pulled the curtain back into place and moved to the duke and duchess.

"Thank you for a wonderful day, duchess," he said to Aunt Prue. "I shall not forget it."

Prue smiled at him, her expression warm. "But it's not over yet," she reminded him. "Tomorrow—"

"I will be leaving in the morning," he cut in, his voice firm. "But I thank you kindly for your hospitality."

Prue's smile dimmed, but she nodded. "Of course. I am glad Jules brought you. I hope you will visit us again."

"You are most generous hosts. Duchess, Bedwin, goodnight."

They bade him goodnight, and he strode to the door, his steps slowing as he passed Georgie. He did not look at her, but spoke quietly.

"Happy Christmas, my lady."

Georgie watched him leave, watched the door close upon him and felt her heart speed with panic. He would leave in the morning. He would go back to Mulcaster and be alone with whatever made him so wretched and no one else would ever be brave enough to get past his defences. That didn't mean she had to, she reminded herself. He was a grown man. He had choices. He did not need to be so antisocial.

Except he did not know how to change, and never would if no one had the time or patience or care enough to show him how.

She swallowed, panic thrumming her blood, her breath coming too fast. Fumbling in the pocket of her skirts, she found the crumpled slip of paper and smoothed it out on her lap, staring down at the words. There was no one else she wanted to kiss under the mistletoe. But there was always next year. She didn't have to do it now. There was time. It wasn't as if she was an old maid. Oh, lud, what was she to do? Between overindulging at dinner and her racing heart, she thought her corset might squeeze the life from her. Pressing a hand to her chest, she felt the too fast rhythm battering against her ribs and caught Aunt Prue's eye. She lifted an eyebrow at Georgie and then stared at the door.

Oh.... To the devil with it.

Georgie leapt to her feet and hurried out. She ran to the great hall. He was there, heading for the stairs.

"Rochford!"

He turned at once, and Georgie gave a little huff of laughter as she saw where he stood. Fate perhaps, for above his head was a kissing bough. The sphere-shaped decoration was made of ivy and studded with holly berries, and beneath, tied with red ribbon, dangled a large bunch of mistletoe.

His grey eyes were wary as she hurried towards him, stopping in front of him, too uncertain to act.

"Georgie," he said, his voice husky. "I'm so sorry. I ought not to have rushed you—"

She didn't let herself think about it, but reached up and put her hands on either side of his face and pulled his head down for a kiss. It was only a brief press of lips and, though the temptation was to linger, she stood back, biting back a smile at the bewildered look in his eyes. Standing on tiptoe, she reached up and plucked a mistletoe berry from the bunch. There were only two left now. Staff and family alike must have stolen plenty of kisses.

"Come to Scotland," she said, her voice breathless, putting the berry into his hands. "And we'll see. Merry Christmas, Rochford." And then she turned and ran back to the parlour.

Rochford blinked, but she was gone. For a moment he was certain he'd imagined it, for he'd spent a distressing amount of time these past days daydreaming such scenes, like some lovesick boy. He'd told himself he was a bloody fool, but it had changed nothing. He'd imagined it over and over. Georgie running into his arms and telling him he was forgiven, that she loved him and wanted him. Ridiculous, romantic nonsense of course, but— Rochford looked down into his hand, and the tiny white berry in his palm. It was real. She'd kissed him. She'd kissed him and told him to come to Scotland. She'd given him a kiss. A kiss *and* a chance.

He let out an unsteady breath and felt the unfamiliar upward curve of his lips. *Merry Christmas, Rochford.* By God. This was the best Christmas he'd ever had in his entire life, and this time, this time, he would not squander the chance he'd been given. This time he would not bollocks it up.

Evie grasped Louis' hand and tugged him into the dark alcove, pressing a finger to his lips to silence his exclamation.

"Shhh," she whispered, as his blue eyes widened in surprise. She heard his breath catch, no doubt shocked by her behaviour again, but she grinned up at him. "Look." She mouthed the word and pointed to the scene in the grand hallway as Georgie ran up to Rochford.

Louis' hand tightened upon hers as they saw Georgie pull the duke's head down for a kiss and then stole a mistletoe berry from the bough. They watched the scene in silence until both parties had left. Rochford walking slowly away, with a wide, dazed smile upon his lips.

"She completed her dare," Evie said, delighted. "I knew she liked him."

"That was her dare?" Louis asked softly.

Evie looked up to see his eyes glinting in the darkness. "Yes. To kiss a man under the mistletoe. She's wanted Rochford from the start, but she's afraid of him, too. I can't say that I blame her, either. He's rather daunting."

"Do you have a dare, Evie?"

Evie shook her head, blushing. "I was too afraid to take one, isn't that ridiculous? I rather despise myself for it. I'm so spineless, Louis. I wish I were braver, but I'm not."

Louis scowled, shaking his head. "You're nothing of the sort. You're brave enough to rake me over the coals when I'm in the wrong, and there aren't many who would do that."

"Because I trust you," she said, giving him a wry smile. "I find other people harder to navigate and the idea of everyone looking at me makes me feel queasy."

She pulled a face and Louis chuckled.

"Not everyone wants to be the centre of attention, at least not all the time. Though I think you enjoyed your time as belle of the ball."

She snorted at the idea she'd been the belle. "Hardly that," she protested. "But yes, I had fun. I've never danced so much in my life."

"And you're not… disappointed?" he asked. "About Rochford."

"Disappointed?" she repeated, puzzled, and then laughed. "You think I was hoping to be his duchess? Good heavens, you're as daft as Georgie. Do you know she was jealous because I danced with him? As if that was ever in the cards."

He shrugged, looking away from her. "He's a duke. You'd have status and wealth—"

"And a man who speaks in grunts and a castle in the middle of nowhere," she cut in, shaking her head. "I think he's a good man, and that perhaps Georgie is strong enough to stand up to him when he's being difficult. She also loves living in the wilds, and stomping miles through mud and rain is her idea of fun. I'd rather read a good book tucked up by the fire with a cup of chocolate in my hand."

Louis gave a soft laugh and reached out, tucking a loose curl behind her ear. "And you need society. You need people around you and noise and bustle so you can arrange everyone and everything just as you like."

"Heavens, you make me sound like a despot," she said indignantly. "It seems I must make many more New Year's resolutions than I had bargained for."

"What ones were you planning on making?" he asked.

Evie considered, growing aware that they really ought not linger in the alcove alone. If it were any other man, he might get the wrong idea, but Louis knew her too well to mistake her intentions.

"To have more fun," she said sheepishly. It wasn't a very noble aspiration after all, when one should probably resolve to do more work for charity, or to improve one's mind, or at least eat less cake.

"I should like to help with that," he said gravely.

Evie nodded, equally serious. "I hope you will."

"What else?"

She hesitated, and Louis waited patiently for her answer. "Not to heed others' opinions of me when my friends like me as I am. And to be more confident, which is perhaps the same thing. I began at the Christmas ball, and you were right, you know. I had a marvellous time, though it was all because of that gown. It made me feel so much more at ease. Silly, isn't it?"

Louis shook his head. "Not silly at all. Clothes are a kind of armour. Knowing you are dressed correctly and well puts you at ease."

She gave him a speculative look. "Surely, you do not need such armour, Louis. You would look handsome wearing rags and, you know it."

He quirked a dark eyebrow at her. "I am far too vain to appear anything less than perfectly attired. Besides which, Elton would likely cast himself into the Thames if I did such a reprehensible thing. He considers himself an artist, you see, and me, his canvas."

"How tiring for you, and you know you're not the least bit vain, so don't give me that."

"Oh, but I am," he insisted. "More than you realise."

She frowned at him, uncertain of his words, which held a private note. "You liked your Christmas present?" she asked him, changing the subject.

"You know I did," he said, touching a finger to the large blue sapphire pin winking in his cravat. "Though you ought not to have bought it for me."

Evie shrugged. "I know, but I could not help myself. I had never seen a stone the exact colour of your eyes before and it called to me. I was there to buy a gift for Jules and pretended it was for him. Mama was too busy with her gifts to notice."

"I suppose I ought to give you a gift too," he said, his eyes dancing with amusement.

Evie gasped, glaring at him. "Oh, you wretch! You waited until now when you knew I was bursting with anticipation."

"Did you really think I had not bought you a gift? How cruel you must think me."

"You *are* cruel for teasing me so!" she reproached him, tugging him out of the alcove. "May I have it now, Louis? Please!"

He laughed and nodded. "I hid it in the library. Go and look among the novels and see what you can find."

With a little cry of excitement, Evie picked up her skirts and ran.

Chapter 19

Mr Lane-Fox,

Your company is requested at:

Cavendish House

For the event of

*The Viscountess Cavendish's New Year's
Ball.*

Cavendish House, The Strand, London.

**—Excerpt of an invitation to Mr August
Lane-Fox from The Right Hon'ble Aashini
Anson, Viscountess Cavendish.**

30th December 1840, Wildsyde Castle, Scotland.

"Georgie!"

Georgie squealed as her father caught her up and swung her around, just as if she were a little girl again, which she most certainly was not.

"Pa!" she laughed, clutching at her bonnet. "I've only been gone a few weeks."

"Dinnae ever go again! Leastways not at Christmastime. Ach, I missed you, lass." He hugged her again and kissed her cheek.

"I missed you too, Pa."

"And do you think I might get to greet my daughter, you big ox. Give me some room," her mother scolded, pretending to push Pa aside, which was about as much use as pushing at the castle walls whether she meant it or not.

"Stop bullying me you dreadful woman. I saw her first," Pa grumbled, but winked at Georgie and stepped aside so she could hug her mother.

"I'm so pleased to see you, Mama," Georgie said with a sigh of relief as her mother hugged her. Mama looked up, perhaps noting the anxiety in her voice, though Georgie tried to hide it. But Mama was perceptive and nothing much got past her.

"Yes, I think we've a lot of catching up to do," her mother said, her eyes glinting with interest as she patted Georgie's cheek. "But first tea. Mrs MacLeod has been cooking up a storm and there're more cakes and biscuits than we can possibly eat in a sennight, so I hope you're good and hungry."

"I'm famished," replied a deep voice from behind her, and Georgie turned to see her brother, Muir. At three and twenty, he was a strapping, brawny young man, and much like his father, with wild tawny hair like a lion's mane and hazel eyes. "Back, are ye?" He was filthy, his heavy boots caked in mud as was the rest of him, his kilt sodden and dirty, and his shirt had fared no better. Heaven alone knew what had become of his coat. He looked like someone had dragged him through a ditch.

"Have you been wrestling pigs again?" Georgie asked, because even for Muir, he was in a frightful state.

"Oh, what have you been doing now?" her mother asked, regarding her middle son with a fond mixture of exasperation and resignation.

"'Twas nae ma fault, Ma," he said defensively.

"This ought to be good," Pa muttered, folding his arms.

Muir returned a reproachful expression. "I'm pure done in, an' me a hero."

"A hero is it?" his father said sceptically.

"Aye. I pulled young Douglas Macmillan out of old Mrs Brown's well. Little eejit's been told a dozen times not to play there. Ach, ye should have heard him holler. Reckon I'm deaf in one ear."

"Good heavens!" his mother said in alarm. "Is the child well?"

"Aye, not the sense he was born with, but nowt but some scrapes and bruises, though his grannie tanned his arse, so he won't sit easy for a day or two." Muir grinned, looking well pleased with himself. "See, I told ye, 'twas not ma fault this time."

"This time," his father said with a snort, but clapped his son on the shoulder. "Ye did good, laddie. Now go and clean up. Ye smell like a dead ferret."

Muir gave his armpit a cautious sniff and pulled a face. "Not that pretty, aye. Good tae see ye, yappy dug."

Georgie rolled her eyes at the insulting childish nickname her brothers had saddled her with, but replied in kind. "I suppose I missed you too, dunderhead."

He grinned at her and strode off into the house.

Georgie was almost ready for dinner before she had time to speak to her mother in private. Meg was brushing her hair out before she pinned it up, but dipped a curtsey at sight of the countess, secured Georgie's hair in a simple knot at the back of her head, and left them alone.

"It's good to have you back, darling," Mama said, resting her hands on Georgie's shoulders.

"It's good to be back," Georgie said, meeting her mother's eyes in the looking glass.

"And so…."

Georgie laughed. "I'm astonished you waited this long."

"Oh, I'm bursting," Mama admitted. She took Georgie's hands and pulled her to her feet. The two of them arranged themselves comfortably on the bed, her Mama's anticipation palpable. "Well?" she demanded.

"Well, what?" Georgie said, all innocence.

"Oh, Georgina! You know very well what," Mama protested. "Did you complete your dare?"

Georgie bit her lip, blushing, and then nodded. "Aye."

"Who? Who was it? What's he like? Will I like him? Will your father like him—no don't answer that, he won't like anyone. Tell me everything!"

Georgie laughed. "I will, if you let me get a word in edge-wise!"

Her Mama mimed buttoning her lip.

"I wonder how long you can stay that way," she said, amused. "Oh, Mama. How I have wanted your advice these past weeks. I do not know if I've done the right thing or not."

Her mother looked like she was about to burst with the effort of not interrupting, but waited for Georgie to continue. Georgie sighed and pulled a pillow into her lap, hugging it tightly. "Do you know anything about the Duke of Rochford, Mama?"

"The Duke of Rochford! The scarred duke?" her mother exclaimed, all the colour leaching from her face. "Oh, Georgie, it wasn't him, surely. They say he's a big, ugly horror of a man who can't keep servants because he terrifies them and disregards every invitation from polite society. Do you mean *that* Duke of Rochford?"

Georgie scowled. "I don't think there can be more than one, but he's not ugly, Mama, and Pa disregards every invitation from polite society too."

Her mother frowned. "Not *every* invitation," she countered. "And his refusals are always very polite, but yes. I take your point. And I should know better than to listen to gossip. I'm sorry, Georgie, I apologise."

"Thank you."

"But tell me about him. Do you mean to say this is the man you kissed under the mistletoe?"

Georgie nodded, clutching the pillow tighter still. "Yes," she said with a sigh.

"So," her mother said cautiously. "I take it he's misunderstood, that he's not so bad tempered and unreasonable as he's made out to be."

Her mother's eyes grew wide as Georgie wrinkled her nose. "Well," she said uncertainly, trying to be fair. "Sort of."

Unsurprisingly, her mother did not look reassured. "You don't sound very sure of that, Georgie."

"I'm not," she agreed. "But I invited him to come here, and I know he will because he wants to marry me."

"Marry you? But you've just met him," her mother protested.

"Ma, you proposed to my father within minutes of meeting him and travelled to Scotland with him, unwed and unchaperoned the next day," Georgie pointed out, because it was true.

Her mother blushed. "That was entirely different, and you know it. I did not have your advantages, and the world was a different place then."

Georgie laughed and took her mother's hand. "I'm not saying I'm going to marry him, though I've known him longer than you think. He was a guest at Beverwyck, a friend of Jules'."

She watched her mother take a breath and compose herself, to listen fairly to what Georgie had to say. "Very well. What is he like then?"

"I spent half the time in his company wanting to throttle him," Georgie admitted ruefully. "And the other half—" She blushed, wishing she'd thought about that sentence before she'd begun it.

"I see," Mama said, one dark eyebrow going up. She reached out and took Georgie's hand, clasping it. "I understand, you know. It was very much that way between your father and I at first."

Georgie nodded. "But how do I know, Mama? How do I know if he's worth taking a chance on? I want what you and Papa have, and even though you have your battles occasionally, there's never any doubt that Pa adores you and would do anything for you. I'm not looking for perfection, I know that's foolish, but I think he's damaged, and the visible scars are not the ones that bother me."

Her mother sat forward, her expression intent. "Damaged how? How did he get those scars on his face?"

Georgie lowered her voice. "His father went mad from syphilis. He attacked Rochford, Mama. The scars are deep and have healed badly. He was just a little boy. What must that have done to him, to have been treated so cruelly? The old duke died not long after, and from what he's said of his mother—well, I don't think he has the slightest idea of what it means to receive love or care, let alone how to give it."

"The poor man," Mama said, pity shining in her eyes.

"Yes," she nodded, feeling her throat tighten with sorrow. "And my heart bleeds for him too, and I want to make it better, to make *him* better, but people can't be fixed like a broken wheel. What if I try, and end up married to a man who is distant, and bad tempered?"

"You've invited him here?" Mama said thoughtfully.

Georgie nodded.

"Good. In that case, he must survive your father and brothers. If he wants you, he'll have to prove himself worthy. For your papa will not let you go if he's not convinced the man is right for you, love. Neither will I, come to that."

"Yes," Georgie said, with a sigh, relieved beyond measure that she would have some help in deciding if this man was the one.

"When did you invite him to come, then? It might be best to wait until the spring when—"

Mama paused as the door flew open and her father strode in. He did not look happy.

"Georgie," he said, his expression fierce. "Why in the name of God is the Duke of Rochford on my doorstep asking to see you?"

Georgie hurried down the corridor, her heart thudding too fast for comfort, very aware of her mother trying to delay her father from following too quickly, their voices receding as she almost ran down the stairs.

There he was. Her breath caught at the sight of him, and she could not deny a little thrill of pleasure at the realisation he must have come directly here.

"Duke," she said, as he turned and saw her. His expression, which was tense and rigid, no doubt a result of meeting her father for the first time, eased at the sight of her.

"Lady Georgina," he said, his gaze sweeping over her. "You are well, I hope. Your journey was not too fatiguing."

Georgie laughed. "No more than yours, I'll warrant. Considering I arrived only five hours before you did."

"Don't be alarmed," he said, his expression grave and holding his hands out in a peaceable gesture. "I took you at your word, it's true, but I'm not staying and—and I do not mean to repeat any hasty words, so there is no need to be uneasy, I promise. I only wished to inform you of my plans, and to make myself known to your parents. Then I shall continue my journey to Wick. By some stroke of luck I have a small property there I have neglected for too long. I mean to attend to its upkeep, which will oblige me to remain for some time, however."

"How fortuitous," Georgie said, quirking an eyebrow at him.

Rochford cleared his throat. "I hoped perhaps we might see each other on occasion, if your parents permit it."

"I'm sure they will," Georgie said, wishing that hadn't sounded so breathless, and wondering at the pleasure she found at seeing him here, in her home, when she had been so very nervous about him coming at all.

"Nonsense," Mama said, crossing the distance between them and giving an elegant curtsy. "Your grace, we are honoured by your presence at Wildsyde. There is no need for you to travel such a distance and in such unpleasant weather tonight. You must stay with us. We would be glad to have you."

"Would we?" Pa demanded, folding his arms and giving the duke a suspicious glare. "Why would that be? What's your business here?"

"Pa," Georgie muttered, giving him a look that pleaded understanding, but her father was hopeless at charades and even if he had correctly interpreted her expression, he ignored it.

"Well?" her father pressed.

Rochford glanced up the stairs to where three large figures had become visible on the landing. The heavy tread of their feet heading downwards announced the approach of her older brothers. Georgie gave an inward sigh and shot a panicked glance at her mother. Mama just smiled and shook her head.

"What's the craic, Pa?" asked Hamilton, the youngest of the brothers, as he came to stand beside their father, flanked by Muir and her eldest brother Lyall, Viscount Buchanan.

"I don't rightly know," Pa said, frowning at Rochford. "You'll take a drink with me, Rochford? Perhaps we can clear this up."

"There's no secret," Rochford said, meeting her father's eye. "Morven, I should like to court your daughter."

Her father stiffened, his eyes narrowing. "I did nae know you'd met my daughter."

"Who is he?" Hamilton demanded of Lyall, in a far too audible whisper.

"It's the Duke of Rochford, ye stoter. Do ye ken anyone else with a face like that?" Muir returned before the eldest could reply.

Lyall smacked the back of his head and gave Muir a warning look to hold his tongue.

"Is Georgie to be a duchess?" Hamilton asked, not taking the hint.

"Not today," her father said darkly, narrowing his eyes. "Rochford, come to my study."

Rochford nodded, apparently undaunted, and followed her father across the hall. Georgie sent an irritated glare at her brothers and hurried after him.

"Rochford," she whispered, making him turn his head, though he did not pause. "Don't mention the ribbons!"

Rochford's face creased in confusion, and she suspected he believed he'd misheard her. Ah well, it was too late now. The door of her father's study closed behind him. Georgie turned back to see her mother watching her with sympathy.

"He looks like the kind of man who can hold his own," she said reassuringly, before turning her attention to her sons. "Where are your manners?" she demanded of Muir and Hamilton.

Hamilton looked indignant, folding his arms and scowling. "What? I only asked who he was," he protested.

"Numpty. A giant with a ragged scar splitting his cheek nigh in two. Who the bloody hell else could it ha' been?" Muir demanded. "You've heard the talk of him. We all have."

"Language!" Mama said, exasperated now. "Lyall, keep them out of the way until we know what's happening, please."

Lyall simply nodded and herded his brothers down the hallway. He never flapped his gums if he didn't need to.

"Mama!" Georgie pleaded. "Won't you mediate, please? I might not be certain I wish to marry him, but I'd like the chance to decide for myself before he's frightened away."

Mama patted her arm and smiled. "He does not strike me as a man who frightens easily, darling, but yes. I will see what I can do."

Georgie sighed and had to be content with that, so followed her brothers down the hall.

Rochford looked about the large and comfortably furnished study. It was a very masculine room, with dark wood panelling and the walls painted a rich deep green. There were bookshelves crammed with titles that looked both loved and well read, rather than merely bought for decoration, and several landscapes, both of the castle itself and the surrounding landscape. From what Rochford had seen of it so far, it appeared as hard and uncompromising as the man before him, but that was fine. He was ready to fight for what he wanted. His gaze drifted to a large stag's head with a fine rack of antlers, and then he blinked as he saw… pink satin ribbons. Someone had adorned the antlers with *pink* ribbons. Tied in pretty bows.

"Whisky?" Morven demanded.

"Yes," Rochford replied, still staring at the ribbons.

"Well. What do you mean by turning up here without a by-your-leave?" Morven demanded, handing him a generous measure in a crystal glass.

Rochford dragged his gaze from the antlers with difficulty. "I'm a duke. I do not require a *by-your-leave*," he replied dryly. He took a sip of whisky, appreciating the smooth, slow burn as it travelled to his stomach. After a cold and uncomfortable carriage ride, it was welcome indeed.

"Ye do if ye turn up at a man's house intending to steal his daughter away," Morven replied, his eyes glinting.

They were the same shade as Georgie's, Rochford realised. Was this where she'd inherited her fierce nature as well? Her mother had not exactly appeared a shrinking violet either, though her eyes had been kind despite the steel he'd seen there.

"I don't think I mentioned running away with her, though as we're in Scotland, it would be an easy enough thing to wed her with no worries about licences and such. Impulsive people, you Scots."

"Marry in haste, repent at leisure," Morven muttered irritably. "I'll nae have my Georgie repent her choice of husband."

"Neither would I," Rochford said, turning the whisky in his hands. "I said I mean to court her. I meant it. I've a place at Wick. It's not exactly on your doorstep."

"An hour and half, if the weather's fine," Morven agreed.

"I'll visit twice a week, at your convenience, *if* Georgie wishes me to."

"Georgie, is it?" Morven demanded, eyes narrowing. "And just how well d'ye know my lass, then?"

"They've been together at Beverwyck these past weeks," the countess cut in.

Both men turned, not having heard the door open.

"His grace is friends with Blackstone, my lord. A fact which must recommend him to us, surely. The Bedwins invited the duke to spend Christmas with them and he and Georgina have spent a good deal of time together. Chaperoned, I'm sure," she added hastily.

"Of course," Rochford agreed, not averse to lying through his teeth to get what he wanted.

Morven continued to eye him with suspicion.

"You must stay with us this evening, your grace, and for Hogmanay too," his wife said, ignoring the look of outrage from her husband. "We would be glad of the opportunity to get to know you better and the roads between here and Wick are not to be attempted in the dark, unless you know them well."

"You are most gracious, Lady Morven. I should be glad to accept, but only for tonight. I do not wish to intrude on family celebrations," Rochford replied politely, knowing well that the earl wanted to throw him out on his arse. Not that he blamed him. If he'd been Georgie's father and a man like him appeared, he'd barricade the doors. Of course, if he ever persuaded Georgie to marry him, he might have a daughter like her. His heart skipped, the image flickering to life in his mind's eye so enchanting he felt a little winded.

"—if that suits you?" The countess' voice pierced his daydream, bringing him back to the here and now.

"Certainly," he agreed, not having a clue what would suit him, having missed the conversation, but he felt certain such a gracious hostess would propose nothing that didn't suit him.

His eyes drifted back to the stag's head and those peculiar pink ribbons. The countess saw him staring, and her lips twitched. "Come, your grace. You must wish to freshen up before dinner. I shall see you to your room."

And with that, she bore him off and out of the study.

Chapter 20

Monsieur,

I never managed a moment alone with you after Christmas day, so I could not tell you how very much I loved your gift, or should I say 'gifts'? I cannot imagine how you contrived such a thing, but I am more grateful than you can imagine. They are simply stunning, and I swear I shall do them justice. You have just made my resolution to be braver a good deal easier, my dear friend.

I hope I shall see you at Lady Cavendish's New Year's Ball, for then you may see for yourself.

—Excerpt of a letter from Miss Evie Knight (daughter of Lady Helena and Mr Gabriel Knight) to Louis César de Montluc, Comte de Villen.

30th December 1840, Wildsyde Castle, Scotland.

Georgie felt very much as if she were sat upon thorns as dinner proceeded with Rochford in position of honoured guest at her mother's elbow. Her brothers had obviously been told to hold their tongues as they were noticeably silent, which did not help the stilted atmosphere one little bit. The devils were doing it on purpose, of course, she fumed. She turned to her mother as the staff brought in the second course, but Mama only bit her lip and stared at her plate, looking very much as if she was trying hard not to laugh.

Strangely, Rochford did not seem the least bit put out or ill at ease, but ate his dinner with apparent contentment. When the meal was over, he wished everyone goodnight before retiring for the evening, only for Georgie to realise she'd barely spoken a word to him all evening.

She glared at her brothers and her father, folding her arms. "Well, thank you very much. If that didn't scare him off, I can only imagine breakfast will put the lid on it."

"Ach, what d'ye want to go marrying a surly munter like that for?" Muir said, shaking his head. "Ye can do better, yappy dug. Don't settle for the first fellow as shows an interest."

"Better than a duke?" Georgie retorted, irritated.

"He means prettier," Hamilton explained seriously. "Ye'd not be wanting to wake up beside that every morning. 'Twould put ye off yer porridge."

"I'd rather wake up beside him than any other man I've met, no matter how pretty," she retorted, fuming at their inconsiderate words.

Then, as she saw them fall about laughing, she realised what she'd said, and that the beasts had goaded her on purpose. Blushing furiously, she scowled at them and flounced to the door, slamming it on her way out.

Rochford was always an early riser, but he made certain he was up and about in good time the next morning, determined to keep his promise and not outstay his welcome. He wanted to do things properly this time, and he'd taken a risk last night as it was, turning up out of the blue. It would be the last. He made his way down the stairs, surprised and pleased to discover Georgie waiting for him.

"Good morning," she said, looking adorably and uncharacteristically shy.

"Good morning," he replied, feeling his spirits lift at the sight of her. "Did you sleep well?"

She smiled. "I think I'm supposed to ask you that as you're our guest, but yes, thank you. I wanted to speak to you though, Rochford, to apologise."

He frowned. "What for?"

"For last night," she said, wringing her hands together. "Honestly, my family is not usually so very difficult. I don't know what's got into them."

"Difficult?" he echoed, his frown deepening in confusion.

"Oh, please don't be polite. At dinner last night, it was so awkward, with no one speaking. Mama tried her best, but Pa was cross, and my brothers were being difficult on purpose. They're protecting me, of course, but it was hardly helpful."

Rochford stared at her with interest. "Georgie, I eat alone most nights. Once a month I steel myself for dinner with my mother, which is an ordeal for both of us endured in silence. Last night was convivial in comparison and I'd have not noticed a thing if you'd said nothing."

"You thought that was normal?" she asked, staring at him in alarm.

"It didn't seem unusual, no. Actually, I rather enjoyed it," he admitted. "You've a fine cook."

"Oh, Rochford!" she said crossly and hugged him, there in the middle of the entrance hall.

Instinctively and with a burst of pleasure, his arms went around her as he gazed down at her in amusement. "What's this for, now? Not that I'm complaining, you understand."

"You need looking after," she wailed, though she'd pressed her face into his waistcoat and the words came out muffled. "Why must you make me want to look after you?"

He grinned, for that had to be a good sign. "I want to marry you. You don't want to be a duchess. I'm not allowed to seduce you, and I've not an ounce of charm. I'll take pity as a motivating factor."

"You're impossible," she grumbled.

He snorted. "This cannot come as a surprise to you."

She shook her head, and he put his hand beneath her chin, raising her face so he could look at her.

"I'll be back on Sunday. I'll take you to church and then we'll go for a walk or a ride if the weather is fine. We'll talk."

Georgie stared up at him and nodded.

Though the urge to kiss her was nigh on irresistible, he forced himself to release her and step back, contenting himself with raising her fingers to his lips.

"Until Sunday," he said, and went out to his carriage.

Rochford was as good as his word. For the next eight weeks, he visited Georgie twice a week without fail. Once on Sunday, and for tea on Wednesday afternoon. He was never late, was scrupulously polite to her family, and kind and attentive to Georgie.

It was a cold, bright February afternoon when Georgie took him for a walk out to the ruins of Bucholie Castle. It was a wild place, romantic, and dangerous too if you weren't careful. But her parents had taught Georgie from a child where was safe to play and where was not, because her mother had almost fallen off the cliffside herself. Her parents had known it was pointless forbidding their children to go somewhere so interesting, and so they'd taught them where the dangers lay instead.

"Christ, it's cold," Rochford muttered as an icy wind whipped about the headland, tugging at his coat. "Should we go back? I don't want you to catch a chill."

Georgie laughed and shook her head. "Not unless you've had enough. I was born here, Rochford. I won't wilt because there's a bit of a breeze."

"A bit of a breeze?" he repeated, shaking his head. "Were you hoping it would blow me off the edge and into the sea so you could be rid of me?"

"There are easier ways to be rid of you, if I had a mind," Georgie shot back, grinning at him.

Rochford paused, his gaze intent as the guillemots shrieked above them, riding the buffeting air currents overhead. "Does this mean you don't mind having me about?"

Georgie stood for a long moment, staring out at the endless expanse of blue as the freezing north sea glittered in the sun. "I would have told you by now if I did, duke, or do you think I'm the kind to toy with a man's affections?"

He shook his head. "No. But I know I'm no prize, Georgie. I'm wealthy and titled, but I'm still me."

She turned to look at him. "So you are," she said softly.

"It's not much of a payoff." His tone was dry, but she saw the anxiety in his eyes.

"But perhaps it's enough of one. I suppose I can overlook the fact you're a duke, after all," she said, biting back a smile.

He moved closer and took her hand, curling their fingers together. "Have I reason to hope, then?"

Georgie reached up and stroked his beard, staring into his dark grey eyes. She was uncertain how much better she had truly come to know him over these past weeks. Her father allowed the visits, but only if they were chaperoned. This was the first time he'd allowed them to walk out alone and only because he'd said even the most ardent lover would rather wait for spring than expose his tender parts to the freezing temperatures outside.

Rochford had been on his best behaviour for his visits, she knew, and that would not be the case if they married, but he had also shown himself to be patient and willing to please her and make himself agreeable. He could do it, if motivated, and that had to be a good sign.

"You have cause to kiss me, I think," she said, her heart skipping as she saw the way his eyes darkened.

She half expected him to grab hold and devour her, his expression was so raw with longing, but he didn't. He pulled her close to him, holding her carefully, and pressed his mouth to hers.

Despite the cold, his lips were warm and soft and, *oh,* she had forgotten just how devastating the touch of his mouth was. Her breath caught, and it was she who deepened the kiss, her heart soaring at the slide of his tongue against hers. She had missed this, wanted this. She could not deny that she wanted him. Her hands caught the back of his neck and she pressed closer to him, wishing the weather was warmer and had not frozen the ground solid. His big hands roamed up and down her back, soothing and caressing and finally settling upon her hips. He pulled her against him, holding her close until a groan escaped him, and he broke the kiss, breathing hard.

"Don't tempt me to misbehave, love. These past weeks have tested my patience sorely when I can think of nothing but how much I want to kiss you."

She smiled, pleased by his words, and relieved that his frustration had been as aggravating as her own.

His gloved hands framed her face, and he stared down at her. "You are the most beautiful sight, Lady Georgina Anderson."

She gave a little snort of laughter. "I can imagine, with my hair blown all over, and a red nose, I don't doubt."

He shook his head. "You look like a wild creature, like you belong here and were born to run free among these ruins. I can see that you're happy here, and I won't make you be anything that you're not, love. I won't ask you to be the Duchess of Rochford in the way my mother has been, but only to be you, and to be happy with me. Do you think those two things are possible?"

Georgie stared up at him and touched his cheek, stroking the ragged scar there as his dark brows drew together.

His voice was hesitant, rough. "I know it's ugly. It won't get any prettier either. Do you—"

"Shut up, Rochford," she said, and rose on her tiptoes to press a kiss to the tortured skin. Gently, she traced the line of his scar with her lips, from his hairline down to his mouth. He was very still, only his chest rising and falling with increasing speed.

She pulled back and cupped his face within hers, as he had done. "I think I begin to see you, Rochford, and I see the beauty here." She took one hand from his cheek and placed it over his heart. "If you can trust me with the rest, if you can let me in. I think I could trust in you too."

"I am trying," he said, and the admission was uncertain, but there was hope in his eyes.

"That's all I ask."

"Georgie…."

She heard the tone of his voice, knew what he wanted to ask her, and pressed her finger to his lips, silencing him. Not yet.

"It's my birthday next week," she said. "Will you come for dinner, to celebrate with us?"

He nodded, and though she saw disappointment in his gaze, he didn't push her. When he replied, his words were warm. "I'd like that. And what would you desire for your birthday? I shall bring you a gift."

Georgie pursed her lips, considering this. "I would like you to choose something you think will please me."

He snorted. "That's not much to go on."

She shrugged and gave him a teasing look from under her eyelashes. "How much depends on how well you know me, I suppose."

"Ah, a test. I see. And if I fail?" he asked lightly, though she heard his nervousness all the same.

She smiled at him, not wanting him to fret. "If you fail, try, try again. You know that much, surely, Rochford?"

"Alden," he said, looking somewhat abashed. "My name is Alden."

Georgie watched him, wondering what he preferred. "It's a nice name, but I'm not sure I can think of you as anything other than Rochford. Not yet, anyway. I shall grow accustomed if you like it better. Which do you prefer to hear?"

"I like the way it sounds when you call me Rochford, but… I should like sometimes to hear you use my name."

Georgie considered his words and nodded. "Alden when we are alone, then," she said softly. "Would you like that?"

"I would like that," he agreed, his gaze falling to her mouth again. "I like you."

She let out a breath of laughter and was about to let him kiss her again when a loud shout broke the moment.

"Yappy dug! Rochford! What the devil are ye doing out in this perishing weather? Come to the castle and get warm."

Georgie sighed. "Damn you, Muir," she muttered.

Rochford gave her a rueful smile. "Don't be too hard on him. He's only protecting you from the wicked ogre, come to steal you away from home. It's what brothers do, isn't it?"

She snorted at that. "Brothers are annoying from dawn till dusk. *That's* what they do. Just wait until he's courting," she muttered crossly, but took Rochford's arm and let him escort her back home.

"Are you certain she didn't mean diamonds?" Joe asked for the fifth time. "Everyone loves diamonds."

They sat in the private parlour of an inn by the fire, nursing a mug of ale each after an abortive shopping expedition. Rochford harrumphed and folded his arms.

"Well, give me a clue. We've visited every jeweller between Wick and Inverness, and we need time enough to travel back again. It's her birthday at the weekend."

"I am aware," Rochford muttered, glowering. "She wants nothing expensive. Georgie knows I'm rich. That's too easy. It's a test, don't you see? It must—"

"It must be romantic and personal," Joe said, frowning over his mug of ale.

Rochford nodded.

"Well, then. I can't help you there," Joe said with a shrug.

"Why not?" Rochford protested, frowning at his valet. "I didn't bring you all this way just to look decorative."

Joe shrugged. "No, you get that for free, but what I mean is, it has to be something significant for both of you. Something that no one else knows about. A shared memory that will make you smile in twenty years when you think of it again."

Rochford considered this and drained his tankard. He thought back over the time he'd spent with Georgie these past weeks, and before at Beverwyck.

"What?" Joe asked.

Rochford's gaze drifted back to him, and he grinned.

"What?" Joe demanded again, sitting up straighter.

"I've got it," Rochford said. He laughed, and hope to goodness he had guessed right, because he couldn't help feeling the rest of his life was riding on it.

Rochford paced Morven's study. If the bloody man didn't arrive soon, he'd have worn through the carpet. He wiped his clammy palms on his coat and raked a hand through his hair and then muttered a curse because Joe had made him swear he wouldn't mess it up. Joe wasn't here, though, sweating his bollocks off, waiting for Georgie's father to appear.

Finally, the door swung open, and Morven appeared with the customary scowl upon his face, Rochford had become used to seeing it over the past weeks.

"You're early," he barked, glowering at Rochford. "She's not here yet. You were told to come for dinner—"

"I know. I came to speak with you first."

Morven's face darkened further. "Oh, damn you. Must we do this now?"

Rochford nodded, though his guts had twisted into a knot and the idea of putting it off a bit longer seemed less impossible than it had an hour ago.

Muttering, Morven went and sat behind his desk and waved an unenthusiastic hand at him. "On ye go then. Gie it laldy."

Rochford stared, uncomprehending.

"Gie it yer best shot," Morven said irritably. "Yer from Cumbria, man. Can ye nae remember yer blood was Scottish way back when?"

"I was not allowed to pick up the local dialect. My mother considered it ugly," Rochford said, his lips quirking with amusement. "Ironic, really, as things turned out," he added with a snort.

"Well, at least ye dinnae blether on like some Englishmen, I suppose. I appreciate that much," Morven said with a shrug.

Rochford blinked, surprised to have been given anything positive. "Thank you."

"Take those words to heart, aye," the earl warned him.

"I will, because there's not much to say," Rochford said. He took a breath and said what he'd come to say. "I want to marry your daughter, Lady Georgina. I know you are aware of the advantages of my title and wealth, and I've also seen enough of this family to know they're not worth a button to you."

"Ye catch on quick, Sassenach, I'll give ye that."

Rochford snorted. "I know she could marry someone else, someone nicer and kinder and more patient, and prettier, by God. But she'll find no one else who will look after her like I will. I believe I understand her now, the things that are important to her, and I will hold those things dear, and make sure she always has them."

"Fine words," Morven said, nodding. "But what are these things, the things she values?"

"You, her family, above all things. She'll need to see you often, and so we must spend a fair amount of time here, if you can stand it. We have the house in Wick, so she may be comfortable and close by."

"But so we're not on your doorstep."

Rochford shrugged. "You can't blame me for that, but you'll need to come to Cumbria too and visit her at Mulcaster."

"If ye can stand it," Morven said dryly.

Rochford rubbed the back of his neck and nodded. "She'll want society. Not all the time. She likes the peace of the countryside, she'll be happiest there, but she'll want to visit her friends, to go to parties and the theatre during the season."

"Your worst nightmare, aye?" Morven said, sitting back in his chair and studying Rochford. "All those people staring at ye, whispering and dredging up the past."

Rochford shrugged. "I'm used to it. I'd prefer to protect her from such… discomfort, but it comes with me. I can only hope in time people will grow used to seeing us and tire of repeating themselves when they gain no reaction."

"They will, and Georgie's nae milk and water miss, as I think you ken by now. She'll nae need protection, though ye may need to hold her back if she thinks anyone's disrespected ye. She's a temper on her."

Rochford's lips twitched. "I am aware," he said softly.

"Aye," Morven said, watching him closely. "Reckon so. What else, then?"

"A family of her own, a home, a place to belong, and a husband who will honour and protect her, and always take her side."

Morven nodded and got up, going to the decanter and pouring out two generous measures of whisky.

"You forgot something," he said, handing the glass to Rochford.

Rochford couldn't breathe. He knew this wasn't the end of the matter. Even if he crossed this hurdle, he still had to convince Georgie she was right to trust in him. But if he couldn't convince her father, he didn't have a hope. She would not go against the earl's wishes, he felt certain.

"Have I?" he asked, forcing the words out.

"Aye, the most important thing of all."

Rochford regarded him, feeling he stood on a cliff's edge. "What's that?"

"Love, ye bloody fool, or d'ye mean to tell me ye dinnae love her?" Morven's voice was harsh, his tawny eyes, so like his daughter's eyes, burning with intensity.

Rochford shook his head, trying to find the words to explain. "I'm not… I…." He cleared his throat. "I can't do poetry and soft words and—it's not me, Morven, but she knows that I-I care—"

"Caring's not enough. Not for my lassie. She'll want ye to love her. She needs it, for if she marries ye she'll give ye her whole heart, whether or nae ye deserve it, and she won't stop until she has yers in return. Are ye ready for that?"

Rochford stared down into the glass of whisky and then took a large swallow, grateful for the shot of heat into his blood. "What if I can't? It's not that I don't want to, I just—"

"Ye father did that, aye?" Morven said, gesturing to Rochford's face.

Rochford felt his face burn and his jaw tightened. What the hell did this have to do with anything? He couldn't help how he looked and, if Georgie had accepted he was far from handsome—

The earl seemed oblivious to his growing tension. "My Pa was a wicked auld bastard. He hated me more than anything else in life. Beat the living daylights out of me too, whenever he could lay hands on me, though he never left a permanent reminder. Of course, I wisnae his get but the earl's bastard son. Not that he could bear for anyone to know that, so he acknowledged me publicly as his own."

Rochford stared, uncomfortable with the confession and uncertain of what to do with it.

"I was hateful to my wife," Morven continued. "I married her for her money. Reckoned as soon as she was with child, I'd send her back to England and be done with her."

Rochford felt his mouth drop open.

"A fine prize I was, aye?" the earl said with a mocking smile. "I did all I could to make her hate me, to hate this place and want to leave it, but I did nae reckon with her strength, her compassion, and a will like bloody iron. I had nae choice but to love her. I still fought it tooth and nail for everything I had mind, because I'm a thick-headed gowk, and I nearly lost her because of it."

The earl sipped his whisky, staring up at the stag's head and its pink ribbons. "Ye see those ribbons, aye?"

"I… er… yes," Rochford said, increasingly eager to get out of the earl's company. This talk was not going as he'd expected.

"They serve as a reminder to me, of everything I have, of everything I could lose if I'm a damned idiot again, and of the punishment in store for me should I be so bloody stupid as to let my wife down."

Thoroughly bewildered, Rochford could do nothing but wait for the rest.

"I deserted her after our first night of marriage. I was scared, ye see… out o' my bloody wits, truth be told. I'd not expected to… to feel so much, so quickly. So I ran away like a coward. For weeks, mind. And when I got back, this room was pink."

"Pink?" Rochford repeated uncertainly.

Morven nodded, grinning now. "From skirting to ceiling, everything in here was pink, and not just any pink, a violent, megrim-inducing pink. Every inch of wall was lined with animal heads like the stag there, staring at me with glassy eyes, and every neck, every ear and every bloody antler had a shiny pink ribbon. It was horrifying."

"Good God," Rochford said faintly, suppressing a shudder.

"Aye," Morven said thoughtfully. "I learned my lesson though…. Eventually."

Rochford stared up at the pink satin ribbons with dawning respect.

"Aye, you take a good look at them, duke," Morven said, clapping him on his back. "But ye'll not propose to my Georgie unless ye mean to love her, because she's her mother's daughter, and ye'll have nowhere to hide when she's your wife. Besides which, I'll have yer balls as a table ornament if ye make her unhappy. Don't say I didnae warn ye."

Rochford turned, only realising the earl had left him alone as he heard the door close behind him.

"Alden, are you well? You seem… agitated." Georgie watched him with concern. The duke had seemed somewhat distracted throughout dinner, and less attentive than she'd grown used to of late.

Rochford looked up from the fire he'd been staring into the past five minutes. He stood by the fireplace, his arm resting on the mantelpiece, his head bowed as he stared at the flames. They had been left alone in the parlour mercifully, though only on condition they left the door open, and someone checked on them from time to time.

"I'm fine," he said, though his expression was grave.

He's changed his mind, Georgie thought in despair. After all of this, after courting her and making her see that he wanted to change, that he *could* change if he tried, he had changed so much he'd decided he didn't want her. Perhaps he'd realised what was possible now? For a rich duke, one that could socialise and—

"Georgie."

She looked up, her heart beating too fast and her eyes blurring.

"Georgie? What is it?" He moved at once, kneeling in front of her, taking her hands in his. "What's wrong? Your hands are freezing. Are you sick, love? Can I get you anything?"

Georgie shook her head, staring into his eyes, into the uncompromising face that so many found ugly, but that had become so dear to her.

"Then why do you look so unhappy? *Oh,* " he said. "Oh."

"Oh?" Georgie repeated, truly panicked now. "Oh, what?"

"You've changed your mind."

"Of course I've changed my mind!" she wailed. "You've spent the past weeks doing everything you can to change it haven't you, you great lummox, and now you've changed yours!"

Rochford stared at her, looking utterly bewildered. He shook his head as if to clear it. "Can we start over? I seem to have missed the thread of this conversation."

It was too much. Georgie had spent the entire day in a stew of anticipation and excitement, only to find Rochford distant and quiet, and now all her dreams were coming crashing down. She'd been a fool. Thoroughly overwhelmed, she burst into tears.

"Georgie! Love, what is it? Oh, God, don't cry. I won't propose if you don't want me to." He hauled her off the settee and into his arms and Georgie clung to him, sobbing so hard it took her a moment to understand his words.

She hiccoughed and sniffed and calmed herself enough to speak. "W-What did you say?"

Rochford gazed down at her, his eyes full of sadness, but his expression tender. "Georgie, I'd do anything to make you happy. You are the beat of my heart, but if you don't want me—"

"Don't w-want you?" she repeated. *Oh, the great numpty.* "It's you that's changed your mind about wanting me."

"Who said such a thing?" he demanded.

"You did!"

He opened and closed his mouth. "Unless I missed something, I said no such thing."

She fought back a sob and shook her head. "No, you've said nothing at all, and you've spent all evening looking so grim."

"I always look that way," he protested.

Georgie shook her head. "You don't. It's different. You've been miles away."

He laughed then and reached out to stroke her cheek. "I was, miles away at Mulcaster, trying to imagine you as my wife, as a part of my days, my nights, my life."

"Oh, that's why you looked so wretched, is it?" she retorted, feeling her lip trembling again.

Rochford shook his head. "That's why I was so damned nervous, you little fool. I spoke to your father, and he made me realise what was at stake. Everything I had to gain, yes, but—but everything you would need from me, too. He scared me half to death."

"I'll kill him," Georgie said, struggling up from his lap.

"No, love." Rochford chuckled, holding her tight. "No. He was right. It took me most of this evening to realise it, but he was right to warn me."

"Warn you?" Georgie said, outraged. "He *warned* you about marrying me?"

He nodded, but his expression was fond, which was encouraging. "Yes. He warned me I had better be prepared to love you, because you'd settle for nothing less."

Georgie relaxed, her mouth opening in a silent 'o' as she gazed up at him. She smiled. "He's right."

Rochford nodded. "I know that now, and I don't know how things will go, Georgie. I don't know the first thing about love, or having a wife, or a family, or any of it, but I'm willing to try, if you would give me the chance."

"I would," Georgie whispered, feeling her eyes brim again as emotion got the better of her.

He grinned at her, such an unrestrained, happy smile that she felt something in her chest shift, like her heart had taken on a new shape, like it belonged entirely to him.

"You actually have to ask me, though, duke," she said, trying to act as if she were scolding him and only sounding like a besotted fool. Ah, well. True enough.

To her consternation, he shook his head. "Not yet. I haven't passed my test."

"What test?" she asked, frowning up at him.

"Your birthday present."

"That wasn't a test," she said tenderly.

"Yes, it was, and I intend to pass it," he said.

He stood, lifting her as though she weighed nothing. Georgie gasped, never having been moved about with such ease. She felt delicate in his strong arms, something she had never felt in her life before.

It was rather lovely.

He set her carefully down on the settee and pointed a finger at her. "Don't move," he ordered, before hurrying out of the room.

Georgie fidgeted, impatient now, but he returned a moment later, holding a small wicker basket with flaps to cover it, like a picnic basket. He sat down beside her and placed the basket in her lap. It meowed.

"Well, you'd best open it," he said, watching her with anticipation.

Georgie lifted the flap and a pure white kitten with a blue bow around its neck poked its head out. It gave a pitiful mewl and climbed out into her lap.

"Oh!" she said, enchanted. "Oh, Rochford."

"I didn't really mean to make a hat lining out of them. And," he added reluctantly, "they *were* adorable."

Georgie stroked the kitten's soft head and sniffed.

"Oh, you're not going to cry again, are you?"

She nodded as the kitten crawled out of her lap and made a beeline for Rochford. It climbed up his coat, mewling at him.

"No, you daft creature. You're for her. She's the one who'll love you."

"So are you, you big fraud," Georgie said softly.

Rochford waved this away and unhooked the kitten from his coat, turning it to face her. "You've not petted it enough," he complained. "You were supposed to find the key."

"What… Oh." Georgie noticed that a little key dangled from the ribbon about the kitten's neck. Grinning at Rochford, she undid the ribbon and retrieved the key, staring at him expectantly.

"In the basket," he said, sighing as the kitten settled itself in his lap, purring loud enough to wake the dead.

Georgie rummaged beneath the blanket lining the basket and found a small box with a tiny brass lock. With an exclamation of excitement, she undid the lock and opened the box, and gasped.

"Oh, Alden," she said. "Oh, now I really am going to turn into a watering pot."

"Do you like it?"

"I love it," she whispered, taking out the delicate brooch. It was a sprig of mistletoe, the leaves studded with diamonds, with three perfect little pearls in place of the berries.

"I'll always have three more kisses, so long as you have that," he said.

Georgie turned to look at him. "You can have all my kisses."

His breath caught, and he smiled at her. "I passed, then."

She nodded, her heart skipping as he took her hand in his. His thumb stroked nervously back and forth over her skin, and he swallowed hard. When he spoke, his voice was a little unsteady.

"Georgie, you're going to have to teach me a great deal, but I'm ready to learn. I'll do my best for you, love. I'll be the best husband I can be, and I'll keep you safe. I'll honour you, and do everything I can to make you happy, if you would do me the great honour of becoming my wife."

Georgie tried to speak, but no words would come out, so she simply nodded.

"Yes?" he said breathlessly.

She nodded again, and then, just in case he was still uncertain. She kissed him.

Chapter 21

Ladies,

I hope you are all prepared for my elevation to such giddy heights. I will, of course, expect you to genuflect at every opportunity, now I am no longer counted among the lesser mortals.

Oh, good heavens! It's utterly ridiculous, I know, but today I shall become a duchess. I'm terrified. Sick with nerves, and so very happy I could burst.

I would have liked you all here to wish me happy, but I think Rochford might have done himself an injury if I'd asked him to wait until spring. Especially now Papa has given his permission. So the next time you see me, I shall be Her Grace, the Duchess of Rochford.

—Excerpt of a letter from Lady Georgina Anderson (daughter of Ruth and Gordon Anderson, The Earl and Countess of Morven) to the rest of the Daring Daughters.

5th March 1841, Wildsyde Castle, Scotland.

They were married in the kirk at Canisbay. It was a plain building, stark in its simplicity, but elegant too, and bloody freezing on a fresh March morning. The congregation's breath clouded about them as the bride and groom exchanged vows and Lady Georgina Anderson became the Duchess of Rochford.

Rochford had been a bag of nerves all morning and was well aware he was lucky that Joe hadn't beaten him to death with a flat iron. He'd been surly, impatient, and sick with anxiety, until Joe had sat him down with a large glass of whisky and reassured him Georgie was not about to run away at the last minute.

"I've seen the way she looks at you," Joe said, exasperated. "Like you hung the moon, you daft beggar. Now the last time I told you not to bollocks it up, did you listen? No, you did not. So, keep your trap shut and get through the bloody service, and then she's stuck with you, the poor, sweet child. Lord above, she doesn't know what she's getting herself into."

With no one else to talk him down, and no better advice on offer, Rochford had done as he was told and made it to the kirk without anyone doing him an injury. Even the bride's father, which was a miracle.

Now he stood with his new wife beside him, and the minister had told him he might kiss the bride. He let out an unsteady breath and reached for the heavy lace that covered her beautiful face, uncertain if he was eager or reluctant to see her expression. Steeling himself, he drew back the veil with hands that felt clumsy and too large to handle the fragile material and found his wife beaming at him. Rochford was fairly certain his heart stopped beating before restarting with a thud hard enough to break a rib.

"Get on with it, then," she whispered.

Rochford felt the smile curve over his lips, tugging at the scar as his grin widened. Obediently, he ducked his head and kissed his bride.

The wedding breakfast was lavish, merry, and mercifully brief. The Anderson family welcomed Rochford more warmly than he felt he had any right to expect, considering he was stealing their only daughter away. Georgie's brothers did corner him, however, when he left the breakfast to instruct his staff to prepare for their departure.

He was making his way back to the party when the three of them stepped in front of him, blocking the corridor.

"A bit late now," Rochford said dryly. "If you wanted to frighten me off, it would have been better done last week."

"Perhaps we just want to make her a wealthy widow," Muir suggested, smirking.

Lyall glowered at him, and Muir subsided with a huff.

"We've something to say," Hamilton cut in, which was obvious enough.

"Out with it, then," Rochford said, folding his arms.

It was rare to come across men who could look him in the eye, but these three were the closest he'd ever seen. They were built like their father, and like the castle they stood in, ready to endure anything.

The eldest spoke then, his voice soft, but no less forceful for it. Rochford thought it might be the first time he'd heard him speak the entire time he'd been in Scotland.

"Ye had best make her happy, Rochford. She's a good girl, and she's not half so tough as she makes out. Ye'll look out for her, aye?"

"I'd protect her with my last breath. I'll not hurt her. You've my word."

Lyall nodded. "Make sure of it, for if she has any cause for complaint, we'll know, and we'll come for ye."

"I'd expect nothing less," Rochford said gravely.

Apparently, this had been the correct response, as Lyall's grin was quick and rather devilish. Rochford shook his and his brothers' hands, and the four men returned to the wedding breakfast without bloodshed.

Georgie dithered outside the carriage as she said goodbye to her family. For now they were only travelling to Rochford's property in Wick for their wedding night, before carrying on to Mulcaster the next day. Yet it felt as if she were leaving for the other side of the world, her life was changing so profoundly.

Mama had sobbed audibly whilst they'd said their vows and was weeping still, though she swore they were happy tears. Pa was scowling, which meant he was feeling too much to speak and did not know what to do with himself.

Georgie hugged her brothers in turn and endured their good-natured teasing, whilst she stuck her nose in the air and told them they must treat her with respect now that she was a duchess. Naturally, this had them all falling about laughing.

Mama stopped crying long enough to kiss her and to tell her not to forget the advice she'd given her last night… a comment which made Georgie blush and set her brothers off howling again until her father told them to belt up before he made them.

Georgie walked to her Pa, who swallowed hard and looked as if he were facing a firing squad, his expression was so resolute.

"I'll be back in the spring, Pa. Rochford promised," she said, taking hold of his fingers as she had when she was a little girl.

His large hand grasped hers. "Ah, Georgie. I'm going to miss ye something fierce, ma bonnie lass. Be happy, aye? Or I'll have to fetch ye back again."

Georgie swallowed a sob and hugged him tightly. "I'll miss you too, Pa."

He gave her a bear hug, the kind that had always made her feel better as a child.

"I love ye."

"Love you too."

Papa sniffed and cleared his throat. "Away with ye, now, duchess. Ye have a husband, and a new life awaiting ye, and… and I'm so proud of you I could burst," he added, his deep voice unsteady.

Georgie kissed his cheek and turned away before her composure deserted her entirely, to find Rochford waiting for her. His gaze was intent, and Georgie smiled nervously as he held out his hand to her.

"I'll take good care of her," he promised her family, before helping her up into the carriage.

And then they were on their way.

The so-called 'small property' in Wick that Rochford had neglected for so long turned out to be a fine Palladian country house on a large estate about two miles outside of town. It was also in excellent repair, a fact that became evident as the housekeeper greeted them and showed Georgie the main rooms before taking them to their private apartment.

"How strange that I see no sign of extensive building work underway, your grace," Georgie remarked, once they had been left alone.

"I only employ neat builders," Rochford replied gravely.

"And if you consider this a small property, I am quite terrified at the prospect of living at Mulcaster."

"As well you should be," he replied, which was not entirely encouraging. "It's vast, and draughty, and bloody inconvenient, and bits fall off it with alarming regularity."

"Home sweet home," Georgie said wryly.

Rochford hesitated, looking anxious. "I told you Mulcaster was not the most welcoming of homes. It's yours now, though, love. So you must do with it as you wish, but… I wasn't entirely honest about this place."

"Oh?" Georgie asked, though it was obvious there had been no renovation done here recently.

"I only just bought it," he confessed, looking sheepish.

"What do you mean?"

"I mean, I didn't own it when I first arrived at Wildsyde. That was a lie. I've spent the time looking for somewhere close to your parents so you could visit them when you wanted to, but we didn't have to stay with them. Not that I don't appreciate their hospitality, but—"

Georgie burst out laughing. "Oh, Rochford. You wicked man. You made up the entire story."

"Of course I did. I had to have a reason for turning up on your doorstep, didn't I?" he protested.

"I thought I'd given you a good enough reason," Georgie said, walking closer to the window and looking out. It was raining now, unsurprisingly, and a fine mist had covered the landscape, shrouding it in grey smoke.

"For turning up in a month, or a week or two perhaps, yes," he admitted, and Georgie's heart picked up as she heard his steps grow closer to her. "But not the same day."

"You're very impatient," she said, hearing her voice quaver as she became increasingly breathless. He was standing close behind her now, the heat of him warming her back as if she stood before a fire.

"I am," he admitted. "The past months have been a dreadful strain."

"Poor Alden," she whispered. Her chest was rising and falling rapidly now, the pretty corset she'd worn especially for him suddenly far too tight.

"I love the way you say my name," he murmured, nuzzling her hair.

"Alden," she said again, smiling as he breathed in her scent and his arms went around her.

"Are you frightened?" he asked, his voice low.

"Yes. Terrified," she admitted, turning in his arms. "But not of this, not for tonight. Only… well, the rest of it."

He nodded. "I know."

"Are you afraid too?" she asked, surprised to see the understanding in his eyes.

"Scared to death," he said with a crooked smile. "I'm afraid I'll make a mess of things, that you'll hate Mulcaster, that you'll hate me. I don't want you to be unhappy, Georgie."

"Then I won't be," she said simply. "We'll make it work. You and me. We'll figure it out between us."

He nodded. "Let's not worry about all that just now," he suggested, tracing the line of her jaw with a gentle finger. "Not when there are much pleasanter things to concern ourselves with."

"Very well," Georgie said, trying not to sound as though her teeth were chattering with nerves. She'd meant what she'd said. She wasn't afraid of him, or of their wedding night, but that didn't mean she wasn't nervous. "I'd like a bath first," she said in a rush.

Rochford nodded. "Of course. Your maid will see to it. I'll return in an hour, shall I?"

"No."

He hesitated, a crease of concern at his brow as Georgie realised how that sounded.

"I mean. You don't have to go, I… I thought you m-might like to help me," she stammered, blushing scarlet now. "With the bath, I mean."

Rochford stared at her and swallowed, his Adam's apple bobbing.

"If you want to, I mean. Y-You don't—"

"I want to," he blurted. "Christ, yes, please. I want to."

Georgie let out a breath of laughter. "Well. Good."

"Good." He grinned and rubbed the back of his neck. "I'll er… see to it."

Rochford told himself to calm down and stop behaving like a green boy, but he was a bag of nerves. He had been in a stew of anticipation for days now, but when Georgie had asked him if he wanted to help her bathe, he'd damn near expired of shock.

Rochford had skill enough with women, but had only known the experienced kind who wanted paying for their services. The thought of deflowering a virgin had him all on edge, appalled at the idea he might hurt her, that she might scream or cry, or hate him for bringing her pain.

"Bridal nerves, eh?" Joe quipped with amusement as he bent to remove Rochford's boots and stockings.

Rochford glowered at him, about to make some scathing retort when he decided he might be better off admitting the truth. "Yes, if you must know," he grumbled irritably. "Do you think she'll—? I mean, I don't want to—"

Joe sat back on his haunches and gave Rochford an assessing look. "If you're looking for advice, you're barking up the wrong tree," he remarked dryly. "However, she's no shrinking violet, and women have babies, don't they? I know you're built like an ox, but you're not a bleedin' elephant. I reckon she'll accommodate you without bodily harm."

Despite the sarcasm, Rochford relaxed. "That's true. I'm being an idiot, aren't I?"

Joe smiled and shook his head. "No, your grace. Actually, I think you have the makings of a decent husband. Now, give me that waistcoat and go and take care of your bride."

Rochford handed the waistcoat over and padded barefoot to the door adjoining his wife's chamber. He knocked lightly and entered. The bedroom was empty, but the scent of perfumed oil hung on the warm air, and he followed it to the small bathing room. Georgie sat at an elegant dressing table, clad in a silk dressing gown, whilst her maid took down her hair.

"Leave us," Rochford barked at the maid, though he'd not meant to sound so hard.

The woman shot a quick look at Georgie and dipped a curtsey, but Rochford did not miss the quick press of the maid's hand to her mistress's shoulder as she went out. No doubt the woman thought him a brute now, but there was no help for that.

Georgie watched him approach in the mirror. Feeling as if his heart might pound its way out of his chest, Rochford touched a hand to the thick silk of her hair.

"Could you take the rest of the pins out for me? Now you've frightened poor Meg away," she added with a smile.

"Didn't mean to bark at her," he said gruffly.

"I know. It's fine. We all need to get used to each other."

Carefully, Rochford undid each heavy coil, captivated by the way it slid through his fingers as the long locks fell to midway down her back.

"By God, but you are lovely," he said, his voice rough. "I've wanted you since the first minute I saw you. Did you know that?"

"You mean when you knocked me on my arse and left me there," Georgie remarked, quirking one eyebrow.

Rochford hesitated, studying her face to be certain she was teasing him. "Yes. Then."

"Why didn't you help me up then?"

"I was afraid," he admitted. "Afraid to see revulsion in your eyes if you had to touch me, afraid of what you might see in mine. It's one thing to know you're not wanted, it's quite another when the person not wanting you knows you want them more than anything else."

"Oh, Alden." Georgie turned on the seat and stood up. "You are too hard, both on yourself and others. You are everything I want. I think I have known that for a long time. I only feared you would swallow me up, that you'd not make room for me. But you will. You have already, haven't you?"

He nodded, his gaze going to the silk ribbons holding her dressing gown closed and all coherent thought vanishing.

"Georgie," he said desperately.

"Unwrap me, then," she said with a cheeky grin.

Rochford wished he could say something tender or romantic, but his tongue had glued itself to the roof of his mouth and he couldn't even swallow. He reached out and tugged at the first ribbon, and then the second, each breath harder to find than the last, as one after another the bows fell apart and exposed a tantalising glimpse of skin. Finally, they were all undone. Rochford lifted his hands to her shoulders and slid the silken material away. It fell with a soft flurry and pooled at her feet, and what remained of his breath evaporated.

"God in heaven," he murmured, gazing at her.

Georgie let out an uncertain laugh and crossed her arms, trying to cover herself, but Rochford caught at her wrists, stopping her.

"You are perfection. Don't hide, please. I want to look at you."

He stared, unable to believe this woman was not only his, but happy to be so. Life had never been especially kind to him. At times it had been bloody cruel, but now…. Perhaps this was God's idea of balance. Perhaps he'd had to suffer through the past to be worthy of this moment. If he'd known that had been the deal, he'd have agreed without hesitation. It would have been worth it for this moment alone.

He was about to touch a hand to her lovely skin when she shivered, and he cursed himself for an unfeeling devil. She must be chilly, and her bath water would grow cold. So instead, he took her hand and led her to the bath, helping her step in.

She sighed with pleasure as she sank into the warm, scented water and Rochford smiled. "Like Botticelli's Venus."

She laughed and shook her head. "She was fair, and coming out of the sea, not climbing into a bath.

"If I say you're Venus, then you are. I am a duke, you know. You can't contradict me. I'm always right."

"Is that so?" she replied, one dark eyebrow arching. "I may have trouble remembering that."

"You'll prove me wrong every day of our married life, I don't doubt," he retorted.

"I'll give it a good try," she said sweetly, and Rochford laughed, unaccustomed to bantering with a woman in such intimate circumstances, but finding he liked it very much. He was about to reach for the soap and a sponge when her hand touched his arm.

"Take it off, Alden," she said, tugging at his shirt and blushing, though whether that was the heat of the water or embarrassment, he wasn't certain. "You're not the only one who wants to see."

He hesitated, rubbing the back of his neck. "Georgie. I should have said before, but this…." He touched a hand to the scar on his cheek. "It's not the only one."

Her expression softened, and she turned to lean against the side of the tub. "Do you think it will make me want you less? Because you're a fool if you do."

Rochford sighed, but nodded. It wasn't as if he could conceal it from her, and he'd not let her hide from him, had he? Quickly, before he could think any more about it, Rochford stripped off his shirt and tossed it aside. He heard her quick intake of breath and looked at her, wondering if he'd see pity, though he knew better than to think she would revile him. Every part of his body tightened at the look in her eyes, at the desire burning there.

"Come here," she whispered.

He knelt beside the bath and shivered as her hands ran over him, over the scars that no one else got to see. They striped the base of his neck and one shoulder, not so deep and ragged as the one on his cheek, but ugly enough. At least the skin on his body was smooth, the measles scars mostly confined to his face, neck, and a little on his shoulders.

"So big, and hot."

Her voice trembled, as did her fingers as they explored his chest, smoothing through the dark hair that curled there and arrowed down his belly. She looked up at him and Rochford thought he'd die if he didn't kiss her. He ducked his head and took her mouth and she pulled him closer, opening to him at once. She kissed him back, matching his urgency with her own, with breathless little sighs and gasps that lit him on fire.

"I want to get out," she said in a rush, making as if she would stand, but Rochford stopped her. He wanted the pleasure of washing her first, even if it killed him.

"No. Wait. Let me," he managed, fighting through a haze of lust to remember how to speak.

He snatched up the soap and sponge and made a lather, and then reached for her foot. She made a little squeal of protest as he soaped her toes.

"Sorry, ticklish," she admitted, making him smile, charmed beyond reason.

He washed her long, slender leg, fighting not to become distracted when he got to her shapely thigh, but concentrating long enough to reach for her other foot. He repeated the motion, and then soaped her hands, her wrists, moving up her arms to her shoulders and the back of her neck. He watched the rivulets of soap slide down her elegant spine until she lay back again, and he slid the sponge down between her breasts. At this point, he decided enough was enough and discarded the sponge, using his hands instead, caressing the wet, silken skin of her breasts as her nipples grew hard beneath his touch. He cupped and gently squeezed, toying with the taut little peaks as her breathing picked up. She let out a sigh of content, her head falling back against his chest, and he leaned down, pressing his lips to her shoulder.

She'd told him he was impatient, and that was the truth, but he'd never felt such desperate need in all his days. He could not take any more torture. Reaching into the bath, he lifted her up, water sluicing everywhere, soaking him as he stood.

"Rochford!" she squealed, but she was laughing as she clung to his neck, so he ignored her protests. "Don't you dare put me on the bed sopping wet," she warned.

Rochford let out a groan but set her down before the fire, snatching up a large towel and wrapping her in it. He dried her, his movements as slow and careful as he could manage as she turned about for him, her tawny eyes watchful as he attended to her.

"You make a wonderful lady's maid," she teased him.

"I know," he replied, kneeling to dry her feet and then making her gasp by pressing his mouth to her navel and tickling into the little divot with his tongue.

She snorted and grabbed at his hair. "Oh, th-that tickles."

He paused, looking up at her. "What about here? Does this tickle?" he asked, his voice low as he licked along the crease of her thigh where the skin was so very fine.

She gasped, her fingers tightening in his hair.

"Or here," he continued, repeating the action on the other side and then nuzzling into the soft, damp curls between her legs. Her breathing was coming fast now as he pressed a kiss to the seam of her sex. Rochford looked up again, to be certain she was not afraid, or horrified, but her eyes were dark, her lips parted as she stared down at him. He smiled then and kissed her again and then slid his tongue between the delicate folds to the tiny bud hidden beneath.

She made a soft exclamation of pleasure and surprise, and his own body ached with need at the sound. He remained where he was, on his knees, toying with her until she was clutching at his shoulders.

"Can't stand up," she said breathlessly.

Rochford let out a little huff of laughter, pleased with himself, and then stood and picked her up again. She stared at him hazily.

"I have never been carried about so much in my life. I might protest that I do have legs, but they don't appear to be working."

"That's quite all right, duchess. I like carrying you," he said, kissing the top of her head.

"I know."

He laid her down on the bed, giving himself a moment to enjoy the sight of her. Her dark hair spilled out over the white linen, her pearly skin glowing in the lamplight, the triangle of soft curls between her legs drawing his attention. Rochford moved quickly, stripping off his trousers and small clothes and climbing onto the bed.

"Good God!"

He paused, startled at the exclamation as his bride sat up, staring.

"Is something wrong?" he asked in alarm.

Georgie shook her head, but her eyes were on stalks. Realising he was being inspected, Rochford held still, though he was feeling unaccountably nervous. After all, if his face and the scars hadn't put her off, he must be doing fine, because there was nothing wrong with the rest of him.

"Everything as it should be?" he asked, watching her with caution.

She let out a soft exclamation. "Oh, y-yes," she managed, her voice faint. "You are a very fine sight, Alden. Very fine indeed."

Her words and her unmistakable admiration unlocked something inside him, freeing him of some toxic mixture of pent-up anxiety and shame that he'd held close for so long. He smiled, feeling strangely vulnerable, as if this was a first time for him too, though she was the virgin.

"Do you want me then, Georgie?"

She gave him an incredulous look. "Of course I want you. I've wanted you since you ate the shortbread I gave you. Honestly, the look on your face. You looked like you'd died and gone to heaven, but would you admit it was the best thing you'd ever tasted? Oh, no. It was the most adorable thing, watching you try to pretend it hadn't impressed you."

"Adorable?" Rochford repeated with a snort. "You're addled, and it wasn't the best thing I ever tasted."

"Oh, yes, it was," she protested.

Rochford prowled up the bed, pushing her back as he climbed over her. "Not anymore. Not even close," he murmured, staring down at her splendid breasts, the peaks tipped with little rosy buds that made his mouth water.

With a moan of pleasure, he ducked his head and circled her nipple with his tongue and then suckled as her hands stroked down his back and she arched into him. God, but he loved the pleasure sounds she made, all those breathless little sighs and moans. He turned to her other breast and lavished equal attention there before kissing his way back down her belly and between her thighs, where she was already slick with desire. She wanted him. She wanted him badly. The knowledge was a balm to every ragged scar, healing old wounds and soothing his pride, making him feel whole for the first time in his life. He wanted to weep and to laugh and to bellow his triumph like some untamed creature, but instead he worshipped her, this strange, beautiful, fierce young woman who had decided he was worthy of her. He wasn't, not yet at least, but he would be.

Pushing her thighs wide, Rochford settled to his delicious task with one long swipe of his tongue.

"You, duchess, my own sweet, Georgie. *You* are the best thing I have ever tasted."

She cried out as he concentrated on driving her out of her senses, teasing the delicate pearl of flesh, licking and caressing with his tongue until she was clutching at the bed sheets, writhing beneath him as if she were something wild he'd caught and held captive. Her climax made his breath catch, aroused beyond bearing as she cried out with no trace of inhibition, utterly abandoned to pleasure. She didn't even stop to catch her breath before she reached for him.

"Please," she begged, her beautiful face flushed, eyes dark and filled with desire.

Rochford could hardly breathe himself, his body primed, aching with need, and yet still very aware of her inexperience.

"I don't want to hurt you," he said, hardly able to force the words out as he settled between her legs, and she coiled about him.

The desire to simply thrust into her was tantalising, but he'd rather die than cause her pain whilst taking his own pleasure.

"I know. So you won't," she said, smiling at him, reassuring him, when it ought to be the other way around. "I want you, Alden."

He stared down at her and gave a soft huff of laughter. "God. I want you so much I'm afraid I'll be clumsy, that I'll—"

She kissed him, tugging at his neck and Alden was lost in her, discovering with his capitulation that he'd come home, that he was a willing prisoner. His wife welcomed him with no reserve, holding nothing back, her soft hands stroking his hair, his back, giving herself to him with every expression of delight. Rochford groaned as he sank into her, striving to be careful, to go slowly, but she shifted her hips, urging him inside, taking him deep and the pleasure of it almost shattered him. She gave a soft cry of discomfort, the only thing that could have pierced his consciousness and he stilled at once, but she only laughed, her eyes dancing with amusement.

"You're v-very big," she said.

Rochford snorted, helpless with laughter, with desire, with love for this glorious woman. *Oh, God.* With love. He loved her. Strangely, the idea did not terrify him as it might have. For really, what other choice was there? It was what she had wanted from him, and he wanted to give her everything she desired.

"I'm fine," she whispered. "Don't stop."

Rochford stared down at her, at his wife, as he made love to her for the first time, and knew she held his heart. She reached up, her gaze upon him soft as she stroked his cheek and he turned into the caress, kissing her palm.

"Beautiful, Georgie," he whispered, wanting to tell her, to give her the words whilst he was brave enough to say them aloud, but his body had wanted for too long, and the feel of her beneath him, holding him inside her was too good. Though it was too soon, and he did not want it to end, he could not hold on. He shattered with a fierce cry, detonating like a light exploded inside him, sending him flying as his body shuddered with the force of it. She held him tight as he spilled inside her, anchoring him to this world, and came back to earth entirely remade.

Georgie held her husband in her arms, almost crushed beneath his weight and not caring a bit. Oh, Lord, but it had been marvellous. *He* was marvellous. The caring, tender man she had suspected hid beneath the uncompromising exterior had been revealed to her now and she had fallen hard. Not that there had been much farther to fall. She had known each week that he chipped away a little more of her heart and took it away with him, but now there was nothing left. He had it all, for better or for worse, and the thought did not scare her as much as she had believed it would. No doubt they would have their trials. He was still impatient, and she did not doubt his temper would surface eventually, but she did not fear it now, nor him. Because he was not the obnoxious arse she had accused him of being, but only a man with flaws, who could be loving and kind and gentle, and who could recognise when he was wrong.

"Did I hurt you?" his gruff voice brought Georgie back to the here and now and she blinked up into her husband's grey eyes. He had braced himself on his elbows, taking his weight from her, and watched her anxiously.

Georgie shook her head. "No. It was lovely," she said. "You're lovely."

He made a sound of amusement and, rather to her regret, rolled off her. She waited warily, wondering if he'd just fall asleep as her mother had warned her he might. Some men needed to be taught how to cuddle, Mama had said. Apparently, Rochford wasn't one of them. He tugged Georgie close, spooning around her until her big, warm husband enveloped her. She shivered with pleasure as one large hand cupped her breast and he sighed with contentment, his breath hot against the back of her neck.

They were quiet for a long moment, and Georgie was feeling sleepy and pleased with the world when he spoke.

"Are you happy?"

With difficulty, she turned her head so she could see his face, and he shifted to look down at her.

"I am spectacularly happy," she told him, to be certain he had no doubts about her sincerity.

He grinned, looking ridiculously pleased with himself. "So am I," he admitted.

"So you should be," she replied tartly, trying not to laugh. "I'm marvellous."

"You are that," he whispered, touching a gentle finger to her cheek before bending and pressing a kiss to her mouth. "I love you, Georgie."

Georgie stared at him, not having expected that. She had thought it might take her months, years even before he gave her such a declaration. "Oh," she said, blinking as her eyes prickled.

"Don't cry," he warned her, looking alarmed.

She gave a muffled laugh and shook her head. "Well, how on earth do you expect me not to when you are so adorable? If you want me to stop, you'll have to be an obnoxious arse again, because I love you too, Alden. I'm utterly, hopelessly besotted, and you'll find it a dreadful trial, I'm afraid, but it's too late now. You're stuck with me."

He stared down at her, his heart in his eyes, and Georgie wondered if her own heart could contain any more happiness as she saw how her words had pleased him.

His expression was still somewhat dazed when he finally spoke. "Stuck with you, am I?"

Georgie nodded.

"Well, thank God for that," he murmured, and kissed her again.

Chapter 22

Dearest Evie,

I am happy! Ridiculously happy. The kind where I can't stop smiling for no reason. I'm certain I must be revolting company to anyone but Rochford. As we are currently inseparable, I suppose that is not a problem, though, is it?

I will not blame you if you are making retching sounds at this moment. It is nauseating, I know, but all the same, I hope you find someone who makes you feel this way one day, Evie, dear. For it is the most marvellous sensation, to be married to a good man in whom you can put your trust and give your whole heart.

You must find someone very special to be worthy of you, though, my dear friend.

—Excerpt of a letter from Her Grace, Georgina Seymour, The Duchess of Rochford (daughter of Ruth and Gordon Anderson, The Earl and Countess of Morven) to Miss Evie Knight (daughter of Lady Helena and Mr Gabriel Knight).

9th March 1841, Mulcaster Castle, Cumbria.

They only spent the one night at Wick, though it was tempting to linger, but Rochford admitted he had neglected Mulcaster for too long and needed to return. Georgie hadn't minded, eager to inspect her new home and see what she could make of it, for Rochford had painted a rather bleak picture of the castle, and she intended to make it a loving, comfortable home for him, for them both.

Georgie gave a shriek as that new home came into view.

"Rochford!" she exclaimed, grasping his hand and holding on tight. "You'll never see me again."

"Why? Is it that bad?" he asked, frowning.

She shook her head, dumbfounded. "No," she said faintly. "But I've a dreadful sense of direction and I'm bound to get lost. It's—"

"A monstrosity, I know," he said dryly as the carriage rumbled up the driveway.

"Magnificent," she corrected him with a tut.

Rochford laughed and pulled her into his lap. "You have some very odd notions, duchess. Things that most people find ugly and overbearing, you find enchanting."

"It is enchanting," she said, snuggling against his chest as she watched the castle grow closer. He held her tight, kissing the top of her head.

"Well, I expect your mother will be champing at the bit to get my measure," Georgie said, trying to tamp down a surge of anxiety. She had promised herself she would be polite for her husband's sake. He would not want his wife and mother at each other's throats, she knew, but she could not feel kindly towards a woman who had treated Rochford so coldly. If she'd shown him even a scrap of affection, he would have been so much less alone all these years. Georgie turned to look at him, aware he had not answered and that he suddenly seemed very tense.

"Alden?"

He still said nothing, so Georgie took hold of his beard and gently tugged until he looked her in the eyes.

"You did tell your mother I was coming, didn't you?"

Her husband cleared his throat, looking shifty. *Oh, no.*

"Rochford! You told her you were getting married, at least?" she asked in horror.

He shrugged. "It slipped my mind," he said defensively.

"It—" Georgie stared at him. "How could marrying me *slip your mind?"* she demanded.

He frowned, avoiding her gaze.

"Was it so forgettable an event?" she pressed, knowing this would provoke an answer.

"Don't be ridiculous," he said at once. "It was the only thing I could think of, as you well know. It was she who slipped my mind. I didn't think of her. She's barely a part of my life and… and I knew she'd only say something spiteful, so I didn't bother."

Georgie relaxed, her heart aching for him. She could not imagine a life where she did not share her every triumph and happiness, as well as the disasters, with her family. He had been so alone for so long. She could hardly blame him for keeping his happiness to himself, where his mother could not take the shine from it.

"Well then. She's in for a big surprise this morning," she said wryly.

Rochford groaned and buried his face against her breasts. "Shall we go back to Scotland?" he asked, his voice muffled.

Georgie laughed and stroked his dark hair. "Do you think I'd let your mother rout me before we even meet? I think not, Rochford."

He groaned again and held her tighter. "Don't let her change you, or the way you want to do things, love. Promise me."

Georgie looked down at him, surprised that he believed it possible.

"Have you met me?" she asked, quirking one eyebrow. "I'm a graceless, mannerless baggage, remember?"

"Georgie," he said, his dark eyes filled with reproach. "Don't make me remember how ill I treated you, the things I said. I'm so sorry."

She made a very Scottish sound of disgust and pressed a finger to his lips. "I did not say it to make you feel bad, but to remind you that you married that girl. Did I ever back down from you, duke?"

"No," he said, adoration shining in his eyes. "Never."

"Do you truly think your mother will get the better of me?"

Rochford hesitated. "She has a way of saying things, of… pricking your tender parts."

"She's spiteful," Georgie said, unsurprised. "Don't you worry about me, my sweet. I shall do just fine."

"Sweet?" Rochford repeated, a little incredulous.

Georgie nodded, enjoying his dumbfounded expression. "Yes. Sweet. My sweet big bear."

"Ugh," he said, looking askance.

"Don't like it?" she asked, wide-eyed with innocence.

"No I d—"

"Kiss me."

"I like it fine," he muttered, and did as she asked.

Rochford strode into Mulcaster Castle, wondering at how completely his world had changed since he'd left the place so many months earlier. He ought to have returned in October of last year but hadn't had the heart for it then. He'd put it off, and put it off, and then snatched at Jules' offer to come for Christmas, not knowing how fortune was smiling upon him. He owed Jules a good deal, he reflected now. A debt he must repay one day.

He had always dreaded coming back here. Not because he hated the castle. He didn't. Though there were too many memories he'd rather be rid of, he did not blame the ancient stones for his unhappiness. There was a stark grandeur to this ancestral monstrosity that pleased him, and he looked forward to Georgie's help in making it into a home for them both. *A home.* It startled him to realise how desperately he wanted that. He'd thought such things as a home and a family were for other people, not for men like him. His parents and his experiences had made it very clear to him that he was unlovable, but that wasn't true. Not at all. Georgie was right. If you gave people a chance, some of them would surprise you. Not all, but he did not want or need everyone to like him. Even before Georgie, he'd had Jules, and Joe, and even the Duke and Duchess of Bedwin, had made him welcome in their home. Miss Knight had been kind, and so had Lady Rosalind, though he knew he intimidated her. Not everyone judged his appearance and saw a monster.

He held Georgie's hand tightly, aware she was feeling overwhelmed no matter how courageous she was. This huge behemoth was her home now, and his mother didn't even know she existed. Well, that at least was quickly remedied.

"We'll get the traumatic part of the day over quickly," he said, hurrying her towards his mother's apartment. "Like ripping off a plaster bandage."

"That's encouraging," Georgie said dryly.

Rochford shrugged. "I'm not expecting to enjoy this, but it's a big place. I only see her once a month. She rarely leaves her rooms."

"Is she ill?"

"She complains of her nerves a good deal," he said, trying to slow his steps as his wife was having to run to keep up. "But I do not know if she's truly ill. She's always been fragile."

"Says who?"

Rochford paused, frowning. "I don't know. She says it a lot."

Finally, they arrived at the door of his mother's rooms. Rochford knocked once and opened the door without awaiting an answer. He turned back to Georgie.

"Well then," Rochford said, his expression giving nothing away. "Let's tell darling Mama that she's no longer the Duchess of Rochford, but the dowager."

🎩 🎩 🎩

Georgie clung to Rochford's hand. Not for her own comfort, but for his. She was anxious, yes, but not unduly so. Running a household held no fears for her, because her mama had taught her well. Dealing with difficult staff was a skill she had learned at her mother's knee as they had spent their time between the many large properties that belonged to her father. Mama was kind but firm, fair, but with a will of iron. Mama had also often reminded Georgie she was not only an Anderson by blood, but a Stone, and no one could wear away one of those. As for dealing with spiteful women, well, she'd been a debutante, and not one that fit the prescribed mould of what a debutante should be. Being on the receiving end of spiteful comments was hardly new. She could do this.

What she had seen on the way to these rooms had shown her a grand medieval castle that was austere and unwelcoming, but beautiful for all its uncompromising lines. The rooms her new mother-in-law had made her own appeared to have been transplanted from somewhere else entirely.

Georgie blinked, appalled and astonished by the surfeit of frills and flounces and lace and… and cushions. The things were everywhere, overstuffed and embroidered. Pictures hung upon every inch of wall space, many of them bucolic scenes of rustic charm, the others paintings of pug dogs in various poses. Two such pups, overfed and snoring softly, were curled upon a large red velvet bed with golden tassels at the edges.

"Mother," Rochford said, and Georgie followed his gaze to an armchair by the fire where a woman of perhaps five and fifty sat with a book.

Georgie hadn't noticed her before, as she too was dressed in so many frills and flounces that she'd blended into the décor.

The woman looked up, frowning with displeasure at being interrupted. "Rochford. It's not the third Sunday of the month, is it?"

"No, madam."

"And it is not dinner time."

"No, madam."

"Then why are you here? I did not ask for you."

"I am here to present the Duchess of Rochford to you, Mother. I am married."

The dowager's eyes widened with shock, and then she turned her gaze upon Georgie. Georgie endured her scrutiny easily enough, too intent on her own perusal of the dowager duchess. She must have been a beauty once, for her bone structure was fine and delicate, and her faded blue eyes large, like a doll's. Her figure had become plump, though judging from the exquisite portrait on the wall above her of a stunning, slender woman of perhaps twenty years, that had not always been the case.

"Wanted a title that badly, did you?" his mother remarked, raising a gold-stemmed lorgnette to her eyes to get a better look at her.

"No. Not in the least," Georgie returned, holding the woman's cool gaze. "I'm the daughter of an earl. I'm not much of a one for society, and the idea of being a duchess held no appeal, I'm afraid, but it came with the man, and I did want *him*, so…."

Georgie smiled up at Rochford, leaving the words hanging there.

The dowager gave a delicate laugh. "You mean no other gentleman wanted such a large, unseemly creature."

"You'll hold your tongue," Rochford said and, from the way his mother jolted in surprise, Georgie suspected he'd rarely raised his voice to her before.

Georgie squeezed his hand and gave him a reproving look.

"That's true enough," Georgie said with a laugh. "I have been blessed indeed to find a man so big and strong that I have not a hope of intimidating him. We are quite perfectly matched."

She sent her husband another adoring smile and felt his tension ease a little.

The dowager regarded her with a puzzled little frown. "You do not care that the rest of the world pities you for your choice of husband?"

"Pities me?" Georgie repeated, doing her best to look merely surprised and not as if she wanted to throw something at the spiteful old witch. "Why would they pity me? For my happiness? For marrying a man I love and esteem? My friends are happy for me, and I do not give a snap of my fingers for anyone else's opinion."

She held the woman's gaze as she spoke, her voice clear and firm so there could be no misunderstanding her.

"You are outspoken and full of opinions, I see," the woman said, her face creasing with displeasure.

"I am the Duchess of Rochford," Georgie replied.

The dowager's mouth tightened. "You'll never find your place as duchess, not as I did. No one will respect you, as they do not respect him."

"If your place is to be alone in this room with a lot of frills and gewgaws and no friends, then I am of glad of it. My husband respects me, as do the people whose respect matters to me. I am sorry if you do not like the fact that we are happy, or that I am the new duchess, but I am afraid neither your opinion nor your words disturb me, but take heart. I have no wish to disturb you either. I doubt our paths will cross very much. Unless you wish to keep dining with your mama every month, Rochford?"

She turned to him, finding him looking a little stunned but with a smile curving his mouth.

"No, love," he said, the smile deepening. "Mother always made it plain she did not enjoy my company, and I only did it out of duty."

"I think you have done your duty," Georgie said, taking his hand before turning back to the dowager. "Though if you wish for our company, you need only ask for us."

It was clear Rochford's mother was a spiteful woman who delighted in causing her son pain, and Georgie meant to put an end to that. If, however, the dowager wished to make amends, that could only be for the good, but it must be she who made the first move. Georgie would not have her husband feel rejected all over again.

"Well then, that's the introductions done," Georgie said, smiling up at Rochford. "Let's go and make ourselves at home, shall we?"

Which was exactly what they did.

Epilogue

Dearest Georgie,

I was so thrilled to hear of your marriage to Rochford last week. A duchess no less! How splendid you are, and how lucky to be so blissfully happy with a good man. There seem few of that kind around, or at least, few that I do not regard as brothers or dear friends.

Do you know I had seven proposals of marriage last year? Seven! And four of them were over fifty. Disgusting old goats. The other three were acceptable on the face of it, handsome, wealthy, titled – but I did not want any of them. Oh, Georgie, if I don't marry soon, I shall get a reputation for being a flirt or too choosy. No one likes it when they hear a girl keeps getting proposals and refusing them and there are enough among the ton who dislike Mama and me for all the other reasons that seem so important to them.

Only one man has caught my eye and I have decided he must be the one. I think you know of whom I speak. He is kind. I see it in his eyes. Kind and patient and gentle. I am tired of men who look upon me as an ornament, as something to be owned because they covet it. I know he liked me when we first met, and yet he keeps his distance. Indeed, I think he is avoiding me and that will not do.

I am on the hunt, Georgie darling, for the only man I think I could be happy with. Wish me luck.

—Excerpt of a letter from Miss Vivien Anson (daughter of Silas and Aashini Anson, The Viscount and Viscountess Cavendish) to Her Grace, Georgina Seymour, The Duchess of Rochford (daughter of Ruth and Gordon Anderson, The Earl and Countess of Morven).

The following Christmas…

25th December 1841, Wildsyde Castle, Scotland.

"Decrepit!" Mama shouted.

"No, no, wizened. It's wizened," Pa said, but apparently that was wrong too.

"Old!" Georgie said, giving a yip of triumph as Alden straightened with a nod and grinned at her.

His impression of a stooped old man had made them all roar with laughter. He was getting the hang of charades now.

"The old something shop… Oh!" Muir leapt out of his seat. "The Old Curiosity Shop!"

Everyone groaned. Muir kept winning and was far too good at the game.

"My turn," he crowed.

"No! No more!" Pa protested. "I'm famished. It must be time for food."

"Food?" Mama said, staring at him in outrage. "How can you be hungry after that feast you devoured earlier?"

"That was hours ago," Pa said, getting to his feet and smothering a yawn. He clapped Alden on the shoulder and grinned. "Rochford here is about to faint, the poor lad is so enfeebled from lack of food. Ye cannae expect a man to play charades for hours on end on an empty belly, *mo chridhe.*"

"No, I suppose not," Mama said gravely. "I'll see what Mrs MacLeod has prepared for our tea, shall I?"

Pa nodded his agreement with this and gave Mama a playful smack on the behind as she went out, making her laugh and give him a flirtatious smile as she closed the door. Georgie saw Rochford grin as he too noticed, and he was still smiling when he sat down beside her.

"You were very good," she said, taking his hand.

"I felt like a prize idiot," he admitted ruefully.

"That's the fun of games. Everyone here liked that you joined in with them, though."

He nodded and raised her hand to his mouth, kissing her fingers.

"Are you happy, Alden?" she asked him.

"Happy?" he repeated with a huff of laughter.

He took a moment to respond, looking about the room. Lyall and Pa were standing by the fire, drinks in hand, laughing over something. Over the mantelpiece, the Christmas greenery fluttered in the rising heat, sending the scent of pine drifting through the warm air. Muir and Hamilton were bickering good naturedly, and around the room were piles of wrapping paper and ribbons and the many gifts that had been unwrapped and admired. Mrs MacLeod bustled in with Sheenagh to collect the tea tray from earlier and tell everyone that they'd laid out an informal repast for whoever wanted it.

"Can I answer that later, love? When we're alone?" he said.

Georgie gave him a puzzled look, wondering why he didn't just reply, but she nodded, and they went through with the others for tea.

Georgie pulled back the curtain and watched the snow fall, big fat flakes that tumbled with slow deliberation, covering the landscape in a quiet hush of white. Though she loved their house at Wick it was lovely to be back in her childhood home with her family for a few days. She shivered in the cold emanating through the glass and clutched her arms about herself.

"You ought not stand by the window in your nightgown, love. You'll catch a chill," Alden scolded, wrapping his arms about her.

Georgie sighed and leaned back against him, shivering for an entirely different reason as the heat radiating from his bare chest sank into her bones. "Not when I've you to keep me warm."

"Always," he murmured, leaning down to kiss her neck. His hands moved over her, sliding up over the fine material of her nightgown to cup her breasts and gently squeeze.

She smiled, relaxing into his touch. "You still haven't answered my question," she reminded him.

"Ah, yes," he said, nuzzling the tender skin beneath her ear. "Though it was a foolish question, as you well know."

"You'd been playing charades and whatever other daft games my brothers could force you into. It was a fair question in the circumstances," she pointed out.

His laughter was a soft flutter of warm breath against her skin. "I felt like a prize idiot, as I said, but… but I also felt like I belonged. Like they want me here, to be a part of this."

Georgie turned in his arms and rested her hands upon his chest, feeling the strong beat of his heart thrum beneath her palms.

"They do. They all like you. Pa especially. He's seen how happy you make me, and this is the third time we've visited them this year, plus you took me to stay with the Bedwins again, and to balls and the theatre. You've kept your word to make me happy and to be a part of this family instead of stealing me away. They adore you."

"I love you, Georgie, and I'd do anything to make you smile, you know that. But to answer your question, yes. Yes, I am happy, happier than I believed possible. You've given me so much, not just yourself, not just your love—which is more than I ever dreamed of, but you showed me the world is not as cold and unwelcoming as I'd supposed. I have you, I have a family, and… I have friends."

He said this with such a wondering expression that Georgie's throat felt thick.

"You have," she agreed. "And they love you, because they see who you really are now, because you let them in. You gave them a chance."

He shook his head. "It was you that gave me the chance. It was you who saw something in me and wouldn't take no for an answer. My brave, beautiful duchess."

He bent his head and kissed her, and Georgie sighed with pleasure. Straightening he broke the kiss and gazed down at her, his expression grave.

"Tell me, my love. Is there anything else, anything you don't have that you would like me to give you? You need only name it."

Georgie stared up into the face of man she adored, and smiled. "Well," she murmured coyly and reached for the little bit of mistletoe she'd hidden on the windowsill. She picked it up and held it over his head. "There is perhaps… one little thing."

She slid her free hand from his chest, down his belly to lie over the placket of his trousers. His body stirred at once, and she stroked her hand up and down as he stiffened beneath her touch.

"That," he said hoarsely, "is not a *little* thing."

Georgie snorted. "True enough, but it's the thing I want most in the world."

"Is it?" he asked, his voice low as he pulled her tight against him. He kissed her then, a slow, tender kiss that left her breathless.

"Always," she said.

He gave a little growl of approval that had desire blooming inside her and made quick work of stripping her of her nightgown.

"I'm glad the guest rooms are on the opposite side of the castle to the family's quarters," he said, nipping at her ear.

"Why's that?" Georgie asked nonchalantly.

"You know very well why," he said, smirking now. "I love the way you scream my name to the rafters, my love, but I very much doubt your father wants to hear it."

"I'll try to be quiet," she said, trying to look demure.

"Don't bother," he said, picking her up and carrying her to the bed. "We're far enough away and the walls are three feet thick, though I may look upon it as a challenge." He set her down and pushed off his trousers and small clothes, leaving them in a heap on the floor.

"Is that right?" she said, gasping as he climbed over her and cupped her breasts, suckling each in turn.

"It is," he agreed. "Though I'm worn out after all that eating and drinking and merry making. I think you ought to do all the work."

He rolled onto his back and pulled her on top of him, making Georgie shriek. She laughed, righting herself and torturing him as she straddled his hips and settled against his arousal, pressing close. He groaned, a deep sound that rumbled pleasantly through her.

"Take me inside you, Georgie," he begged her, his big, warm hands roaming over her, caressing her.

Georgie slid against him, ignoring his demand for now, enjoying the slick slide of his hot flesh against hers.

"That's cruel," he said, canting his hips up for more.

Georgie leaned over him, gasping as the hair on his chest rasped against her sensitive nipples. She kissed him, slow and deep, still sliding her sex back and forth over him in languid, undulating motions designed to drive him insane.

He grasped her hips, pulling her harder against him as he nudged his hips upwards, seeking entry.

"Please," he groaned. "Please."

"Well, as you asked so nicely," she whispered, and raised herself up.

He thrust into her, so hard and deep that she saw stars. She clutched at his shoulders, holding on tight as he moved faster and harder. Georgie closed her eyes, throwing her head back, letting him pleasure her until her body gathered, tightening, the pleasure rippling through her. She cried out, shouting his name as he'd wanted her to, scaring the bats no doubt and sending them flying into the night as she was flung into the heavens. Gradually her breathing quieted, and she opened her eyes, staring down at him.

"Again," he demanded, knowing she could and would.

He was still this time, letting her do the work, taking him inside her deep and increasingly slow until he was panting, his hands clutching at her hips as though he held on for dear life. She loved to watch him this way, at her mercy, until he couldn't take any more. Soon, he was going to break—

"Enough," he gritted out, turning her onto her back, pinning her hands to the mattress. "Wicked girl," he murmured, nipping at her ear.

Georgie laughed and kissed him, holding him close as he loved her.

"Again," he told her, his voice firm.

"Yes," she whispered. "Oh… yes."

She clung to him, holding her breath as the peak glittered ahead. His powerful body was hard, every muscle taut, his skin sheened with sweat as he began to shudder and jerk, spilling his seed inside her with a harsh cry of pleasure. It was enough to tip her over the edge, and she laughed with the joy of it, holding on tight until every last glorious shiver was done, leaving them boneless and sated.

He rolled to the side, taking her with him, still breathing hard, and they lay together in contented silence.

"What happened to the mistletoe?" he asked, once he'd got his breath back.

Georgie sat up and looked about them and then shifted to one side to discover she was sitting on it.

"It's a bit the worse for wear," she said with a grin, holding the mangled bit of green up to show him.

Rochford took it and snorted, setting it down on the bedside table. "Plenty more where that came from," he said, reaching down and pulling out an enormous bouquet of mistletoe from under the bed, tied with a big red ribbon.

Georgie burst out laughing. "What did you get all that for?"

He shrugged. "A fellow likes insurance."

"Alden, I already told you, all my kisses are yours," she said, snuggling into him.

"I know," he said.

"I think I knew it would be you beneath the mistletoe with me from the start."

"Give over. When I knocked you on your backside—which was not my fault—you hated the sight of me."

"I did not," Georgie retorted. "I was only furious with myself for liking such a dreadful man."

He chuckled. "I'm glad you did. I'm glad you completed your dare with me and didn't leave it for this year. Just think how different this Christmas might have been." He shivered and tugged her closer. "Forget I said that. I don't want to think of it."

"Me either," she said sleepily. "And just think, next year, we'll have a family of our own."

"Well, we might," he agreed. "God willing."

"No, we will. Sometime in June, by my reckoning."

Rochford sat up so quickly Georgie's head thumped from his chest to the mattress.

"Alden!" she protested, blinking up at him, and then she saw the look in his eyes.

"You," he said, sounding breathless. "A baby? In June? You… You never said. Not a word. You didn't tell me. Have you seen a doctor? Are you well? Why didn't you tell me?"

He sounded panicked, possibly rather angry. Georgie sighed. The only time he became unreasonable was if he thought she was unhappy, sick, or in some way at risk. She'd known he might react badly.

"Which question shall I answer first?" she asked wryly, pulling herself upright.

"All of them!" he said, his expression taut.

She reached out and cupped his face, stroking his beard. "I didn't tell you before because I wasn't certain, and I knew you'd fret. Also, I wanted to speak to Mama first. No, I haven't seen a doctor yet, but I will, and yes, I'm very well. I'm fit and strong and very happy, Alden. There's no need to fret."

She watched him carefully as he digested this. He let out an unsteady breath and rubbed a hand over his face. "Christ, Georgie. You might give a fellow some warning. I think I'm having a heart attack." He pressed the heel of his hand to chest and glowered at her.

"I'm not a fragile little slip of a thing, Alden. I've good child-bearing hips like my mother," she added ruefully. "She gave Pa three huge sons before she had me."

"What if it's too big? What if—"

"You're a big man, and I fit you perfectly. So our child will fit me perfectly. There's no problem. Mama isn't worried, so neither must you be."

His expression pinched, his brow furrowing, and Georgie reached out a hand to smooth it. "Now what?"

"I don't know how to be a father," he said, his eyes filled with anxiety.

Georgie gave a soft laugh. "And you didn't know how to be a husband either, but that's going splendidly well. You'll be a splendid father too, my love. I know you will."

"You think so?" he asked, looking dubious.

"I most definitely do," Georgie said, her voice gentle. "Are you still happy?" she asked, cautious now.

He laughed, sounding rather stunned as he pulled her back into his arms and settled them both against the pillows.

"Georgie," he said, his voice low. "Last year, when you gave me the mistletoe berry and a kiss, I thought it was the best Christmas I had ever had. This year… This year I did not believe it was possible to be any happier than I am now."

"And now?" she asked, his dear face blurring as she blinked away tears.

"Next Christmas, with our own child. A son or daughter. My God, Georgie, I am to be a father. I am terrified, but… I cannot wait for that. *That* will be the happiest Christmas ever."

"Yes. Until the next one," Georgie said confidently, nestling herself in his arms.

"Yes, and the one after that," he said with a choked laugh.

"And the one after that," she murmured, yawning as sleep got the better of her.

Georgie smiled as she closed her eyes and her husband's arms tightened reassuringly around her. She still wasn't sure she believed there was magic in that old hat, but she was glad she'd done as her mother had told her to and put her trust in the dare and a mistletoe kiss.

Next in The Daring Daughters…

Just a Little Daring
The Daring Daughters, Book Nine

Their mothers dared all for love.

Just imagine what their daughters will do…

A Determined Daughter…

Snow is cold, water is wet, and Vivien Anson is beautiful. It's an indisputable fact, and one that is becoming increasingly tiresome. Viv has had more proposals of marriage than anyone considers seemly, and she's getting a reputation as an ice maiden through no fault of her own. None of her prospective beaus see the woman behind the beautiful face. None of them understand who she truly is, but Viv is no shrinking violet, and she will not leave the biggest decision of her life in the hands of fate.

A Man Resisting Temptation…

August Lane-Fox is a liar. Despite years of bad-behaviour with his scandalous best friends, the ton believes August innocent of any wrongdoing. After all, how could a man with such guileless blue eyes and lovely manners be a dreadful scoundrel? Little do they know he was often the mastermind behind their most outrageous adventures. With his wicked friends happily married, August is looking for a quiet life, with a quiet wife. Tired of his radical mother and sisters' constant dramas and scandals, the very last thing he wants is a woman who takes risks and invites disaster whenever possible.

An Invitation for Adventure…

If she can't get the right man to propose, Viv will just have to be the one doing the proposing, and she has the very man in her sights. Mr. Lane-Fox appears to be the epitome of an elegant, upper-class gentleman, but Viv doesn't believe it. Surely, if she uses the right bait, she can tempt the deliciously well-behaved, handsome August into revealing the devil lurking inside.

But it might take just a little daring…

Out February 25, 2022

Pre-order your copy here:

Just a Little Daring

Dreams of love are all well and good, but all Prunella Chuffington-Smythe wants is to publish her novel. Marriage at the price of her independence is something she will not consider. Having tasted success writing under a false name in The Lady's Weekly Review, her alter ego is attaining notoriety and fame and Prue rather likes it.

A Duty that must be endured

Robert Adolphus, The Duke of Bedwin, is in no hurry to marry, he's done it once and repeating that disaster is the last thing he desires. Yet, an heir is a necessary evil for a duke and one he cannot shirk. A dark reputation precedes him though, his first wife may have died young, but the scandals the beautiful, vivacious and spiteful creature supplied the ton have not. A wife must be found. A wife who is neither beautiful or vivacious but sweet and dull, and certain to stay out of trouble.

Dared to do something drastic

The sudden interest of a certain dastardly duke is as bewildering as it is unwelcome. She'll not throw her ambitions aside to marry a scoundrel just as her plans for self-sufficiency and freedom are coming to fruition. Surely showing the man she's not actually the meek little wallflower he is looking for should be enough to put paid to his intentions? When Prue is dared by her friends to do something drastic, it seems the perfect opportunity to kill two birds.

However, Prue cannot help being intrigued by the rogue who has inspired so many of her romances. Ordinarily, he plays the part of handsome rake, set on destroying her plucky heroine. But is he really the villain of the piece this time, or could he be the hero?

Finding out will be dangerous, but it just might inspire her greatest story yet.

To Dare a Duke

Also check out Emma's regency romance series, Rogues & Gentlemen. Available now!

The Rogue
Rogues & Gentlemen Book 1

The notorious Rogue that began it all.

Set in Cornwall, 1815. Wild, untamed and isolated.

Lawlessness is the order of the day and smuggling is rife.

Henrietta always felt most at home in the wilds of the outdoors but even she had no idea how the mysterious and untamed would sweep her away in a moment.

Bewitched by his wicked blue eyes

Henrietta Morton knows to look the other way when the free trading 'gentlemen' are at work.

Yet when a notorious pirate bursts into her local village shop, she can avert her eyes no more. Bewitched by his wicked blue eyes, a moment of insanity follows as Henrietta hides the handsome fugitive from the Militia.

Her reward is a kiss, lingering and unforgettable.

In his haste to flee, the handsome pirate drops a letter, a letter that lays bare a tale of betrayal. When Henrietta's father gives her hand in marriage to a wealthy and villainous nobleman in return for the payment of his debts, she becomes desperate.

Blackmailing a pirate may be her only hope for freedom.

**** **Warning**: This book contains the most notorious rogue of all of Cornwall and, on occasion, is highly likely to include some mild sweating or descriptive sex scenes. ****

Free to read on *Kindle Unlimited*: The Rogue

A Dog in a Doublet
The Regency Romance Mysteries Book 2

A man with a past..

Harry Browning was a motherless guttersnipe, and the morning he came across the elderly Alexander Preston, The Viscount Stamford, clinging to a sheer rock face, he didn't believe in fate. But the fates have plans for Harry, whether he believes or not, and he's not entirely sure he likes them.

As a reward for his bravery, and in an unusual moment of charity, miserly Lord Stamford takes him on. He is taught to read, to manage the vast and crumbling estate, and to behave like a gentleman, but Harry knows that is something he will never truly be.

Already running from a dark past, his future is becoming increasingly complex as he finds himself caught in a tangled web of jealousy and revenge.

A feisty young maiden…

Temptation, in the form of the lovely Miss Clarinda Bow, is a constant threat to his peace of mind, enticing him to be something he isn't. But when the old man dies, his will makes a surprising demand, and the fates might just give Harry the chance to have everything he ever desired, including Clara, if only he dares.

And as those close to the Preston family begin to die, Harry may not have any choice.

A Dog in a Doublet

Lose yourself in Emma's paranormal world with The French Vampire Legend series…..

The Key to Erebus
The French Vampire Legend Book 1

The truth can kill you.

Taken away as a small child, from a life where vampires, the Fae, and other mythical creatures are real and treacherous, the beautiful young witch, Jéhenne Corbeaux is totally unprepared when she returns to rural France to live with her eccentric Grandmother.

Thrown headlong into a world she knows nothing about she seeks to learn the truth about herself, uncovering secrets more shocking than anything she could ever have imagined and finding that she is by no means powerless to protect the ones she loves.

Despite her Gran's dire warnings, she is inexorably drawn to the dark and terrifying figure of Corvus, an ancient vampire and master of the vast Albinus family.

Jéhenne is about to find her answers and discover that, not only is Corvus far more dangerous than she could ever imagine, but that he holds much more than the key to her heart …

Now available at your favourite retailer.

The Key to Erebus

Check out Emma's exciting fantasy series with hailed by Kirkus Reviews as "An enchanting fantasy with a likable heroine, romantic intrigue, and clever narrative flourishes."

The Dark Prince
The French Fae Legend Book 1

Two Fae Princes
One Human Woman
And a world ready to tear them all apart

Laen Braed is Prince of the Dark fae, with a temper and reputation to match his black eyes, and a heart that despises the human race. When he is sent back through the forbidden gates between realms to retrieve an ancient fae artifact, he returns home with far more than he bargained for.

Corin Albrecht, the most powerful Elven Prince ever born. His golden eyes are rumoured to be a gift from the gods, and destiny is calling him. With a love for the human world that runs deep, his friendship with Laen is being torn apart by his prejudices.

Océane DeBeauvoir is an artist and bookbinder who has always relied on her lively imagination to get her through an unhappy and uneventful life. A jewelled dagger put on display at a nearby museum hits the headlines with speculation of another race, the Fae. But the discovery also inspires Océane to create an extraordinary piece of art that cannot be confined to the pages of a book.

With two powerful men vying for her attention and their friendship stretched to the breaking point, the only question that remains…who is truly The Dark Prince.

The man of your dreams is coming…or is it your nightmares he visits? Find out in Book One of The French Fae Legend.

Available now to read at your favourite retailer

The Dark Prince

Want more Emma?

If you enjoyed this book, please support this indie author and take a moment to leave a few words in a review. *Thank you!*

To be kept informed of special offers and free deals (which I do regularly) follow me on *https://www.bookbub.com/authors/emma-v-leech*

To find out more and to get news and sneak peeks of the first chapter of upcoming works, go to my website and sign up for the newsletter.

http://www.emmavleech.com/

Come and join the fans in my Facebook group for news, info and exciting discussion...

Emma's Book Club

Or Follow me here…

http://viewauthor.at/EmmaVLeechAmazon

Facebook

Instagram

Emma's Twitter page

TikTok

http://viewauthor.at/EmmaVLeechAmazon

Can't get your fill of Historical Romance? Do you crave stories with passion and red hot chemistry?

If the answer is yes, have I got the group for you!

Come join myself and other awesome authors in our Facebook group

Historical Harlots

Be the first to know about exclusive giveaways, chat with amazing HistRom authors, lots of raunchy shenanigans and more!

Historical Harlots Facebook Group